LAST ORANGE TREE

A Phoebe Moon and Louie Dawes Mystery
(Number 2)

LAST ORANGE TREE

A Phoebe Moon and Louie Dawes Mystery (Number 2)

Barbara Curbow

ISBN 978-1-62806-480-3 (print | paperback)
ISBN 978-1-62806-481-0 (ebook)

Library of Congress Control Number 2026907232

Published by Salt Water Media
29 Broad Street, Suite 104
Berlin, MD 21811
www.saltwatermedia.com

Cover image via licensed permission from istockphoto.com

Interior image via licensed permission from istockphoto.com

For those who teach to transform

CONTENTS

Acknowledgements

This book is a work of fiction. None of the characters are real people nor are they representative of real people. The town of Lower Sierra is not a real place and the horrible crimes depicted did not occur. That being said, every day countless people are made to feel degraded and demeaned by the words and actions of others. This book is for them.

There are many terms from the social sciences that can be used to describe the processes applied to people who are considered outsiders. Negative stereotypes, prejudice, stigma, shaming, just world belief, self-fulfilling prophecy, victim blaming – take your pick. While multiple personal and social characteristics can be used to justify mistreatment, in this book I focus on social class divisions. The American Dream is the titular cultural pathway to erase or decrease class differences, but only a proportion of the citizenry will have the resources needed to bring about this reality.

Most important to me are my family members, my husband Bruce and my daughters Caitlin and Oksana. More and more, I also depend on my grandchildren who are wise in their observations and advice. This group of people supports me unconditionally and I draw from their collective strength on a daily basis.

As I noted in my first book, I made two excellent decisions when I decided to write. The first was to take writing courses, first through Stanford University's continuing studies, with Ellen Sussman. I needed to take her course on writing a novel in a year three times, but I did produce a series of novels I enjoyed writing. Ellen is able to unlock the writer in her students and to nurture the growth of their ideas. My second decision was to work with Reedsy to identify a professional team to enhance my work. I am grateful to Anne Brewer for her developmental editing. I feel like she can see inside my head and know what I am trying to do with a character or a scene. Jamie Thaman provided excellent editorial assistance. She goes way beyond the concepts of accuracy and consistency. For this book, for a number of reasons, I am working with a team from a local company, Salt Water Media on production and marketing. In true small town style, their office is next door to my haircutter. However, both of my daughters researched my writing needs and they both recommended Salt Water Media.

If you are in a situation such that you are not able to be your true self or live your fullest life, find a mentor. It may not be the first person you ask, or even the tenth person, but I know help is out there. Sometimes you have to fight to take ownership of your own identity.

Prologue

Lower Sierra, 1960

The girl was small for her age, a good four inches shorter than her classmates. She hung back from all the excitement around the jump-ropers. She loved all the games they were playing, especially red hot chilies. Her natural shyness was compounded by an unfortunate clothing situation. She had begged her mother to buy her the bright blue tights they had seen at the store. Even as she begged, she knew she was being selfish, but her need to fit in was much stronger than her conscience. Yesterday she had come home from school and found a pair of blue tights on her bed. They weren't in any type of packaging, and like all her clothes, they looked used.

Her mother had done her best, so she felt she had to wear them to school. But when she put them on, she found that they were too small. No matter how hard she pulled, the waistband only came to her hips. It was uncomfortable to walk, with the crotch of the tights hanging low. So, she stood off to the side, watching as her classmates moved from one game to another. She heard her name and suddenly her only friend at this new school was running toward her. Her friend grabbed her arm and said excitedly, "Let's jump pairs!"

Outwardly she smiled but inwardly she knew she was headed for trouble. She hoped she'd be able to keep her skirt from flipping up and showing everyone how small her tights were. *Please let me get through this,* she thought. *I will never beg for anything again.*

She was pulled into the center of the ropes as the other girls chanted the pairs song. She was lost in the rhythm until suddenly the chanting stopped and the laughing and pointing began. She looked down—her skirt was caught on the ropes, and everyone could see the large gap between the top of her tights and her waist. The next thing she knew, she was being hugged by her friend, who was jumping up and down laughing. Her eyes were burning; why was Maggie laughing at her? She was supposed to be her friend.

Finally, Maggie wiped her eyes and practically shouted, "Silly Nina! Did you accidently wear your little sister's tights today?" Maggie pulled her close and whispered in her ear, "Play along."

She realized what Maggie was doing, and she said, loud enough for all to hear, "Yes! I pulled them out of the laundry without checking the size!" Then Nina started laughing too. And that was enough to shut down the mean girls . . . this time.

As Maggie and Nina walked away, the mean girls followed them with their eyes. One of them whispered to herself, "White trash. You'll never belong here."

A short distance away, a girl with bright blue eyes had taken in this entire scene as she sat drawing intricate chalk patterns on the blacktop. When she went home that night, she talked it over with her parents—what she had seen and how it had made her feel.

On Sunday morning, when Nina's family got home from church, they found a welcome basket on their doorstep. Buried under the canned fruits, jams, and household items were two brightly wrapped packages, each of which held five pairs of tights. There was a one-word note with the basket— *Welcome!* —but no return address.

CHAPTER 1
A Reunion of Sorts

Newport Beach, Present Day

I had just sat down at my desk on the first Tuesday in October when Pauline, my assistant, called to tell me I had a visitor who had only given her first name: Maggie. I knew exactly who she meant, and in a vague way, I had been expecting her. I opened the door and we both stood there, not knowing how to address each other. I touched her lightly on her shoulder and asked her to come in. I steered her over to the small round table in my office and offered her a chair. After we both sat, she looked at me, seeming to study my face—searching for traces of my mother, I suspected.

I thought about what I knew of Maggie's life—maybe a bit more than I should. On the surface, I knew that Maggie Stewart had been the lifelong friend of my mother, MG. She had helped nurse MG through the stage 4 cervical cancer that eventually killed her while I was away at boarding school. Beyond this, I learned some things during our last case that I probably shouldn't have. Primarily, I learned that her college friends thought her daughter's father was disgraced professor Peter Sampson while her hometown friends thought it was her high school boyfriend, a decorated pilot. We found out the truth when we compared DNA; it was Peter Sampson.

I hadn't seen Maggie in a long time, and I couldn't conjure an image of a younger version of her in my mind for comparison. Being my mother's age, Maggie was around seventy, and she had let the aging process occur naturally. Her long curly hair was steel gray, her eyes were hazel, and there were deep lines in her face. She had that sinewy look that some older women get when they exercise a lot or do heavy chores on a regular basis.

Looking at her made me feel a bit uncomfortable because her face and body told different stories. Her body looked strong and steady; her face looked as if it had seen a thousand sorrows. Mostly, though, I felt curious. Why was she here?

After a minute or two, she met my eyes, and I asked, "What can I do for you, Maggie?"

She sighed and said, "I guess we have a lot to talk about, but most urgent to me is learning about the body they found buried on your ranch."

This did surprise me. In late summer, I had received an anonymous tip that the body of Sally Garrett had been buried on my family's ranch in the low ranges of the Sierras. Sally had been my mother's college roommate, but she had suddenly disappeared from her apartment near UC Berkeley in 1976. Sally, along with a half dozen other young women, had been manipulated into attending a party that turned out to be what was essentially a gang rape of those same women, including my mother and the woman sitting across from me. Immediately after the party, or even during it, Sally had disappeared and had never been in touch since. The pressure to investigate the rumor of her burial was intense, and an exhaustive search of the property was conducted.

"Yes," I responded, "they did find a body, but dental records conclusively confirm that it was not Sally's."

"The coroner is an old friend, and she told me that it was a young female who died about fifty years ago. What she wouldn't tell me was whether there was evidence that the young woman had been pregnant when she died," Maggie said.

It was my turn to study her face. "Why do you suggest that?"

"If you think about people and relationships in those days as a Venn diagram, your mother and I were in the overlapping area, but we each had separate groups of friends and acquaintances. A large part of your mother's circle was filled with people from wealthy, stable families, and mine was filled with people who were more transient in their jobs and living spaces. Over the years those lines have somewhat dissipated, but not entirely. For example, regardless of what I have accomplished as a teacher and administrator, some peers still see me as the raggedy child I was in elementary school."

She continued, "Anyway, one girl in my circle was Nina Scott. Nina became pregnant during the summer between our junior and senior years, and then in mid-October, when her pregnancy started to show, she disappeared. In the beginning, I figured she was either staying under wraps at home or her parents had sent her away. At the time, our school did not accommodate girls who were pregnant; in fact, as soon as the school would find out, they'd suspend the girls.

"After about two weeks, I went to her house and asked her parents, and they said they thought she had run away with the boy who'd fathered her child. I knew that wasn't true. She wouldn't tell me who the boy was; she only told me he was popular and a football player. All the boys that fit that description were still very much in school, playing football and having active social lives. I told her parents what I knew, stressing that she had not run off with the father. So at that point Nina had been missing for two weeks, which is when they finally told the sheriff. The sheriff's office made a brief attempt to find her, but then they let it go."

Now finished with her part of the story, she looked at me expectantly. After a moment, I took a breath and reluctantly said, "Yes, it appears the girl was pregnant."

I had been told about the pregnancy in confidence by my almost cousin, Alex Boas. Alex was a lieutenant in the Tulare County Sheriff's Office. After telling me that the body was not that of Sally Garrett, he provided no further information. All he would say was that the body had been defiled in a gruesome way, but he wanted to gather more information before he filled me in. Right now, I was glad not to know because I didn't want to have to tell Maggie that her friend had been mutilated.

Instead, I asked a question: "Does Nina have any family living in the area who could give a DNA sample for comparison?"

"Her younger sister, Faith Scott Hobson; she's a librarian in the county and on the verge of retirement."

I called Alex and left a message about the possible identity of the body and who to contact for a DNA comparison. While it seemed like a wild guess, you never knew about life in rural areas; there were always hidden relationships.

Pauline tapped on my door to tell me my next appointment had arrived. I hated to leave Maggie hanging, so I asked her to come over for dinner that night. We made plans to dine at 7 p.m. in my backyard.

▲ ▲ ▲

The next appointment was with a student who had a quick question about an assignment for my poverty seminar. I took care of that and then sat looking out my window at the ocean view. That view had been one of the things that had lured me to my job, and yet I seldom allowed myself the time to look at it. It was too mesmerizing and distracting.

My first summer as a department chair at the Carson Institute of Lifelong Health, just north of Newport Beach on the California coast, was both physically dangerous and emotionally torturous. We had uncovered a treacherous extortion and theft scheme, which had begun in the mid-1970s as payments for pictures from the gang rape party and continued through this summer, when academic theft was uncovered. Stealing other people's work had proven so lucrative that uncovering it had resulted in five known deaths, missing people, and at least three arrests. And it was not over; the trials were still to come, and I had no idea if we would ever find those who were still missing. Searching for Sally's body on my family's ranch was just a single step in the process, but even that small step seems to have generated more havoc.

Both my mother and my biological father had been victims of the scheme. In the process of identifying the extortionist, Carlton Richmond, I learned a lot about my mother's life and the decisions she'd made to keep me safe. Learning about her life included meeting many of her friends, most of whom knew one another from college.

My next-door neighbors, Colette Mason and Abe Rossman, were among the UC Berkeley group who were victimized by Carlton. Their payment to him included his withholding information about their kidnapped infant daughter's whereabouts. As I thought about the reality of having dinner with Maggie, I decided it might be more comfortable to include Abe and Colette, as well as my father. With all of us gathered around the table, we should be able to keep the conversation going. Besides, it would be a kind of tribute to MG, as Maggie and Colette were two of her closest friends.

I called the catering service, which specialized in impromptu gatherings, and made dinner plans for six people—I had already invited my friend Louie Dawes for dinner. Louie and the employees at his cybercrimes detection agency had spent much of the summer focused on finding the identity of the extortionist.

When I first met Louie and he took me on as a client, he told me he never dated clients or the police. When we came to a respite in the case last summer, he asked if we could go beyond our friendship. I said yes, and as a recent widow and widower, we had been proceeding very slowly over the past two months.

▲ ▲ ▲

I left work at five so I could get home, shower, and dress before the caterers arrived at six. I had ordered the Coastal California Most Deluxe Food Bar, which came complete with two servers and consisted solely of ingredients produced in the state. Not only did I enjoy the pretentiousness of the name, but as part owner of a ranch, it appealed to me to eat local, however far the distance might be in such a huge state.

Louie and the caterers both arrived at six, and while the caterers did all the work, I told Louie about Maggie's suspicions that the body found just inside the property line at Canton Moon Ranch was someone she knew. Louie was eager to talk with Maggie about the body. I wondered if he wanted to be involved, given the body was found on my family's land.

The guests started to arrive at seven. Colette, a former professor of nursing, and Abe, a retired adolescent psychiatrist, got there first because all they had to do was walk through a door in the wall that separated our properties. They had aged more gently than Maggie. Colette had long white-gray hair that she kept piled on top of her head. She had an array of beautiful combs that she used to secure it; usually they matched her flowing and vibrant gowns. Abe had a collection of retro Hawaiian shirts, complete with coconut shell buttons, that he wore on a rotating basis. He wore his thick gray hair long as well. Together they looked quite regal.

My father, followed a few minutes later by Maggie, came through the gate on the street side of the yard. I had only recently been introduced to my father, one of the positive outcomes of the extortion case. He was a handsome man, and I actually resembled him quite a bit. We both had blue eyes and silly grins, and we were both tall and athletic looking. One difference, though, was that he was tan, while I still had my East Coast pale. We first met when I was a child and then he was going by the name Jackson Redman, but his real name was John Redman Summit. After the reveal, I had started referring to him as Jackson/John, but my son, Will, quickly put an end to that, dubbing him JJ.

As the boomers hadn't seen one another in an exceptionally long time, there were hugs all around, and the conversation sparked right away. Louie and I were superfluous, and that was OK, as we had forgotten to discuss the choice of music. Louie and Will were determined to bring me up to date with current musicians, and Louie had refused to let me play oldies during dinner. I reluctantly agreed to country as long as he mixed in Willie Nelson. It really didn't matter, though, because the guests didn't seem to be paying any attention.

At 7:30, the caterer told me it was time to start serving the meal. I looked at the food that was set out for us, and it was pretty deluxe. Each dish had a card that listed the ingredients and where they came from within the state. The protein options were various seafood and legume dishes, and there were bountiful salads and a fruit display. Dessert included pecan and peach pies with vanilla bean ice cream. Even the selection of beer and wine was from California. We eventually convinced our guests to serve themselves and come to the table. As I'd expected, after the guests had their drinks, the first action was a salute to my mother by each person there. In their pre-dinner conversation, they had agreed to tell a funny MG story, and when it was time, they each tried to outdo one another as we went around the table. It was charming and a bit naughty at times, but it was enough to make me briefly reevaluate my beliefs about boomers. Louie was laughing loudly along with the others.

I didn't have to worry about any stiffness or awkwardness. Before I knew it, it was time for dessert and coffee and then it was last call on drinks. Colette could see that I was fading, so she asked discreetly if she could move the party to her house. I gave her a grateful yes, and within five minutes the boomers had gone through the back wall, and I could hear Crosby, Stills, Nash, and Young's version of "Woodstock" and smell pot. Louie and I sat back down at the table and looked at each other.

"Do you think they liked the country music?" I asked. He rolled his eyes at me.

"Did you learn anything new about the case?" he asked. I shook my head no.

Then I added, "But I did feel like I had a boomer cultural experience." I didn't add that I'd learned a bit of generational humility.

▲ ▲ ▲

It was a beautiful fall evening and Louie and I had planned to spend it outdoors, but there was so much noise coming from Colette and Abe's house that we gave up and went upstairs to my home office. Even while we were in a professional relationship over the summer, it had not escaped me that Louie had many positive attributes. But I had stayed true to my word that I would not think of him as dating material. In fact, when he told me he wanted to see if we could be more than friends, I was genuinely surprised and needed time to get used to the idea.

My husband, William, died three years ago from colon cancer. His death sent my relationship with my son, Will, into a downward spin. Will had depended on his father to be his rock, and when he died, Will didn't want a substitute. He wanted to make his own decisions and took his independence to extremes, possibly to test me. That relationship was slowly getting back on track.

I tried to suppress it, but I let out a big yawn. Louie gave me a pretend offended look, then pulled me up and gave me a long hug and a short kiss. That is where we are. It was superficially comfortable, but looming overhead was the "more than friends" component. I hadn't dated since my husband died, and Louie had not been in a meaningful relationship since his wife died. I think we both felt a heavy dose of approach-avoidance anxiety. We had a strong friendship and definitely found each other attractive, but I wasn't sure it was worth another source of disruption in my new life.

Louie said good night, and we made plans to talk the next day. I forced myself off the couch and headed toward my room. I was exhausted both mentally and physically, and I fell asleep with my clothes still on. My last thought was about the body and the strong possibility that it was Maggie's friend Nina. Would I be dragged into a complicated investigation? Would I see and learn things I'd rather not know?

CHAPTER 2
More About Nina

Wednesday morning, I had my graduate seminar on child poverty from 9 to 11:45 a.m. I enjoyed the seminar, as it was basically the only time I got to engage in professor-speak, meaning I could expound on almost anything, including things I knew little about, for an indeterminate amount of time. Because it was a seminar, however, I tried to keep my own talking to no more than five minutes at a time. Monica Moreno was serving as my graduate assistant, and we walked back to the office while discussing her dissertation proposal. I was trying to assure her she was ready to defend her proposal, but her four years of collaborating with my deceased colleague, Peter Sampson, had left her with a very low reservoir of self-esteem. I told her that I knew it was hard, but she had to trust me that I knew what I was talking about and that she was ready.

It was in the middle of this discussion that I walked into my suite and saw Maggie and Pauline laying out a small lunch buffet in the conference room. Pauline had texted me during class that Maggie had dropped by, and I suggested that she use my credit card to order enough lunch to feed whoever was around. Teaching always makes me hungry.

About ten people had been around, so we all filled our plates and sat down to talk. I liked these informal chats, as they helped me get a sense of issues going on in the department. I introduced our guest to everyone and told them she had been a lifelong friend of my mother. They were all too polite to ask any of the questions I would have wanted to ask, so we kept the conversation light throughout the meal.

▲ ▲ ▲

After we cleaned up the conference room, Maggie came back to my office with me. We sat down at the small table again, and she started talking right away.

"I want to apologize for just showing up yesterday and for being so single minded. I didn't know what you would be like because you've been away for over thirty years. I didn't know if you would remember me or care about my need to understand what happened to Nina. Then you gave such a lovely dinner for me and your mothers' friends. I ended up spending the night at Colette's, but when I woke up this morning, I was drenched in sweat and guilt. I guess the guilt comes from forgetting about searching for Nina for so many years." She finally looked up at me and took a breath, giving me a chance to talk if I did it quickly.

"Maggie, I know how you cared for my mother and how close you were to each other. I consider you family, and I will help you in any way I can. Maybe you can go back over Nina's story and tell me about it in more detail?"

An odd look passed quickly across her face. I thought she was going to dispute my picture of her friendship with MG, but she just continued her story instead.

"I met Nina in about the third grade; actually, it was the summer before. At the time, my dad was overseeing the picking crew on one of your grandfather's peach orchards in the west side of the county. Nina's parents had just moved the family to the area, and they were part of the group picking the peaches. To save money and because they had no family nearby, Nina and her little sister, Faith, came to the orchard with their parents, and they spent the day playing in the mud and the small pools of irrigation water. I remember they would make boats and houses of leaves, twigs, and mud. I couldn't believe the fun they were having without there being any real toys to play with.

"I met Nina and Faith one day when I went to the orchard with my dad. I had to go for my back-to-school physical in the afternoon. At that time, my mother was working full-time as a nursing assistant in what used to be called a convalescent hospital, and she couldn't leave to take me. Usually, I would have stayed with my grandmother, but she didn't have a driver's license, so she couldn't take me either.

"I was walking through the orchard with my dad, and I saw these girls having so much fun that I begged him to let me play with them. He stopped, got down on one knee, and looked me in the eyes. 'Maggie, these people are trying to earn a living. If they spend time looking after you, it could mean they don't make enough money this week to buy food or pay their rent.'

"I knew the seriousness of this because although we always had enough money for food, there was rarely money for luxuries like ice cream or soda pop. Looking down at my feet, I saw one of those luxuries, new white canvas shoes, and I said, 'What if I promise to stay clean and just watch them and not make any noise?' He said he would ask their mom and dad if I could stay for a half hour.

"The parents said it was OK but that they could not slow down from their picking to watch me. My dad then walked me over to the girls and asked if I could watch them play for a little while. He told them I couldn't get muddy because I had to go to the doctor later. They said OK, and he brought over a wooden box for me to sit on. The box was used to hold the picked peaches, so it was made of rough splintered wood. Before he left, he reached in his pocket and pulled out two pieces of penny candy for each of us. It was like the greatest gift to the girls, and they ran over to their parents and gave them each a piece. When they got back, I gave them mine, telling them I didn't like that kind of candy.

"And that is how it started. Every day I would beg to go to the orchard with him, and every day he said no. After a week or so, he told me that my mom said it would be OK to ask the family over for a cookout on the weekend so I could see them. After that, the girls would come over most weekends to play while their parents went grocery shopping.

"At the time, the Scott family followed the crops to make a living. People called them migrant workers, while others called them white trash and much worse things. My family had come to California in the mid-1940s and had picked fruit too. By the mid-fifties, they had managed to get a leg up and find full-time jobs. But social class in rural California was very visible, and everyone knew the order of things: landowners, professionals, other white-collar workers, manual workers, and at the bottom, fruit pickers.

"That fall I looked for Nina every day in school until my dad found out that they had traveled to Oregon to pick pears and would be back in late September. When Nina got back, she was placed in the same class as me; MG was in the other class with most of the kids from wealthier families. I found out right away how smart Nina was, and instead of me explaining assignments to her, she explained them to me—especially when it came to arithmetic.

"Over the years I bounced between MG and Nina and my other friends. As we grew older, MG was invited to parties and on weekend trips, and I spent most of my weekend time with my own circle of friends. MG went on elaborate summer vacations, and I had a weekend at Pismo Beach and a week of church summer camp. When we got to high school, teachers assigned us to groups by ability, so I was usually in classes with both MG and Nina. Nina had the best grades of all of us, while taking the hardest set of classes.

"The summer before our senior year, Nina took a job at a nursery, and she mostly worked as a cashier inside the building with the indoor plants. She was saving money for college; she and I had decided we wanted to go to San José State University. We would be near the beach, which was just over the hill in Santa Cruz, and not far from San Francisco, but we wouldn't have the pressure of earning top grades on a University of California campus. We both intended to major in education and see where it would take us.

"MG had taken a study abroad trip to Europe with two of her friends that summer, so I had more time to spend with Nina. At first we had fun together, but after about a month Nina became 'unavailable.' She admitted she was dating someone, but she wouldn't tell me who. She said he was a football player and that he loved her.

"When our summer jobs ended, we went back to school, and it looked to me like her body was changing. She was in all my classes except electives and physical education. At the beginning of October, I heard girls gossiping about Nina—that she must be pregnant because her boobs were huge. Another girl reported seeing her throwing up in the bathroom. And that was it, the rumor was everywhere, and I was sure it had gotten back to her. In the classes we shared, people giggled when she walked by, and they pointed her out to others.

"One evening, I borrowed my mother's car and went to see Nina at home. I took her out for a milkshake. She stayed in the car while I went up and ordered, and we took off right after I paid for them, but even within that short time, people had rapped on her window and mockingly asked how she was feeling. We drove out to the orchard that my father supervised. At that point we were living rent-free in the house that had been built on the land. As soon as we got there, she burst out crying and admitted that she had not seen a doctor, but she hadn't had a period since early July. The one person I knew who would help her was MG's mother, but she said she was too embarrassed to talk to her, afraid she would be disappointed.

"Nina was beautiful as well as intelligent; when she was with people she knew, she was also funny. She had curly blond hair and an angelic face. She was petite, so the changes in her body were easy to see. I could tell that the strain was breaking her down. She confided that the father of her child was now dating one of the girls who had gone on the European trip, and she suspected she had been nothing more than a summer replacement. In all her pain, she refused to give me any names. I remember hoping she wasn't the replacement for MG, but I doubted it, because MG rarely dated. She thought the boys in our class were immature.

"I begged her for over an hour to let me help her come up with a plan to continue her life, but she refused. Eventually, although it broke my heart, I took her back to her house and dropped her off. I never saw her again. That was Saturday, October 14, 1967, at around ten thirty p.m."

"What did you do to follow up?" I asked.

"I tried to talk with MG about it, but she refused to say anything. I thought she might know something—and she never denied that she did—but she wouldn't discuss it. However, as time went on, she seemed to distance herself from everyone, spending time on her art projects and preparing her art portfolio for her applications to college.

"I then tried the next best thing: I went to your aunt Beatrice. Beatrice was the same age as Nina's younger sister, Faith, and they were close friends. Beatrice never seemed to have any conflicts about social class, and she did what she wanted to do. Apparently Beatrice and Faith had overheard girls gossiping about Nina in their gym class. Beatrice said Faith started to cry, but she quickly pulled her away from the girls and into the showers. By the time they had showered, the gossipers had moved on. Beatrice told Faith she absolutely could not cry at school because that would start a feeding frenzy on her. She kept Faith close to her until things started to die down and gossip drifted to the next person. Faith did confirm that Nina was dating someone with a nice car, but he never came into the house, and they had stopped dating when school started back up.

"Beatrice's next idea was to sneak a look at MG's journal. MG was on a Saturday senior trip, I think visiting a college, so Beatrice used the time to sneak a quick read. She wrote down a sentence she thought might be about Nina, which was along the lines of, 'Something horrible has happened, but I have to let it go. I won't be writing about it, but I will say that I didn't know my classmates at all.' I'm not certain, but maybe she wrote more about it in her journals as she was dying? The rest you know."

Her comment about the journals made me pause. Was she fishing for information about their content? Instead of asking Maggie what she meant, I said, "I can see how you might think the body is Nina's—but maybe you pray that it isn't. During the summer, we found all of MG's journals, and we put them together chronologically. We skimmed some journals from her college years, but I have been too overwhelmed by all the new information I have about MG to read them all. We have the journals she wrote before she died, but no one has opened them. I suppose they belong to me and it's my responsibility to read them, but I don't know how quickly I can do it. They bring up so many emotional issues for me."

Maggie said, "I could read them for you."

I thought about Maggie's devotion to MG—a devotion MG may not have deserved. What if MG had written something demeaning about Maggie? Truth was, I didn't trust MG completely to be kind. But I also had a sense Maggie was overstepping the bounds of our relationship.

"No, I'll have them sent to me, and either Louie or I will read them first. Louie can do it with an informed yet uninvolved eye, and he can indicate if passages might be too painful for me or Aunt Beatrice."

Something had been troubling me as I listened to the story, and I had to ask about it: "Maggie, why did you stay and take care of MG, given that she refused to talk with you about Nina?"

"Please realize this is something I asked myself as well. In fact, MG asked me too. She didn't refer to Nina specifically but to how she treated me in general. During certain periods in our lives, it did feel like MG had abandoned me. She got to do amazing things, and she never invited me to join her. I am thankful for my other friends, who opened their arms to me and who treated me as their equal. By the end of her life, MG really didn't have anyone close enough to just stop what they were doing and care for her. I know that both Jackson and Colette would have stepped in to help, but she didn't want them to know about her illness; I had to tell them after she had passed.

"All I can say is that I had a bond with your mother, which started in first grade, when she pulled me away from two of her friends who were bullying me. And she continued to stand up for me for the rest of my school years and I was never bothered again.

"She never did anything intentionally to hurt me. It's just that everyone wanted to be her friend. She never felt the shame of exclusion, so she didn't know what it felt like. Imagine a life where you are never picked last and you always have people who want to sit by you. Imagine a life where you are good enough at everything, so you never feel inadequate. That was MG's life experience, and she let herself enjoy it in high school. After Nina's disappearance, she turned her back on the popular kids, and for the rest of her time, she kept a tight circle of friends she cared about. I was part of that circle."

I knew there would be more questions, but we were finished for now.

I made it through the rest of the day—meeting with students and faculty, signing papers, and trying to make sense of faculty recommendations for the redesign of our department. I left for home with a feeling of heaviness pulling at me. I was worried that my image of my mother could be tarnished or even shattered. I also worried that Nina could quickly turn into another soul that I grieved for.

▲ ▲ ▲

I called Colette on my way home from work to ask if she could meet me in my backyard. I walked through the house to the kitchen, poured two glasses of white wine, and walked onto the patio. Just as I did, I heard Colette's knock on the back door. Sort of spooky, I thought.

I opened the door for Colette, and we walked over to the table with the wine glasses and sat down. I didn't know where to start, so I chatted with her about the impromptu get-together she had had at her house after dinner last night. She said that she enjoyed catching up with everyone, and even though they were all retired, they each led very involved lives.

She said, "I know people think that boomers were all talk with no sustained action. Some people think we are phonies with a false sense of pride in a lifestyle that ultimately did more harm than good. I admit that both good and bad came from our generation, but I see examples of people who are still living value-driven lives, and they will continue to promote those values until they die."

I couldn't help but think she meant me in the group of boomer critics, seeing as how I had basically said this exact thing to friends for the past twenty years or so. I needed to change the subject, so I asked her if Maggie had told her about her missing friend from high school.

"Yes, she told me about Nina's disappearance and the fact that there is now a body that could possibly be hers." She studied my face intently and said, "To answer your silent question, you want to know if I think MG could have been involved. My answer to that is yes. As part of MG's legacy, I do think it is our responsibility to understand what happened and try to make it right."

I gasped, never expecting to hear this response. "Colette, you can't possibly think my mother would kill someone."

"I don't think she would do the actual killing or even condone it. If MG were involved, I suspect that she was possibly holding on to information that could help solve it. One evening, your mother's women friends were gathered at her apartment and Sally, her roommate, wanted to play truth or dare. Your mother's dare was to tell us her worst secret. She was drunk enough to say something like, 'I helped hurt someone.' That was all she would say, but I got the impression she didn't mean 'hurt' in an emotional way."

She quickly drank the rest of her wine and said, "I can see you need to think about this. I will leave you be." And then she left.

Chapter 3
Moral or Personal Dilemma?

I couldn't sleep that night. Eventually, around midnight, I grabbed a bottle of wine, went outside to the patio, and stretched out on the lounge chair. This is what I knew: A body was found on the ranch, the body may belong to Nina, the fetus may belong to Nina and some unknown football player, and my mother and her former friends may be involved. Outside that general description of the situation, my mother may have left clues in her final journal entries. Opposing this general description was my personal situation: I did not want to read the journals, I did not want anyone else to read the journals, and I wanted to protect my mother.

Now that the sheriff's office was involved, the case would move along on its own. People would be interviewed, and because it was common knowledge that my mother kept journals, the notebooks might be subpoenaed and then I would lose all control over sharing the content. It should be fairly easy to identify the body, but doing DNA analysis might be harder for the fetus. If there was viable blood from the mother, they might be able to identify the fetal DNA if the fetus was far enough along from the mother's blood sample. Or they might be able to use the skeletal remains of the fetus to analyze DNA. It all hinged on the quality and viability of the samples.

At the core of my angst was my anger with my mother. Why had she kept so many secrets? Did she realize those secrets would float to the top and blow up in my face? Was she afraid of her secrets coming out, and if so, why? I realized that my mother's later secrets were meant to protect me and keep me away from her enemies. What was her motivation to have secrets around Nina?

In the end, I would just keep reassessing the situation and see if I needed to jump in. I was comforted by the fact that only Louie knew the exact location of the journals, and it would take a while for people to figure that out. I still had issues from the date rape case to investigate and resolve. I didn't want to start something new.

The morning sun woke me. I tried to get up out of the lounge chair but felt something heavy weighing me down. I gave myself a few moments to wake up fully and then I looked around. Sometime in the night, Colette had placed a thick hand-knitted blanket over me. I knew it was her because I recognized the blanket from her patio. Either she was a light sleeper or I was a loud snorer. Maybe both.

▲ ▲ ▲

I made it through until Friday with no added information popping up, and I was grateful for the time to gain a bit of distance from the decisions I knew I would have to make.

I was spending my time analyzing the preliminary data from the study of educational interventions among poor preschool children. To keep continuous funding of one's research, investigators have to write their next grants while in the middle of current projects. It's a bit tricky, and I didn't enjoy working this way. Around midway in a study, I would peek at early results and see how the study was doing. In this case, I was comparing the pre-intervention data to the data collected one year into the intervention to see if children had improved across any of the three study groups compared to the control group. In the full study design, we would collect data at three years, and findings at one year may not be the same as at three years. So, we called it preliminary findings and hoped for the best.

The direct line in my office rang. This didn't happen very often—friends called my cell, and most work-related calls went through Pauline. Curious, I answered the phone. It was Alex Boas, from the sheriff's office, on a line I had not seen before. After catching up, he told me that something involving the ranch had come up and asked if I was free to talk. It occurred to me again that I was running out of time to make my decisions, but I said, "Of course. I am in my office alone, so could I put you on speaker?" He gave his OK to do so.

"First, I appreciate your suggestion about the DNA comparison. We drove the samples up to the Fresno Regional Office of the Bureau of Forensic Services. In confidence, the body was wrapped in a very particular way. On the outside was a layer of heavy black plastic. Inside that was a sheet, and then the body. I hate to tell you this detail, but the fetus had been cut from the womb and placed in a small white crocheted bag lined with foil. The bag was in the mother's right hand, and a sealed envelope was in her left hand. We couldn't read whatever was in the envelope because they took it to the forensics lab. We will learn what it says eventually, after it has been processed."

I pictured the crocheted bag in my mind. I recalled seeing one among my mother's high school home economics assignments. The bag was roughly four by three inches, and MG's was red with green trim—maybe she'd meant for it to hold a Christmas present? I had asked Beatrice about it, and she said the project had been mandatory for the home economics class for years. She also remembered that at the time, older women in crafts groups made them to put stocking stuffers in. Was the bag meant to hold the dead girl's last present? Was it meant to be a present to her or from her?

"Comparing DNA from the body with DNA from the sister, Faith, showed a match. We know this is the body of Nina Scott. Analyzing the DNA from the fetus will take longer to do if it is even possible at this point. This is a verification of identity that leaves us with questions involving your mom. Things got stranger, however, when we extended our cadaver search into the field across the street from your ranch. I know this is going to hurt, but we found two more bodies of teenage girls. The reason I gave you details on the first body's wrappings is because the other two girls were preserved in the exact same way, with a fetus in one hand and an envelope in the other.

"I am calling to see if you have any other thoughts on who the women might be. To our knowledge, there were no more missing pregnant girls in the two years before or after Nina's disappearance at Lower Sierra High School."

"I'm sure you are thinking you need a broader timeline or a broader geographic search," I said.

"Correct."

"Three months ago, while working on the Carlton Richmond case, I went through MG's high school files and saw that she was invited to join some sort of intra-county club for daughters of farmers at the end of her junior year. I thought at the time it was strange because my mother was not much of a joiner, and it seemed so random. You probably know from Carlos and Beatrice that MG's passion was her art, and later on, it was politics, and she rallied on behalf of farm workers. So, it seemed so out of character to join what she would later think of as the oppressors. I guess what I'm saying is maybe look for disappearances across the county within that same period. The other thing I would suggest is that you bring Maggie Stewart in to help you. She knew my mother better than anyone."

"Those are great suggestions," Alex noted, "and I will follow through. I was also wondering if you had plans to come home anytime soon."

"What do you mean by soon?" I asked.

"Actually, I was thinking tomorrow, since it's Saturday."

"OK, I can do that."

As I was saying yes to Alex, the rest of my being was shouting no. The case from the summer had drained me in every way and had kept me from doing my academic work. On the other hand, the body was found on family land, and my mother may have had a role in Nina's disappearance and murder. I needed to know what happened no matter what, and this need far outweighed my need for safety and a peaceful life. And so, I jumped in.

I figured that if I was making the drive to the ranch tomorrow I should leave the office by six, so I could pack. I called Louie before I left and asked if he wanted to go with me; he said he did and told me he would pick me up at seven the following morning. As an afterthought, I asked him to bring the journals my mother wrote during her bout with cancer but to hide them from me until after I had met with Alex. I wanted to deny knowing where they were until I read them myself.

CHAPTER 4
The Process Begins

We drove directly to the Porterville substation of the Tulare County Sheriff's Office on Saturday morning, and we found Lieutenant Alex Boas waiting for us. It was a bit early, but he suggested we talk over lunch so we would have a bit of privacy. I remembered Alex from visits with my grandparents before I left for boarding school in Baltimore. My mom and my grandparents had all died while I was away at school, so I hadn't seen him much since. I remembered him as a tall gangly boy who was always showing off on his bicycle or skateboard. Now that my aunt Beatrice was living at the ranch, there was a possibility that a relationship might bloom between her and his father, Carlos. If the two married, Alex would be my cousin—my first and only cousin. I liked the thought of that, and I vowed not to be snarky with him.

He asked for my preference for food, and I said Mexican with great enthusiasm, so he took us to a small authentic-looking place north of town. Alex was still on duty, but Louie and I had just been in the truck for three and a half hours, so we ordered beers, promising we would only have one, then switch to iced tea. Alex rolled his eyes to that and said, "Hey, cuz, it's been a long time! I hope you decide to hang out at the ranch; it has been so deserted and lonely for my dad."

"What do you mean? You have other cousins in the area," I bantered back.

"Yeah, but none as kick-ass as you—and I can honestly say you are the only one who gets involved in murder cases," he teased. Then he looked at Louie and said, "I'm not sure how you are related to Phoebe."

I explained that Louie was on retainer by MG's company, MoonShots, to conduct any investigation that might involve her interests and that the service had been incredibly helpful to the police last summer. I also told him that Louie's company could supply any needed assistance if Alex wanted it. Then Louie told him about his company and their capabilities, one of which was tracking down people who didn't want to be found. He added that he had references from police officers he could provide.

That was enough information to win Alex over and treat Louie as a colleague. He began, "I don't know if it is luck or not, but you've given me three good tips already—the DNA match with Faith Scott, talking with Maggie Stewart, and looking at other county high schools in the late sixties. You know we found two more bodies close to your ranch. But in addition to Nina, there were five missing girls in Tulare County: one from Lindsay, one from Woodlake, one from Exeter, and two from Porterville, all from the 1967–68 school year. They were not exactly clustered, but they almost form a line on the east side of the county, close to the mountains. The similarity should have been noticed at the time. Of course, back then we had no computerized systems, but I don't think that was the problem. All the missing girls were from low-income families, all were white, and all were above-average students.

"You haven't been around much lately, but the 2023 Tulare County poverty rate was about 40 percent higher than that of the state and the country; the rate of people with a college degree is less than half that of the state and country. Poverty and environmental hazards cause low health and social well-being outcomes. Sometimes I don't even see the point of attacking crime rates without attacking poverty rates at the same time."

"I sense a political statement coming," I said.

"Well, look at Carlos. He taught all of us to see the bigger picture, whether it be in supplying food or educating children or fighting crime," he said. "Anyway, it would be great if you could both provide access to resources I don't have and skills my team doesn't have. Phoebe, you can help by giving me a better perspective on your mother and her friends. Louie, you can help by tracking down living relatives of the missing girls. That way we can try to match DNA to the names of the girls we have identified. Then we can build profiles of each girl and possibly identify their killers.

"We were able to find the mother of one of the girls from Porterville—she's in her nineties now. She told me that her daughter was the second girl to become pregnant in fall 1967 at Porterville High School. Her daughter, Amy, knew the other girl; they were both juniors, and after she went missing, Amy became very anxious and was convinced someone was watching her. They decided, as a family, to drive their daughter to an aunt's house in New Mexico."

Alex continued with his story. "Amy had the baby in New Mexico, then changed her and the baby's names to her mother's birth name, which was White. Then she waited a year and moved back to town, where she lived with her maternal grandparents, who helped with the baby while she attained her GED then took classes at Porterville Community College. Eventually, she earned a nursing degree and was able to work and support her child; years later, she married and had two more kids. So, we know we can cut the list by one, and I hope we can locate some of the others. The question is, would Amy have been safe if she hadn't gone into hiding?"

Louie said, "In order to see if there's a connection, we first need to identify those two other bodies."

Alex replied, "That's right. We don't have any samples to compare DNA against, which is why we could use your help in tracking down any known family members." He paused for a moment, then said, "I am a bit worried about tracking down siblings. If you have always been on the bottom rung of the social ladder, you want to get away. Then you have a sister who disappears, and you have a double stigma. You are poor and you have a pregnant, unmarried sister. People want to be normal, right? It's easier to be seen as normal when people are not comparing you to their image of the past. For me, it has always been fighting the stereotypical image of a Latino, but Carlos never let me dwell on it or use it as an excuse. I didn't like it at the time, but now I'm glad."

We sat for a while. I was thinking about all the obstacles kids can face in reaching adulthood and the importance of raising resilient kids, like we want to raise resilient crops. After a moment, Alex said he needed to get back to the station, so could we summarize where we were? Louie agreed to run the names of the girls identified as possibly missing and get back to Alex. Alex promised to update us when possible. I promised to help interview family members and friends of the missing girls.

▲ ▲ ▲

When we got to the ranch, everyone was waiting for us, and there was a spread of sandwiches, salads, and cookies. Because Carlos believed in sharing the food grown on the ranch, he supplied lunch each day to anyone who was around and wanted to join in. Sometimes people brought their kids, and they swam in the pool. Sometimes he would bring his agriculture students from Porterville College who were there on a field trip. He had a full-time cook who prepared lunch, cleaned up, and occasionally started dinner. Dinner was family time, but family was broadly defined. I liked this about Carlos, as I am sure my aunt Beatrice did. My mother was raised this way as well, and so living on the commune was an easy transition for her.

After we had our second lunch and swapped stories, Carlos and Louie rode horses out to where they had found the bodies. Will was on a hiking and camping trip with JJ, his newly identified grandfather. After a chat with Beatrice, I took my mother's last journals up to my room to read. I had no idea what to expect.

There were three journals MG wrote while she was being treated for cancer. It looked like the front inside cover, carried through to the back if needed, of each journal was a list of dates, doctors' visits, and her functional abilities. I had been sent to live with Aunt Beatrice in June, and the cancer care had started right afterward. She lived until the following January. A case summary was included in the beginning of each journal as well, so that her progress could be tracked. Diving in, I started with the opening summary:

> *I hadn't had a Pap test in over five years, I don't know why I put it off. Maybe I thought I was so healthy from all the herbal teas I consumed that I would stay safe. One day, I had heavy bleeding, but I knew it was not from my period. The bleeding continued on and off for a couple of weeks and then the bloating and cramping started. I grew so weak I couldn't drive to work each*

day, so I made an appointment with an OB-GYN in Eureka. She suspected right away from the pelvic exam that I had cancer. The bottom line was I needed to have surgery to find out the extent of disease: was it contained in my cervix, or had it spread to my uterus, fallopian tubes, and beyond? The next questions were where to have the surgery and where to recuperate? After discussion, we decided I would have the surgery at a cancer center in Fresno and if the results were horrible, I would be sent down to the ranch in an ambulance for my convalescence. If the surgery turned out to be less extensive, I would travel by car to the ranch. I knew my mother would never give up the caretaking role. Then, the hardest decision of all, what should I do with Phoebe? I didn't want her to experience my decline, and I didn't want to lie to her. Hoping someday she would understand and not judge me too harshly, I sent her to live with Beatrice on weekends and vacations and attend a boarding school during the school year. I believed the school that would challenge her to grow. Phoebe is gone, and my surgery is tomorrow. I am in the hospital to prepare for a 6 a.m. start. I feel my heart is too burdened to pray for my own well-being, so I pray for the medical team and what they have to do.

This description filled in holes for me. It bothered me that MG felt she needed to wait to start any treatment until I had left town. I couldn't get through that never-ending flow of what-ifs. I appreciated that Alex had not asked for the journals outright. I decided to read ten or so pages a day so I could digest them, ending with one more entry for the day:

I am ten days out from surgery, and starting today, I am making myself continue to write. The surgery showed stage 4 disease, meaning the cancer had spread outside the pelvic area. In my case, it had spread up to the edges of my bladder but not to my lungs or bones. My surgery turned out to be an abdominal radical hysterectomy with a little extra tissue removal. It was uncomfortable, but I was able to go home to the ranch by car. There are treatments I could try, but from my readings it was clear that any success would serve only to add weeks or months to my life. Through that brief extension I would be experiencing the effects of chemotherapy and/or radiation therapy, which were my treatment options. I have chosen not to have any curative therapies; I will stick with palliative care because I understand I will lose the battle in the end, and I want to have a few good months to address my business and personal issues.

Maggie is here with me, even after the pain and trauma I have caused over the course of our lives. I would like to be able to say it was all inadvertent, but I can't make that claim. I am curious to know if I am brave enough at the end of my life to be honest about how I have treated her and why I have done so. Maggie appears to be a good person. She will jump into any battle to protect the underdog or to support a principle. So many times growing up my mother would praise Maggie's strength or character. Maggie is an angel, and she is proving that by being here with me. I am not, nor have I ever been, an angel. Being a good person has always been a struggle for me, and I have had to fight against myself to do the right things, to try to act more like Maggie. I have found that I do better when I am out of sight and just doing my art, then I am not faced with day-to-day interactions that tax me to stay upright in my beliefs. Maggie can be herself no matter who is around her.

She is here every day between four and seven. She gives my mother a respite so that she can cook and do other chores. She sits quietly by my bed and reads. If I feel like talking, we talk; if I feel like looking out the window, she moves me over. She doesn't ask for anything in return, just like my mother. When I went through my teenage rebellion phase, maybe I was rebelling against Maggie as much as I was against my parents. I will think more about that.

As I reached the end of the passage, I was thankful I had said no to Maggie's offer to help read the entries. Somehow, my mother's decision to die without trying treatment was too personal. I didn't want Maggie to see that vulnerability in our lives. Also, reading through the lines, MG was expressing that Maggie was somehow more connected with her mother, or maybe she was more the kind of person her mother admired.

Then I thought about MG's comment that Maggie "appears to be a good person." Was she implying that maybe Maggie was not genuine in her actions? What would that be like for MG to have someone acting as graciously as Maggie while wondering if that behavior was real or contrived? Or was it that Maggie knew MG so well that she knew her darkest parts? Somehow, the Maggie-MG relationship was off-kilter, but I didn't know how or why.

I didn't know whether I should feel grateful to Maggie or wary about her motivations. All I could do was keep an open mind for now.

I heard a lot of noise downstairs and realized that I needed to get outside my head. I ran down the stairs to see what was happening.

▲ ▲ ▲

The hubbub downstairs was because Will and JJ had gotten home from their overnight camping trip and were talking about fishing the North Fork of the Tule River around dawn. They had brought home a half dozen sizable trout and were discussing how to cook them with Louie and Carlos and if there was enough to feed everyone with Beatrice. They decided to cook the trout on the grill with lemon and spices. At the last minute, they put chicken thighs on the grill to round things out. This turned out to be a great idea because not only were all the men big eaters, but Alex dropped by for a "taste." It turned into a raucous evening, with everyone telling their fish stories and nobody wanting to be outdone. I don't know what got into him, but Louie invited everyone out on his boat next Sunday, and we planned to grill fish at my place (with a backup plan in place, I thought, but didn't say out loud). Everyone would come down Saturday night and stay with me or JJ and then set off early Sunday morning.

Later on, I saw Louie and Alex having a serious talk, probably about police business. After Alex said good night, Louie and I took our almost routine evening walk. Louie began by telling me about the list of names Alex had given him. Up to this point, in addition to Nina, five other girls had been identified as missing, but one of them, Amy, was found to be alive. So we had four girls to account for and two bodies to identify. It made me wonder if Alex had been thorough in our search for the girls and if there were more out there. Louie suggested we search for the four and then maybe go back and look for additional names.

We walked for a bit in silence and then he said, "Maggie told Alex about the journals, and he asked me in a rather offhand cop way if they were accessible. I told him I wasn't sure because they were being used in the Carlton Richmond case, and he seemed to accept that for now."

"I did start reading the first cancer volume, and as I suspected, Maggie cannot read them for us," I said. "MG seemed to have a very conflicted attachment to Maggie, as one might with a sister you believe your parents love more than you—or maybe respect more than you would be closer to the feeling. I think MG is working up to making some confessions about times she let friends or family down in some way. I did learn that MG chose palliative rather than curative care so that she might be more comfortable in the time she had left."

After we walked about a mile down the path, we turned back toward the house. Louie took my hand, and we discussed my mother's decision and what we might do in her situation.

▲ ▲ ▲

I woke up around five the next morning and decided to read more of the first journal before going down to breakfast.

MG wrote that news of her recuperation at the ranch was out, and people began stopping by to leave food, flowers, and notes. She had been able to find a local oncologist who stopped by once a week to see her and to adjust her medicine if needed. Amazingly, he, Dr. Daniel Roan, was a couple of years ahead of her in high school and had also gone to Berkeley. After college, he headed off to UC Davis for medical school. Knowing the poor state of cancer care in the area, he came back to Porterville after his training to practice. As the weeks following MG's surgery passed, he scheduled her to be his last patient of the day and often stayed for a while to talk with her.

About midway through the journal, she went back to the theme of mistakes she had made in her life:

> *Often Maggie and I talk about the people we have known throughout our lives. It reminds me that two of the three horrible decisions I have made in my life involve Maggie, and I can't understand how she can treat me with such kindness. Sometimes I long for her to not come, to just let me slip away, but I could never tell her that. Sometimes I wonder if she is waiting for me to let something slip about what happened to Nina. I pray I never do.*
>
> *When I went abroad the summer before my senior year, we had get-togethers with other schools who were studying in the same country. Sometimes we had trips to experience regional foods or attend a museum. Once we took a weekend trip to a beach in Spain, and we divided up the roommates so that six of us, three from each school, stayed in one large room. One of the roommates from the other school was an attractive blond girl who was physically big, loud, and domineering. Also, she was the president of the Intra-County Farm Group I had been invited to join. The entire weekend she hounded me about getting involved until finally she wore me down and I agreed to go to their first meeting.*
>
> *I admit now that I was scared of her because no one had ever talked to me in such a rough way. I guess I was flattered, too, because it seemed I was important to her agenda. The other two girls from my school who were sharing the room were also invited to join, so at least I would already know people.*
>
> *Upon reflection, I think there were a few reasons why I didn't*

want to go. Most importantly, I wanted to focus my attention on building my art portfolio for college applications. Not only was that important to my future, but it was what I enjoyed most. But even if that were not true, I didn't feel comfortable being around that clique of girls. I didn't want to try to live up to their expectations.

The first meeting was in early September and then they were once a month after that. At the first meeting we went over the rules, one of which was secrecy, then we discussed the farm-based beauty pageants coming up throughout the year. It seemed like our real agenda was to supply girls to the pageant organizers. No, it was not girls in general but preselected girls, the girls the group thought to be deserving of the title. Basically, girls whose families had been in the county for a long time. That is why I had been invited.

After the formal part of the meeting, we sat around talking, and one of the girls from my school started ranting about how her boyfriend had dated a "white trash" girl over the summer. She could have been talking about Nina, but I didn't know for sure. I also didn't know who the boy was. From my perspective, there seemed to be pretty quick turnover among couples at my school. This started a discussion among the girls as they claimed the same thing had happened to them, and they started bad-mouthing girls they considered lower class. After I'd heard enough, I stood up, mumbled I had homework, and left. No one even noticed.

The atmosphere was tense at school the next week, and I felt uncomfortable with everyone, including Maggie. I struggled with whether I should tell her about the meeting, but I had been sworn to secrecy, and if anything got out, everyone would suspect me because I was the only one not going along with the discussion. The alleged cheated-on girl acted like she was glued together with her clique of friends. In class, I sometimes saw her glaring at Nina, who always looked straight ahead or at one of her friends. It felt like our classes were split down the middle, and I was floating somewhere in between. As we got closer to our October meeting, rumors about Nina started to swirl, with nearly everyone talking about her pregnancy, and half of them wanting her out of the school.

I could feel myself detaching from the wealthy kids, but I wasn't brave enough to support Nina in public. I started spending my free time in the art room, helping out and working on my college portfolio. The day of the meeting came, and I didn't want to go, but I didn't know what to do. The club secretary called the night before and reminded me I needed to be there, as they had a pageant lined up for me and she wanted to give me the details. The meetings rotated around the schools, and this week it was at my school, so I had no real excuse.

There were low-level pageants coming up in the fall, so we discussed them and who we wanted to enter each. Again, at the end, there was the social period, and the talk turned to Nina's pregnancy and what should be done about it and to everyone involved. Someone added that the boy had said he wanted nothing to do with Nina. After that comment, the talk ran largely toward running Nina out of town and making it clear she should never come back. Again, I left early, and no one noticed.

When I went back to school on Monday, there were whispers that Nina had run away to have her baby. Things were quietly tense until Maggie convinced Nina's parents that she really was missing and was not with the baby's father. The police got involved but did very little. They came to school and talked to my class as a whole and then to her best friends. There were no leads because the kids who had information were never asked about it.

I couldn't bring myself to go back to the club even though I had taken a vow to go the entire year. The secretary called repeatedly, and finally I asked my mom to tell her I was swamped with college applications and chores and could no longer attend. I hated to bring in a parent, but it worked, and they left me alone. I don't know what was told to the other girls, but my popularity dropped at school, and I wasn't invited to any more parties the rest of the year. That was fine with me, and I felt like I had escaped from catastrophe, but I knew in my heart that somehow Nina had not escaped.

I put the journal down, sickened by my mother's behavior. She was complicit in Nina's murder, complicit due to her inability to speak up. It was this same inability that had led her and her friends to be at the gang rape party after college. I could understand this inability at age seventeen better than at age twenty-five. It occurred to me that all of MG's yearbooks were in the barn, and maybe there was a picture of the club members; I was doubtful, however, because the club was not affiliated with any single school. I dressed quickly and went downstairs, found that everyone was up already, and chipped in to make breakfast.

As I looked around the kitchen, it was obvious that JJ was thrilled to be on the ranch among family, and he and Will acted like they had known each other all their lives. In one respect they had; they shared 25 percent of their DNA, and Will looked and sounded like a younger version of JJ. My relationship with JJ, while warm, was not developing at high speed. I was content to take it slow and get to know him before I gave him my heart. They both kept glancing at me during breakfast, and I got the feeling they wanted a family talk.

As I got up to fill my coffee cup, Will asked if he could talk with me alone, and we slipped around to the front porch and sat in the rocking chairs. He looked a bit nervous, so I just waited for him to start.

"Mom, I've been talking to JJ about the University of Florida and whether it is a good fit for me. I've been thinking about whether I will like it enough to make a four-year commitment, and I realized the only way I'll know is if I try it out. JJ has been looking around at options, and he found a sublet for me for November and December. I can do my classes anywhere, so I could just go down and get a sense of the campus and the town and see if I like it. Of course, I'll come home before the holidays. What do you think?"

My first thought was that Will hadn't asked my opinion about a major life event in a long time. He had been so determined to go it alone after William had died. I realized I hadn't really been there for him either. We had both been traveling our own roads alone. I wondered about JJ's influence on this change. Was he quietly putting our family back together?

I reached out and gave Will a hug, then said, "That sounds like a perfect idea; go with my blessing!"

He hugged me back and then ran off to tell JJ. It made me think about how he had missed having a grandparent around, especially one with JJ's smooth touch.

I went back in, filled my coffee cup, and joined the family. When the lively conversation began to die down, I slipped out to go to the barn to find MG's yearbooks. Louie noticed and followed me out. With so many people around, we hadn't had much time together. He put his arm around me, and we went in search of the yearbooks. We found them just where I'd left them, along with the invitation to join the Intra-County Farm Group. Unfortunately, the letter was signed by the faculty advisor, who rotated among the schools every year. I scooped everything up, and we went back to the house to help clean up and pack for our trip home.

Chapter 5
Distillation

We left right after lunch to make our three-to-four-hour drive back to Newport Beach. My bag was full of yearbooks and other mementos from MG's high school days. I filled him in on what I had learned so far from the journals, and we agreed that I would tell Alex as much as possible but in a distilled format. My concern was that if we told Alex everything, he might share it with someone who didn't necessarily prioritize confidentiality.

I pulled out MG's senior yearbook, found a picture of the group who had taken the study abroad trip to Europe, and wrote down the names of the six seniors and six juniors. I looked through to see if any of the girls were tagged as being in pictures with boys who were on the football team. This task basically took me the rest of the trip home. By the end, I had a list of two senior girls who had dated senior boys on the team, one senior girl who had dated a junior boy on the team, and three junior girls who had dated senior boys on the team. I would start with the couples that consisted of two seniors. As I flipped through the pictures, I could see that couples were fluid and there were changes throughout the year, but we had a solid group of suspects to start with.

We got back to Newport Beach around five. Louie wanted to go surfing, so he dropped me off at my house. I put my bags in the kitchen and took the yearbooks with me out to the backyard, along with a glass of white wine. I picked up MG's sophomore yearbook to see if there were pictures of Daniel Roan, my mother's oncologist. I found his individual picture among the other senior class members. He was quite handsome, in a swoony kind of way. He had signed his picture "MG, we will always be connected, Danny." That was much too prophetic for my tastes, not to mention a bit eerie. I looked through the rest of the yearbook and found pictures of MG and Daniel hanging out around campus and a couple of them dancing at prom or some other special occasion dance. In a couple of the pictures, Maggie was watching them with an unreadable look on her face. There were also a couple of pictures of Maggie with a petite blond girl, who I figured must be Nina. They looked relaxed and happy.

I suddenly realized that someone was tapping on the door of the back wall, and it was getting progressively louder. I went to open it and found Colette, carrying two brownie volcanoes with whipped cream. She knew my weakness.

She said, "This is a peace offering of sorts. I know I was a bit short with you last time we talked."

I welcomed her in and told her there was no reason to apologize. As we ate our volcanoes, I told her about the cancer journals. "My mother did make a confession about Maggie and Nina early in the first cancer journal, and I have to say your assessment was correct. My mother played an indirect yet critical role in Nina's death, and it seems to have bothered her."

Then I asked, "Did she ever mention a man named Daniel Roan?"

She started laughing. "Ah, the doctor! Yes, he was a recurrent theme. At the time I met her, he was at UC Davis in his last year of medical school. She was dating Jackson fairly regularly, but she and Daniel saw each other every once in a while, when he wasn't researching residencies in cancer. Daniel was a nice guy, but because of his looks, he got a lot of female attention, and he often gave in to it in a flirty way. It didn't seem to bother MG; she always found time for him."

She looked at me expectantly, waiting for an explanation as to why I asked. "I can't talk with you about Nina yet, maybe never. I have to find a way to deal with it on my own. But I can tell you that Daniel was MG's oncologist, and he stopped by the ranch to see her once a week to check her medicine. I'm not sure if you know that MG chose not to have any curative treatment after her surgery; instead, she basically chose limited pain management that would not keep her in a stupor or feeling too sick."

Colette nodded. "That doesn't surprise me. She often talked about quality of life over quantity of life and how she wanted to be creative until the day she died. I don't blame her; you look at the fine print on the cancer drug commercials and they often report only three to six months' extension of life. But you pay so much in terms of finances and your physical and mental health. I think of the people I have known who have had advanced cancer; those who have chosen aggressive treatment sometimes do it for the sake of their families and friends.

"I wouldn't be surprised if MG kept everyone away because she didn't want them to argue with her or try to talk her into taking experimental drugs or doing clinical trials. And maybe she sent you away for that same reason, so she didn't doubt her decision every time she looked at you. Knowing the friendship she had with Daniel, I would guess that he respected her treatment wishes and maybe even helped her along when it was time."

She saw the shock on my face and continued: "You never know what you will do until it is your turn to face the end. I don't judge or blame your mother for the decisions she made; she was using her own particular type of moral reasoning. In fact, your mother was challenged many times in her life, and most of the time she made decisions based on her values, but a few times she made them to avoid conflict and arguments. She didn't like the negative emotions that came from arguments, and she would drag herself through life for days after what others might see as a minor skirmish among friends. She learned to keep a positive or equanimous disposition to avoid negative emotions. Strangely, there are artists who thrive on pain, but your mother thought it negatively affected her work."

She continued, "Abe told me there is a word for it, emotophobia."

I must have given her a confused look, because she continued: "Often for children, especially girls, there is an expectation that they always be nice, happy, and gracious, no matter how they really feel. For some people, this can become an obsession to never show negative emotion."

Suddenly a memory of my early life emerged. In about the first grade, a mean girl in my class ran up to me carrying a cup of red punch. She bumped right into me, and suddenly there was red punch all down the front of both of our dresses. Then she threw the cup on the floor and started screaming that I had ruined her dress. Later, when her mother started yelling at MG, instead of defending me, MG tried multiple soothing strategies on the woman until she found one that worked. I think MG offered to buy the girl a new dress. The next day, I subtly tripped the girl when we were playing outside in a large group. She tore her dress that time. I didn't feel bad about doing it, but once was enough. I was never mean to her again. It just didn't feel good to me.

I didn't have an answer for why we were so different in some ways and so alike in others, but then I realized that not all my characteristics came from my mother. I never ran away from conflict, and I knew feeling bad was a part of life. Did I stand up to conflict because MG allowed me to express my true feelings as a child?

Later, as I sat down for a quick dinner from the freezer, I thought about what Colette had told me. Using my mother's own words, she had failed to warn Nina to get away. This then led to Nina's gruesome death because of her need to avoid negative emotions due to conflict. I think MG saw this as a grave character flaw, but did she also see it as an excuse for her behavior?

Maybe I would understand my own identity if I thought more about the ways MG and I differed.

CHAPTER 6
No Let Up

I went to work the next morning and realized that I liked both my new job and my new life. I felt stronger and more open to challenges; even the ones that seemed minor to me were life-changing for others. I gave each issue my full attention and made the best decisions I could. Sometimes I even felt I had found my niche in the position of chair, but I didn't want to count my successes too soon.

After a couple of hours spent on administrative tasks and a couple more on my research, I reached a lull in my day. I found my curiosity about Daniel Roan breaking through my thoughts, so I looked him up online. I easily found the website for his practice, and someone had done an excellent job of keeping it updated.

As with JJ, he was a good-looking man for his age. There was a collage of former patients over the years, and near the beginning was a picture of my mother, sitting at her chair with the mountains behind her. The message associated with the collage was that cancer treatments had changed over his career, but the quality-of-life needs of patients had stayed the same—and they would until treatments became more successful and less toxic. He noted that he looked forward to the day of having better detection options so that cancer could be found and treated at its earliest stages. I looked at other pages and saw that he was associated with regional and state cancer organizations, and he was on the board of directors for a national cancer group.

I debated whether to call him or not. Was he really such a humanitarian? Would he remember my mother? I had to know. I called the number listed for his office and reached a receptionist. She told me, of course, that he was with a patient, but I could leave a message. I told her to tell him that Phoebe Moon had called and would like to speak with him about MG

Moon when he had time. Barely three minutes had passed when my office phone rang. The receptionist told me he had a break in his schedule so he could talk with me now.

Before I could back out, he came on the line. "Phoebe! I am so surprised and happy to hear from you. I haven't seen you since you went away to boarding school. It was decades ago but seems like an instant in time!"

I was overwhelmed by this level of friendliness from someone I didn't remember even knowing. I told myself that this is the reality of small-town life. The characters may evolve and transition, but they remain the characters of people's lives forever.

I thanked him for remembering me and for agreeing to talk with me, and then I started in on my topic. "Dr. Roan, I wasn't there when my mother went through her surgery and cancer treatments, so I know little about that time in her life. I understand that you had been a friend to her since high school and that you were her oncologist after her diagnosis. I was wondering if we could meet for coffee the next time I am at the ranch and talk about her frame of mind during her care. I would also like to hear any stories about her that you think would help me know and understand her life."

He hesitated for a moment, then said, "You know, MG was the best friend I ever had. We were different in many ways, but we complemented each other's strengths and weaknesses. So yes, I would be happy to talk with you about her life. She was, for such an unassuming person, a lightning rod for chaos. I have heard through gossip that you are in Newport Beach now; I'm actually coming down for a cancer conference in a couple of weeks; can I call you then?"

We agreed to this, and he promised to call a couple of days ahead of time, because he never knew when or where he was going unless his assistant told him. I smiled at that and looked forward to getting to the point where I could let go of that responsibility too.

That done, I did what I did well: made a list of leads I could follow about Maggie and Nina. Alex and Louie were tracking down the people in the international study group and the football players. Who else was there, and was there anything I could do from here? I could read the journals and keep a list of people who were mentioned. That is what I continued to do for the rest of the week. That and plan for the family company we were to have on the weekend.

Friday morning, I had just started reading student papers about the lasting effects of policies from the Great Society era when my direct phone rang again.

"Phoebe," Alex gasped out, "Maggie is dead! It looks like a break-in, and Maggie got the worst of the struggle. First look suggests she was hit over the head and left to bleed out."

I hadn't sorted out my ideas and emotions about Maggie yet, so I was slow to respond. Maggie was definitely an important force in my mother's life—but what kind of force was she? Could I even respond to her death without knowing her role in my mother's life?

I took a deep breath and tried to focus, as I knew Alex was waiting for my initial shock to pass. Although I felt confused and in a bit of a fog, I managed to ask Alex if he could see any materials she had been working on. What I really wanted to know was whether she was working on Nina's case.

Alex put the phone on mute, and when he turned the volume back on, he said, "Phoebe, I thought you had the single existing copy of MG's journals. It appears Maggie had a set here too. They have been photocopied and stapled together. She was apparently going through them, looking for relevant passages, which she underlined."

I told him I had no idea of when or why she copied the journals but that I would look into it and be up to the ranch soon. I couldn't wrap my head around why Maggie would have copies of the journals with her, journals which so far did not put her in the most favorable light. Journals MG had made clear were private and only to be opened by me sometime in the future.

He looked around some more and then said, "Maggie had a full investigation going on Nina's death—pictures, news stories, and a few documents she must have stolen somewhere. It's all very creepy."

After Alex promised we'd talk later, I called Louie to discuss what to do. As much as he was looking forward to it, he suggested we put the fishing trip off and go back to the ranch this weekend. This time, however, he would see if the company helicopter was available.

▲ ▲ ▲

As soon as I got home from the office, I took the cancer journals and a glass of wine out to the backyard and settled in to work. I was only about halfway through the first one, so I switched to skimming less relevant material, keeping a list of names, and reading the relevant sections.

As I read, there was one curious thing I had not noticed earlier: while MG wrote that different people had stopped by, she never reported that she actually spoke with them. Did she send them away? I decided that after I got all the way through this first journal, I would go back and put all those people on my list. I skimmed another ten pages and found this: Two high school friends, Deborah Sutton and Pricilla, had paid her a visit. This time, she explicitly said that she asked her mother to tell them she was too sick for visitors. They left her a note, but she never mentioned that she read it.

Her next story was about Maggie:

> *Daniel came to see me unexpectedly this afternoon because he had just upped my pain medicine and wanted to know if there were any negative effects. I was asleep when he arrived, and he caught Maggie reading my journal. I had told her previously I was documenting things for Phoebe and whomever she wanted to read them. Of course, they were open to Daniel as well because I might need his help later.*
>
> *Maggie's excuse to Daniel was that I had kept secrets that affected her life, and she deserved to know what they were. This infuriated Daniel so he grabbed the journal, drove into town, and bought me a lockbox for it. He put the key on a ribbon that he later tied around my neck. When he returned, Maggie was gone and I had woken up. He told me what had happened and, without prying, told me that I would need to be more careful if I didn't want Maggie or others to know things. He also told me that I could tell him anything at any time.*
>
> *Daniel had never liked Maggie. He thought that she wanted to be me more than she actually liked me. I didn't feel that way*

and always thought he might be jealous of her—but I did feel violated. I had no way of knowing how far she had read in the journal. Had she read about Nina? Was my choice to either not write about the things I have held close or risk having them read by the wrong people?

She continued on with the story the next day.

When Maggie came in today, I asked her about it. She said that the journal slipped from my hand when I fell asleep, and she had just picked it up so she could put it on the table and Daniel had walked in then. She said it was no big deal, and she would never violate my privacy. However, when she saw that Daniel had bought a lockbox for the journal, she was offended and told me she needed a few days off and left. I didn't know quite what she meant by needing days off—was I a job or a chore? I hadn't really asked her to be there anyway.

I wasn't sure which secrets Maggie wanted to know about, but I was almost positive that some of them were about Nina. I think she also had suspicions that I had a role in Sally's disappearance. I need to think about what else it might be. I did know Maggie's secrets. I knew why she got married and who her daughter's father was. I would never speak of it unless she brought it up.

The rest of journal one was about her art projects that she wanted to finish and who she was talking with at MoonShots to make sure the company was solvent. She was concerned about ultimately passing the company on to me and Beatrice and making sure the Boas family was compensated. She also wrote about the regular news Beatrice sent about me.

My overall sense was that MG was trying her best to give honest explanations about these mysteries in her life. Maybe it was the drugs, maybe it was the disease, or maybe she was just trying too hard, but I was having a tough time understanding her stories. MG was my mother, and I would love her no matter what I found out, but would that come at the cost of hating other people in her life?

Chapter 7
Maggie's Death

Carlos left one of the ranch trucks at Porterville Municipal Airport for us, and we drove to see Alex at the Tulare County Sheriff's Office. He invited us to take a seat in his office in order to fill us in on things and to share what we had found. Alex went first: "The evidence at Maggie's house looked like a staged robbery—nothing of value was stolen, but things were tossed around. Interestingly, the copies of the journals were not with her case notes on the kitchen table. The journal copies, along with the neatly written notes on them were stored in separate file folders hidden in her attic."

I looked around Alex's work area. There was a thick file with my name on it, including notes from the earlier talk Maggie and I had in my office. Alex let me look at the journal pages he had—they were in a large sealable bag. I couldn't manage to see every word, but it looked like the last page of the photocopied version was toward the end of the first volume of the journals. I wondered, did Maggie come back while MG was sleeping and ask my grandmother if she could copy the journal? Or did she ask at a later date?

Alex pointed at the pages. "Have you read these?"

I nodded my head and said, "I believe so, and I think there are a couple of passages that might be helpful to the investigation. There seems to have been a falling out between MG and Maggie because Daniel Roan, MG's oncologist, found Maggie reading the journal one day while MG was asleep. Daniel got MG a lockbox and put the key on a ribbon around her neck. Maggie was insulted and stayed away for a while."

Alex then asked, "Did you know Maggie had a copy or where it came from?"

I looked him in the eye and said, "No, I did not know, but I suspect she must have either stolen the original or given a phony reason to my grandmother for needing it. Then she made a copy. MG was adamant that I was the only one who should read it, so I have no reason to believe she gave it to Maggie willingly. Plus, there appears to be a dispute about the relationship from the writings and conversations. It appears that Maggie was a complex person with a tangled relationship with MG. Somehow, MG was bound to Maggie by guilt. I did call Dr. Roan, and he has agreed to talk with me about MG's cancer care when he comes to the Orange County area for a conference within the next couple of weeks. He wasn't sure of the dates, but if you have any specific questions, just let me know."

Alex then turned to Louie and asked what he had learned.

Louie responded, "Here is a list of all the public high schools that were active in the county in the 1967–68 school year. After making the list, we looked for missing person cases within each school's boundaries. Putting all of the work together, we believe there is a total of six missing girls, and we have numbered them by their dates of disappearance.

"Girl number one is Nina, from Lower Sierra, and we plan to reinterview her sister about her final days. Girl number two is from Porterville; her name is Vickie, and she was never found. Girl number three, Amy White, is also from Porterville; as you noted, she got spooked and moved away to have her baby. We looked for her, and we found her living in Pismo Beach. She's a retired nurse but does occasional shifts when needed. She has agreed to talk with us, and Phoebe and I plan to see her tomorrow. Girl number four is Karen Jennings from Lindsay. We will set up an interview with a family member as soon as possible. We currently don't have any information on what happened to girl number five, now known as Lorie Winter from Woodlake, or girl number six, Sharon Lane from Exeter.

"We would not have found Amy White so easily if her mother had not pointed us in the right direction, since she lives under a different name. I hope that is true for the other missing girls and that there are no other graves."

Alex congratulated us on our progress and told us that he had to put Maggie's case first because of its recency; we could pursue the old cases at our own pace for the next couple of weeks. He also told us that they had not found any leads on Maggie's break-in; the house had no extraneous prints, and no one saw anything. Caroline, Maggie's daughter, and Parker Sampson Montgomery, Maggie's grandson, both took off right after the funeral, so he did not have a chance to question them.

I said, "Maggie was focused at this point on identifying Nina's killer. There are people who might want Maggie to go away, starting with Nina's killer. Or possibly the baby's biological father. I don't think it is going to be easy to identify the people who might want Maggie dead, because they might not be obvious."

We agreed that we would talk regularly and share information as it came in but also schedule regular conference calls starting Monday at 1 p.m. Louie and I had decided ahead of time to head straight back to Newport Beach and spend the weekend working our leads. Before we could slip away, Alex said he had one more thing to tell us.

He didn't make eye contact for thirty seconds, and I was starting to prepare myself emotionally. When he was ready, he said, "I have the results back on the note with Nina's body. I am deeply sorry that I know what the note said, because it is hateful and alarming. The note read: *"Proud to be taking out the trash."*

We drove to the airport and made the short flight back to Newport Beach. The level of hate associated with Nina's death was overwhelming, and it left me feeling depleted. The thought that these young women could be called trash as they were being murdered was beyond comprehension to me. For quite some time I had kept a mental list of things I couldn't comprehend because I had no personal experience with which to frame them. I understood the meaning of the word *trash*—just not when it was applied to a human life. These deaths would certainly go on the list, and I knew they would rise up to haunt me for the rest of my life. I needed something simple and positive to balance it all out.

▲ ▲ ▲

Louie and I sat on the patio, thinking through what we knew. Something was bothering me about the Maggie story, and on a whim, I called

Colette and Abe and JJ and invited them over to remember Maggie. I put together platters of cheese and crackers, fruit, and cookies and took them, along with a couple of bottles of wine, out to the patio table. While I did that, Louie picked flowers from the garden and set the table. Our guests joined us just as we were finishing up.

To get us going, I raised my glass of wine and said, "To Maggie and her life spirit. I didn't know her well, but I know she influenced lives—especially those of her students—during her long career in education. She gave back more to the world than she took." The conversation started flowing then, and my guests praised their old friend, showing great kindness toward her memory. The conversation slowed down after a while, and people drifted off in their private thoughts. Then I spoke again.

"Maggie died a violent death, and there was little to no evidence left behind. And although she was a largely admired person. We have started to produce a list of people who might have a grudge against her. On that list might be Nina's killer or other people involved with Nina; her daughter, Caroline, for lying about her father's identity; friends or relatives of the man Maggie claimed to be Caroline's father; or even Daniel Roan, in an effort to protect MG. We hoped that you might have memories or comments that you can share that might lead us in a particular direction."

After a while, Colette spoke: "I have been trying to remember specific conversations we had, but she was a person who was generally in the background. During the period that we knew her, she visited MG regularly at UC Berkeley, but somewhere along the way, she started seeing Peter Sampson. Toward the end of 1974, when Maggie came up to Berkeley from San José, she spent more time with Peter than with MG and MG's other close friends. People in Peter's group might know her better. Of all the people you mentioned, they all seem plausible except for Daniel. I'd pay special attention to the fact that by claiming Kent, the marine she married, was the father, she defrauded the government out of eighteen years of benefits for Caroline because Peter was paying her as well."

JJ commented next: "I agree about Daniel. As much as Maggie tried to create ill feelings between Daniel and me, neither of us felt that way. I can imagine what he might not have wanted revealed about himself, but I can guarantee it doesn't matter anymore. Now that I'm thinking about it, I'm remembering how often Maggie got involved in dramas around MG and her other friends. All the other scenarios seem plausible, but my vote would be on Nina's killer, especially if someone is now in politics or trying to promote a certain image."

I found JJ's comments interesting and asked, "How did she try to stir things up?"

He chuckled and said, "Well, every time MG saw Daniel, Maggie would find a way to work it into a conversation with me while MG wasn't listening."

He looked at my suspicious face and said, "I guess I may as well tell you, but be discreet. MG was Daniel's cover date, and she had been since she was a sophomore in high school. Daniel is gay, but during that period of time, the discrimination and hostility were over the top—people had the wildest ideas about gay men, and then when HIV/AIDS appeared, it was near hysteria. MG's gift to Daniel was to always be there if he needed or wanted a female companion. His gift to her was undying devotion and free tutoring if she needed it. He extended that gift to me as well. But ultimately, he gave her the gift of dying in a way she wanted, giving her control over the process."

That pretty much stopped the conversation, because I, too, had been wondering about MG and Daniel's relationship. We chatted for another half hour or so, had some more wine, and then everyone left.

As I stretched out on the lounge chair to enjoy the moonlight, something came together for me when I was just on the verge of sleep. Parker Sampson Montgomery is a student in my graduate seminar.

CHAPTER 8
A Trip up the Coast and Back

Our meeting with Amy White was at one o'clock on Sunday. Louie picked me up at seven, and we drove the four hours up the coast to Pismo Beach—a beautiful but exhausting drive. We had planned to get there a bit early so we could explore and have a nice lunch. Our first destination was the beach. We took a relaxing walk out on the pier and spent time watching the fishers and surfers. Our stomachs were growling after half an hour, so we looked for somewhere to have lunch—my criteria were an ocean view and tasty food. After asking around, we walked to a rustic seafood restaurant and were able to get a table with a view. I could have eaten my way right into dinner, but 1 p.m. was closing in, and we didn't know exactly where Amy's house was located.

After plugging Amy's address into the navigation system, we found she lived across the highway and halfway up the hill, supplying a panoramic view of the ocean and all the colorful plantings. Her house was a single-story rancher with a deck off to the side, also with a view. There were ice plants everywhere we looked, and on the deck were large containers of vibrant flowers. We knocked on the door, and after a moment, it opened. Amy was a tall, trim seventy-year-old with short white hair, who exuded energy and confidence. She greeted us warmly and walked us out to the deck. She then slipped inside the kitchen door and came back with a tray of iced tea.

Louie and I had decided beforehand that he would take the lead in the interview, and I would observe and take notes. After we had chatted for a while and asked about her gorgeous home, which she and her husband had bought thirty years ago, Louie brought the conversation around.

"Amy, thank you so much for talking to us about your friend and your own experience being pregnant as a teenager. This case came to us in a roundabout way when a body was found buried on Phoebe's family ranch, and then further searching found two more bodies across the street from the first.

"We received a tip about the identity of the first person, a teenage girl named Nina, and through further investigation we found that two other teenagers disappeared from Porterville at about that same time. We located your mother, and she told us the wonderful news that you had survived your disappearance and had had a fulfilling life. Unfortunately, your friend Vickie has never been heard from again. I would appreciate it if you could take us back to 1967 and tell us what you remember about Vickie's disappearance and what made you believe you were in danger."

Amy looked out over the ocean, then began to tell her story. "Vickie and I lived down the street from each other in a rather, how should I say this, neglected area of town. Our parents were farm workers when we were young, and sometimes our families would go out of town to work together. Other times, we would stay in the same area but carpool to orchards across the county. All our parents eventually got full-time jobs that were low-paying but secure. Given our circumstances, we didn't have money for nice clothes, shoes, or makeup, so we didn't fit in with the wealthier kids. I guess that in some ways, it was like two different worlds in school. When we were with the kids in our social circle, we felt comfortable.

"But we were smart and attractive, and we had dreams of going to college and making a life for ourselves. When we turned sixteen in the second half of our sophomore year in high school, our parents said we could get jobs as long as it didn't hurt our grades. We started looking, and right away we were both hired at a drive-in restaurant on Main Street that used carhops on skates. Skating was a cheap activity compared to other things, and we had been skating around the neighborhood since we were six or seven. Still, the work was hard because the trays of food could get heavy, and people were always walking in our path. After three or four paychecks we bought makeup, and after more checks we had our hair professionally cut. Then we started buying clothing and nice shoes.

"But looking more normal came at a price, because people started to notice us, including boys. We got asked out on dates. At first we said no;

then we only agreed to double dates. But after we both found guys we liked, it seemed more natural for us to go out on single dates, and things got steamy for both of us. We were naive and we were flattered, so although we asked the guys to use condoms, sometimes they didn't have one. I think they figured we would go along with it anyway, and we did. These were our first boyfriends, both of them seemed to be popular at their schools, and we thought what we were doing was normal.

"By the end of the summer, it was pretty clear that Vickie was pregnant and that it was time to have a serious talk with her family. She kept putting the talk off, and after about a month, a group of senior girls started coming in every day when Vickie was on shift and making comments about her body changes. At first they were nice to her and would talk about what they would do if they were pregnant. They never directly asked her if she was pregnant; they just assumed, correctly, that she was.

"One Sunday afternoon our boss called both of us and said he urgently needed us to come into work. Two girls from the afternoon shift had not showed up. We had planned to do homework, but we wanted to keep our jobs. That night, some kids I didn't recognize came in. There were three girls, and they were all wearing senior rings from other schools. One of the girls was with a big guy I had never seen before. The two of them were trying to chat with Vickie. When our shift was over at nine, my father came to pick us up, but I couldn't find Vickie anywhere. My father used the pay phone to call Vickie's parents, but they hadn't heard from her. I never saw her again."

Louie asked, "Do you remember what the girl and guy who were trying to talk with her looked like?"

Amy closed her eyes and said, "The girl was tall and bulky. Not fat but like she was an athlete. She had shiny blond hair in a ponytail and a kind of angry face—I guess now we would refer to that as a resting bitch face. She had a loud voice and seemed to talk over everyone else in the group. At one point, she and the guy got out of the car, maybe to intimidate Vickie, and they fake lunged at her every time she skated by. They would miss her and then laugh when she lost her balance and almost fell. The guy was about the same height as the girl, but he was even bulkier, like a football player.

The guy's facial features were squished in, like he had broken his nose at some point. They looked like they were related, but he was unattractive compared to the girl."

"So how did you come to think they were after you?" Louie asked her.

"About three weeks later, I realized I was pregnant too. A few weeks after that, the same girl and guy came in. I noticed they were watching everything I did. I was worried so I went inside and told the manager I was ill and needed to leave. I called my father and asked him to pick me up in front of the diner, not in the back, where cars parked for service. On the way home, I told him about the pregnancy and my worries that I would disappear like Vickie. Although my parents were disappointed in me about the pregnancy, they believed me, and we took off the next morning to my aunt's house."

I thought about what Amy had told us so far, and I couldn't help but ask, "Your memory of the time is so clear and detailed; what's your secret?"

She blushed and said, "I should have mentioned this first: During junior year, my A-level English class included a yearlong assignment to keep a journal. I dug mine out of a box of keepsakes from school right after you contacted me. Let me get it for you, so you can see I had a lot of help in remembering."

She went inside for a moment, then came back carrying a worn blue spiral-bound notebook. She said, "I kept the notebook for the entire school year, during my pregnancy, and through the birth of my daughter. I clipped together the pages that pertain to me and Vickie. Feel free to read those pages; the rest is personal, and I don't think any of it will help you."

I looked at the clipped-together pages—there were around ten total, and they were written in loopy teenage script with hearts over the i's. I scanned through the pages, and close to the end were two drawings, a young woman and man, and a list of characteristics about each: hair color, eye color, etcetera. The drawings showed details, enough so that if you knew the person, you would recognize them. I asked if we could have a copy to share with the sheriff's office. She offered to scan them, then got up to do so.

At that point Louie remembered to ask about potential genetic matches. He said, "Amy, do you know if Vickie has any genetically related relatives living in the area?"

She seemed surprised. "Oh, sure, they mostly stayed in the area. Her brother is Larry Miller, and she had a sister too."

I thought about the fact that we didn't know who killed Maggie, and I certainly didn't want anything to happen to Amy. When she came back from scanning the drawings, I suggested she put the journal in a safety deposit box at a bank and not mention to anyone that she had taken notes from that time. Amy had learned how to hide early in life, so she told me she would do so at once, and she would not tell anyone why we were there. If a neighbor asked, Amy would tell them we were life insurance salespeople.

Before we got up to leave, I found I was compelled to ask one more question, "Amy, can you tell me the name of the boy you were dating then?"

For the first time, she looked embarrassed. She said in a voice I could barely hear, "He told me his name was Reid Miles and that he was a senior at Lindsay High School. I didn't know anyone from that school, so I just accepted it was the truth. I struggled about whether I should tell him about our daughter, so one day I drove to the Lindsay library and looked him up in their collection of yearbooks. There was no Reid Miles listed, and there were no boys who looked like him. So recently I looked on the internet and found he was a graphic designer who started designing album covers in the 1950's. I told you—I was naive"

I hugged her and Louie and I told her goodbye.

▲ ▲ ▲

It was midafternoon by the time we got on the road. I felt gratified by the latest information but anxious because I had a new person to worry about.

We drove out of town, enjoying the scenery of the valleys and glimpses of the ocean we saw along the way. As we passed through Santa Barbara, we turned west on State Street, and after a few turns we ended up at Santa Cruz Market. Louie came back in a couple of minutes carrying a cheap Styrofoam ice cooler and a couple of reusable grocery bags. I raised an eyebrow, but he gave me his warning look that I should not ask. We drove through the city and down the coast past Carpinteria. Louie stopped at a beach that was uncrowded, and we carried the bags, the cooler, and a blanket down toward the shore. He spread out the blanket and opened a bottle of wine—just in time to see the sun starting to set. Then he said, "I am so glad today isn't cloudy."

I laughed as I thought of him carrying this secret of a sunset picnic around all afternoon. We drank wine and ate the gourmet salads and other contents of his bags of groceries until we got to the chocolate extravaganza that was our dessert.

I felt relaxed and happy, even though there was chaos in our lives. After we ate, Louie took my hand and told me he had an ulterior motive for the picnic and sunset. "We've had the opportunity to spend more time together as friends and work partners, but I thought it might be time to think about where we want our relationship to go before we are too emotionally invested. One thing we have not let ourselves experience is whether there is any passion between us. Our kisses have been chaste and short. I need to know if the passion is there for us."

We had gone through all the early relationship stages, but I still felt unsure about my ability—or readiness—for a romantic relationship. In fact, it was hard for me to imagine being a couple with anyone other than my deceased spouse. Instead of sharing my fears, I said, "How soon can we get away for a sail to the Channel Islands on your boat?"

He laughed and said, "Saturday morning at sunrise."

Then I remembered, Louie had promised to take my family out fishing last weekend, but it had been canceled. Surely they wouldn't just show up this weekend.

We walked down the beach holding hands, intermittently discussing the possible nature of our future together and the case. We shared this duality of romance and murder all the way back to Newport Beach.

CHAPTER 9
A Different Portrayal of Maggie

I got to the office early on Monday. I felt invigorated by the evidence we'd received from Amy and the talk I'd had with Louie. It was getting easier for me to think about moving on and starting a new relationship. I was developing new relationships and friendships with people who were encouraging me to live in the present and to have a more balanced viewpoint about my family and the past.

Before I got down to work, I pulled up the roster for my seminar and scanned the students' pictures. *Ah, there it is, Parker Sampson Montgomery—he looks so much like Maggie that I should have known he was her grandson!* I made a note to give him my condolences when class met.

The rest of the morning went by quickly, as the paperwork was never ending.

Louie picked me up at noon, and we stopped and bought deli sandwiches and drinks on our way to the beach. The stretch of beach we chose was right across the street from Louie's building, so we could be sure not to be late for our call with Alex.

We carried our lunch and blanket down almost to the edge of the water, where we could sit and enjoy the view. After we ate, we both dozed off a bit and were saved only by the ten-minute warning alert on Louie's watch. We threw everything into the basket and ran across the highway to Louie's office building. I had to say, all of this rushing around was not fitting my image of the California lifestyle.

We made it to the top floor of the building with one minute to spare, and we headed straight into a secure conference room and called Alex. Before I told him anything, I informed him that we had very sensitive information that absolutely could not go into a file at this point. He agreed to protect our sources.

I told him that I was worried about the safety of Amy White, and that her name should not appear anywhere in his notes. I ended by telling him that she had made a great life for herself, and I hoped it could stay that way.

Louie then took the lead in telling him about the meeting itself. Our intent was to have Amy tell us what she knew about Vickie's disappearance and how that compared with what happened to her and Nina. Louie went through their stories and then summarized the essence of what we'd found out so far: (1) Vickie's experience closely matched Nina's; (2) Vickie came from a family named Miller, and she had multiple relatives still in the area, including her brother Larry; (3) the descriptions of the unknown girl and guy matched what we had read in MG's journal about the girl who invited her to join the Intra-County Farm Group, plus Amy had given us the added bonus of her sketches of the potential suspects; (4) Amy left town after the same two people showed up at her job and watched her.

As we were reporting to Alex, I heard his fingers tapping the keys of his computer. Just as Louie was finishing, Alex yelled out an enthusiastic "Yes!" then continued, "We have the DNA of Larry Miller on file. He's kind of an old guy now, but he had a fistfight with a much younger neighbor over property lines. He accused the neighbor of killing an entire row of his garden with an illegally placed fence."

"Is that his only incident?" I asked.

"Seems so. His neighbors say he's grumpy but harmless, and he donates the excess food from his garden to a food bank."

"Do you have someone who can compare the DNA results?" Louie asked.

"Yep. The Fresno lab has the results of DNA profiles from the bodies, and I will email Larry's DNA results as soon as we finish here. If I beg, maybe we can get the results tomorrow."

With that, he started to sign off until I said, "Wait! I realized that Maggie's grandson is a student in my graduate seminar. Did you talk with him about Maggie's murder yet?"

"No, his mother said he was away at school," Alex replied.

"Do you want me to talk with him after class?" I asked.

He paused a moment before answering. "I would rather you didn't. Just let me know if he is in class this week, and I will decide what to do."

We hung up from our call with Alex, and by now Louie was fully awake. We talked about the new leads we had and where we wanted to go next. Louie suggested that he have a staffer go through all the 1967–68 yearbooks from Tulare County High Schools to see if we could find the suspicious male and female by using Amy's drawings. Louie would also have his company do a deep dive into Parker Montgomery and his mother, Caroline, for background on Maggie's murder. After this analysis, Louie drove me back to work so I could pick up my car.

I was in a somber mood when I got home and was not hungry yet, so I dug out MG's second cancer journal. As with the first journal, it opened with an overview of her status and the medicines she was taking. It appeared from her status report that sometime in early fall, Daniel had wanted to check to see how the cancer around her bladder was behaving. He took MG back to the cancer center in Fresno, and a surgeon used laparoscopic surgery to see if the cancer was spreading. It appeared that her bladder had been invaded by the original cancer and there was a growing tumor. The surgeon they trimmed some of the tumor away, but that was all they could do. After staying in the hospital for two days, Daniel drove MG back to the ranch.

When she started her journal again, she had apparently decided to include intimate stories about her friends, though there was no explanation as to why. She began with a story about Maggie:

> *I am not sure when Maggie started dating Peter Sampson. Most people, including her family and her hometown boyfriend, Kent, thought Maggie and Kent were informally engaged. Kent and Maggie met when he was home on leave from the Air Force. It was the summer after our senior year of high school, and she was missing Nina. Kent was an easy replacement, but then she met Peter Sampson a few years later at a party. It soon became apparent that she was no longer coming to Berkeley to see me. The truth of it was that on more recent trips, she didn't even stop by—she went directly to Peter's house. She and Peter were an item, and as she got closer to him, she also got closer to the people he associated with, including Emma Bell, Edward Block,*

and Cary Richmond. By the time we were in graduate school, they had rented a big house close to school, and all the students in their clique lived there, along with a couple of other students and part-time guests. It didn't make me sad or angry that she had changed groups, but it did worry me. Peter seemed like a fairly good guy, but there was something dark about the others. I never really understood how Peter became involved with Emma, Edward, and Cary, but I think he may have mentioned playing high school football with Edward.

One of the secrets I have kept is that it was not just Emma who tried to persuade me to go to the graduation party she'd planned, the one where we were raped; Maggie tried to convince me too. She intimated that she had helped plan the party, and she was convinced I would enjoy it. She even told me we could invite Daniel and not Jackson and no one would know. What I can't really remember is if Maggie knew Peter before Emma tried to infiltrate my group of friends or after. At any rate, I took on the burden of guilt for Maggie being at the party and what I assumed happened to her. I know that this doesn't make any sense because (a) she had gone to the party with Peter, and (b) she had persuaded me to attend—even insisting that I stay for at least a drink or two. Maybe it was because her dad worked for our family, but I had felt responsible for Maggie for as long as I could remember.

Either way, I never saw Maggie again once I had been drugged. To be fair, I don't really remember seeing anyone after my first drink.

By the time I came back around, Maggie had gone back to her home and eloped to Las Vegas with her high school boyfriend. She did not have anyone attend the wedding—I think that Kent was due back on base a week after the wedding, and they wanted a honeymoon. This was in 1976, and although the war was officially over in Vietnam, Pol Pot was committing genocide in Cambodia and the US had a clandestine hand in his regime. Kent was on a plane that was shot down in Cambodian air space while trying to gather intelligence. His death came about six months after the marriage. I came home for the funeral and Maggie was very pregnant; in fact, she delivered Caroline days later, blaming it on the trauma of Kent's death. She told everyone that Caroline, who weighed a full seven pounds, was "several weeks early."

Intellectually I know that friendships often have a stopping date, and if they go too far beyond that date, they can become toxic. On the other hand, when you end an old friendship, it can leave you feeling untethered and alone, especially if you haven't yet grown into new ones.

I sent a present to Maggie when Caroline was born, and she never acknowledged it, but then when I got sick, she was at my door. Nothing in between. Looking back, I think Maggie was ashamed of having her Berkeley friends think Caroline was Peter's baby, when she was telling everyone at home she was Kent's. I don't think her secret really got out, though, as I didn't tell, and as far as I know, no one else guessed. To my knowledge, Peter never married, but I think he remained committed to Maggie and Caroline, and he visited as much as he could.

I found this passage particularly sobering. We often think we know what our relationships are based on and how the other person truly feels about us. Sometimes the relationship gets tested, and we get a peek inside the other person's true feelings. Maybe we feel disappointed that someone didn't stand up for us at a meeting or didn't invite us along to something we wanted to go to or didn't help us get accepted into a group. We have this peek inside, and then we spend nights debating the meaning of the action and whether it was purposeful. And if it was purposeful, we wonder what it meant for the long-term quality of the relationship.

This weighty thinking came from my indecision about Maggie's character. It was dawning on me that Maggie was neither good nor bad. She seemed to be driven by values that could place her on either side of the morality line. To be her friend would mean accepting both of those sides. Was it better to have an informed or a loving heart? But then again, can you love without being informed?

▲ ▲ ▲

Louie was waiting for me Tuesday when I got home from work. He had been in touch with Alex, who had requested a secure call for 7 p.m. Apparently he had some updates for us, and wanted to see if we had acquired any new information. We drove out to Louie's offices for the call. Alex sounded excited to talk with us, and after all the greetings, he said, "First off, we can definitively ID one of the bodies as Vickie Miller, as the DNA showed a familial overlap with her brother. I spoke with members of her family, and although it has been over fifty years, they are happy to have the opportunity to give her a proper burial. Please let Amy White know. So, I am assuming we next try to identify victim number four, Karen Jennings. Not only is she the next to go missing, but her school is the next closest one to the ranch. So please move on to her, and we will follow up on Vickie. Second, I tried again to talk with Maggie's grandson, Parker, but Caroline is insistent that she will not bother him. She threatened to involve her attorney for harassment. I will drive over later this week and hunt him down. Can either of you put me up?"

Louie told Alex about his mini-suites for out-of-town clients and said he could use one for as long as he needed—and that he would take him out for a nice dinner too. That made Alex less cranky about the drive over. He also asked me if I could try to find Parker's class schedule. I told him that would be a conflict of interest, but I also told him who to call to get it.

He continued with his report: "Caroline has a nice house close to the Tule River, right above Springville. I can't tell exactly what she does for a job, some kind of consultant for startup businesses. She appears to work mostly from home, but she flies out regularly to meet with clients. That's it for me."

Louie reported in next. "One of my staff members went through all the yearbooks for 1967–68. Comparing senior pictures to the drawings from

Amy, she found three women who are similar in their basic bone structure and are hair- and eye-color matches, all three from different schools. Our next step is to call in a professional to use facial recognition software to compare the yearbook pictures to the drawing to see if there is any overlap in facial structure. She did not have any luck with the male—any ideas?"

I thought for a minute and said, "The male is described in a way that made me think he might be older. Starting with the same schools, could you have her go back two to three years and look for his picture? My bet would be he was either a wrestler or a football player." We all agreed that would be a good tactic.

I finished up by reporting how Maggie's friends had described her and what I had learned about Maggie and Peter Sampson in MG's journal. "People described Maggie in ways that were vastly different from what I had expected. First, she was much closer to Peter Sampson, and for a longer period of time than I was aware of. In fact, by the time of the infamous gang rape party, Maggie was going to Berkeley to see Peter, not MG. MG wrote that Maggie started going directly to the house where Peter and the suspects for last summer's crimes all lived together. Most damning, it was Maggie who insisted that MG attend the party, saying that she could bring Daniel Roan instead of Jackson. According to her friends, Maggie was someone who liked to stir up trouble for MG by telling Jackson—er, JJ—about her outings with Daniel Roan."

By this time, I was really getting hungry, so I asked if someone could summarize. Alex did the summarizing and then gave out assignments: (1) Alex would get Parker's class schedule and pay him a visit at the end of one of his classes; (2) Louie had found family members connected to Karen Jennings so would interview him and take a DNA sample; (3) Louie would have his team conduct a closer investigation of Maggie, Caroline, and Parker, with a special emphasis on finances; (4) Louie's staff would continue trying to identify the male and female in Amy's sketches; (5) I would continue reading the journal and interviewing people who might be relevant. I thought my task was the hardest. Who knew what more I would learn about these people who had taken on such significance in my life? Would they disappoint me further?

CHAPTER 10
Where's Parker?

I raced to get to the institute early on Wednesday morning, as it was my first seminar since learning Maggie was Parker Montgomery's grandmother. I wanted to go through my slides one more time and think about how they flowed and how each might be interpreted. The slides could be painful to read, given the level of deprivation in parts of the country, but they were based on statistically sound data and told a compelling story.

Monica came to my office, and we walked down the hall to the small seminar room together. There was the usual chatter going on as I prepared my slides on the in-class computer. I was set to begin, but I always took time to check in with students about the seminar and any other issues about their training or life in general. As we started to chat, I looked around and noticed that Parker had not come to class. I didn't really know how to interpret his absence. Was he sick? Was he grieving?

I realized that the anticipation of seeing him had made me tense up with my students. I stopped, allowed myself a "be here now" moment, and started over.

After class, Monica and I walked back to my office for our debrief. When that was over, I asked Pauline if she had heard from Parker; there was nothing on her end either.

The phone was ringing on my desk, so I slipped back into my office and saw that the call was from Alex. He was clearly excited about something. "Hey, cuz. Parker has a graduate seminar on Thursday from nine to noon. I plan to be there well before class is out." I told him that was great, but he could hear my lack of enthusiasm. "What's wrong, Phoebe?"

I said, "I don't want to overreact, but Parker did not show up for my class today. I know there are reasons why that might be, but I'm worried you will drive all the way over here, and he won't show for that class either."

After a moment, Alex asked, "Do you know where he lives?"

"I don't," I said, "and any attempt by me to find out could be viewed as harassing him for not coming to class. I need to treat this as I would any absent graduate school student: send an email and give him instructions for next week."

"Understood," Alex said. Then, "OK, Phoebe, I will call you back shortly; stay close to the phone." Alex has more options than me, so I was happy to leave it in his hands.

I settled in to work and I was deep in research and writing when my desk phone rang again. It was Alex, so I picked up the phone.

He went right into his findings. "I asked for a welfare check on Parker, and according to two separate interviews with roommates, Parker has been gone since 'the day his grandmother died,' and no one knows where he went. All that is missing is his backpack and the usual things students keep in it. I don't know about his car yet. Police there will search for his car, and I am going out to his mom's house again."

I suddenly felt a chill run through me. "Take someone with you; this all seems a bit too familiar, given how Maggie was killed."

"I will. I'll call you later."

"Call my cell phone, Alex, as I might be leaving the office."

"Will do."

I called Louie to tell him about Parker and Alex, and then I asked if I could drive over to his business offices. Maybe they would have more tools to use in tracking Parker down.

Alex called right after Louie and I had sat down to discuss the case. It was good timing, so we put Alex on speakerphone.

Alex began, "I am here at Caroline's, and no one is coming to the door, so we will ask to do a welfare check. Her car is here on a pad behind the house, but Parker's car is not here."

"OK," I said. "I am meeting with Louie, and I have you on speakerphone. Louie was just about to catch me up on what his team found, so you're timing is perfect."

"Hey, Alex," Louie said. "The girl sketched by Amy White has been identified as Denise (Deni) Copeland. She often goes by the nickname

Clover. Her family used to own Copeland Dairy, which had the catchphrase 'From our clover to your table.' At the time of the murders, Deni/Clover was a senior at Tulare High School, where she was head cheerleader and president of the Intra-County Farm Group. Based on MG's journal, we know Clover is the same girl that caused trouble for MG and guilted her into joining the ICFA,

We took Phoebe's advice and looked backward for the male. We think he is Jay Schmidt, and you were right, Phoebe: he was a varsity wrestler and still holds a couple of standing records. He was some kind of cousin to Clover, and he hung around her so he could have access to high school girls.

"When we tried to locate Jay, we were told he died in prison about ten years after he graduated from college. At the time, he was serving a twenty-year sentence for manslaughter for running down his wife with his truck while she was six months pregnant. Apparently, the aggression he demonstrated in his successful wrestling career, which carried him through college at Fresno State, did not serve him well in the real world. And because he's already dead, it might be hard to prove he had any involvement in the murders. We would need Clover to name him or find some strong tangible evidence. Remember, we don't have any physical evidence yet."

I was astounded. "How were you able to get such detailed information?"

"Well, he was kind of a legend, so old-timers and classmates talked about him. We found guys who had been on his high school and college teams, and they had no trouble telling us what he was like. Also, there were newspaper stories about him in the archives, and they included more personal information. The good news is that his fingerprints are on file in the unlikely event we find any evidence."

"What about Clover?" Alex asked.

"Clover's nowhere to be found—yet. We employed all the usual methods for tracking someone down, but then we hit a dead end. Turns out she went away to Cal Poly San Luis Obispo, and a few months after she graduated, she just disappeared."

"What about the dairy?" Alex asked.

"The dairy was sold to a large agribusiness conglomerate in the late 1980s. Clover's parents retired, and they died about a decade after that. I don't know who the estate went to or how the money was divvied up. But that is one thing that might give away Clover's location."

Alex said, "Now I know why you have such a good reputation for finding people. Oh, here comes the approval for the welfare check; stay on the line with me." There was silence as the team prepared to enter the house. Then we could hear them going from room to room, clearing the place. Alex came back on the phone.

"There is no one home, but there is evidence that the residents packed in a hurry, and the safe was cleaned out and left open. On top of that, it looks like someone else came later and went through all the rooms, including the attic. The contents of all the boxes have been dumped on the floor in the attic and in other storage areas. It will not be a fun place to come home to. I'm guessing Parker Montgomery was here as well, and they left together after the funeral. Both sets of toiletries have been picked over, and the ones not needed are scattered on the counter or on the floor. Pretty much the same with the clothes. A locked gun box is also standing empty. Anyone know what kind of car he drives?"

Louie answered quickly, "Yes. I wanted to know if he was trailing Phoebe, this is normal surveillance of all people involved with a case. He has a low-key but tricked-out Chevy Colorado, with a crew cab. I'm guessing it was priced out at around forty thousand. Not bad for a student. However, he didn't do anything to make it stand out, just a standard silver color that you see everywhere."

"Yeah," said Alex, "I see truck tracks in the dirt by his mom's car. I do think they took the truck and left together. We don't have any evidence they are running from someone, so I think I have done all I can do. Let's talk tomorrow morning at eight."

It was already late and I was tired, so I spent the night in one of Louie's mini-suites. There were three suites, each equipped with anything a guest might need—for me, it meant I even had a couple of work outfits. Louie had to go back to his boat because he wasn't sure if he had secured it. I felt OK being in the building alone because of the layers of security. I picked out a snack, watched the late news, and fell asleep on the couch.

Louie fed his employees breakfast and lunch if they wanted it, so when

I left my suite the next morning, there was a full breakfast spread, and a bunch of people were milling around it. Louie gave me a hug and suggested I fill my plate and cup and take it to the conference room. The conference room phone rang, and after a few preliminaries Alex asked, "Any ideas on where to search?"

I thought about it and said, "I don't want to waste our time chasing things down, but I know that Peter Sampson, the grandfather, left at least two properties when he was killed. He had a beachfront condo, which might be difficult to sneak into, and he had a small house by the 405 freeway near the Costa Mesa border. When we last checked, no one lived in the house. He also was part owner of a large yacht, but I suspect that is still impounded by the police as evidence."

Louie suggested we drive by the house to see if they were or had been there and, if necessary, snoop around the condo. We signed off with Alex and drove Louie's truck to Sampson's old house, a small white and green rancher on a road running parallel to highway 405. The last time we were at the house, we found that no one had actually lived in it for many years, but a service company maintained the yard and kept the outside clean.

The first thing we saw when we turned the corner onto his street was a large silver Chevy truck in the driveway. I remembered I should not be there because it would look like I was stalking my student. I stayed behind in the car when we reached the house, and I was ready to drop to the floor of the cab should anyone answer the door. I kept my window rolled down so I could hear.

No one came to the door after extensive knocking by Louie. As he turned away, a neighbor drifted over to the fence and called Louie over. I think he mistook Louie for a cop because he started chatting right away.

"Are you here about what happened the other night?" the man asked.

"Yeah, can you tell me about it?" Louie responded.

"Well, around two a.m. Sunday morning, I noticed that truck pulling alongside the curb; it woke me up because the headlights shone into my bedroom. Few people are around that house, especially at night, so I got out of bed and looked outside. I saw a woman and a man open the garage and pull the SUV that was parked inside out onto the street. They took all the stuff from the truck and packed it in the SUV. Then the man backed the truck up the drive as close as possible to the garage door. They locked the truck up, then took off in the SUV."

"Did you do anything about it?" Louie asked.

"I reported it to the police the next morning. They ran the license plate on the truck and said it looked legitimate, and it was possible the owner of the truck was a relative of Dr. Sampson. So I let it go."

He looked expectantly at Louie, so Louie said, "Dr. Sampson died this past summer, and he left the property to his heirs. I imagine it was a relative, but I agree it was an odd time to drop by."

The man looked as though he had not heard anything after the part about Sampson being dead. He genuinely looked sad when he heard the news, and from where I sat, it looked like he might be crying. Then he said, "I was away all summer at my son's lake house. When I got back, the neighbors across the street thought he might have had trouble, but I didn't follow up on it."

He looked uncomfortable and finally asked Louie, "Was he killed?"

Louie said, "Yes, he was run down in a parking lot. What made you ask that?"

"Well, the professor and I used to be friends when we were younger. We used to go out on fishing boats together. We helped each other out with our yards and with house projects. We even kept each other's dogs when we went out of town. I was really sad when he moved to his condo, but we stayed connected for a bit after he left. Sometime in the spring, he stopped by and asked if he could take me out to lunch. I told him that would be great, so we drove down to the beach and had lunch at a nice seafood restaurant.

"Peter acted strange, almost like he knew he was telling me goodbye. He told me that in addition to being a professor, he had been involved in a publishing business for a while but that it looked like the business might be in trouble. He gave me a notarized envelope and told me if he ever died due to foul play, I should give the envelope to the police. If he died from natural causes, I should burn the envelope. I think it might be his will. I guess I should hand over the envelope to you?"

"No, no," Louie said. "The person investigating his death is Detective Fraley. I am going to call him right now and ask him to come out. How about if you go get the envelope, and I will stay here and wait with you?"

The neighbor went into his house to get the envelope, and Louie drifted back to his truck to call Fraley. He told him he had accidentally discovered a piece of evidence about the Sampson murder while working on a different case. When he finished, Louie walked back over to chat with the neighbor and keep him calm.

Fraley was at the house within fifteen minutes. He greeted Louie warmly, and Louie was able to escape with just a brief explanation because Fraley immediately focused on the neighbor. Louie ran back to the truck, and we took off, not exactly having a plan. He pulled over a couple of blocks later. I turned to him and asked, "Weren't you even a little bit curious about what was in the letter?"

He smiled and replied, "My guess is that it is evidence helping to convict Carlton Richmond and the others, if we're lucky."

He really knows his business. I thought for about the hundredth time.

"Can I drop you at work?" Louie asked.

"OK—as long as you pick me up after work too."

▲ ▲ ▲

The next morning, Louie dropped by and I was already dressed for work.

"So, what do you have planned for today?" He asked.

"Just the usual...read things, write things, sign things."

He continued to look at me.

"Wait," I said. "Is today Friday?" He nodded his head yes. "Oh, I took the day off so I could get ready for an overnight trip." He looked pleased that I was taking our weekend away so seriously.

Louie looked at me and said, "The boat is stocked and ready to sail—we could go today."

Thanks to my great need to plan, I was packed and had no real reason, except nerves, to say no. I thought about the last time I had been spontaneous, and it was probably when Will was little. As he looked at me, I realized he thought I would say no, so in that moment I made up my mind and said, "Let's do it! But I do need to eat and pick up a few items at the grocery store." Emotions passed over his face, too fast for me to interpret, but I suspected I would find out what they were eventually.

CHAPTER 11
Down by the Bay

When we got back to my house a couple of hours later, there was a large Canton Moon Farm truck parked in front. We walked into the living room and heard voices coming from the backyard. We walked out and found Aunt Beatrice, Carlos, Will, and Alex on the patio, and JJ greeting Abe and Colette at the door in the back wall.

Beatrice shouted out, “We were so excited for our boat trip and fishing we came early! Hope you don’t mind!”

Louie and I looked at each other and laughed. Aunt Bea not only spent most of her life on the East Coast, but she’d also not acclimated to different customs. Because uncertain weather conditions on the East Coast meant that most events had an alternative rain (or snow) date, she would have assumed the canceled trip would just be pushed back a week—just as I’d hoped she wouldn’t. Looks like our romantic getaway would be postponed for at least another week.

I waited to see how Louie would respond. “You know, that is perfect! I just told Phoebe the boat is ready, and she took the day off to get packed. We were just thinking it would be great to have an extra day!”

JJ looked around and asked, “How many people can you fit on your boat, Louie?”

“Six comfortably, seven in a pinch.”

“How about if I take my boat too?” JJ offered. “Then maybe we could convince Colette and Abe to go too!”

The boomers all squealed excitedly. *Maybe we can put them all together on one boat,* I thought, then said, “That will be so much fun!”

JJ glanced at me, then said, “How about if all the old-timers come with me?” I gave him a grateful smile, which he acknowledged with a slight wink.

Beatrice came over to me and gave me a hug. As she did so, she whispered in my ear. "I hope you don't mind but I brought Faith with me. All the news has stirred up talk about Nina's murder, and it has been hard on her."

That was my kind and loyal Aunt Beatrice. I hugged her back and told her I was really happy to have the opportunity to get to know Nina's younger sister better.

Just then, Faith walked through the back door of the house. Beatrice took her by the arm and walked over to everyone standing around. She said, "Hey, everyone, some of you already know her but for those who don't, this is my friend Faith. Faith was my best friend from kindergarten through high school, and I begged her to come with us this weekend."

▲ ▲ ▲

It turned out that JJ's boat was docked just a few hundred feet from Louie's, so it was easy for us to meet up and divide people and supplies. As decided, all the boomers went with JJ, and Alex, Will, and I went with Louie.

Fortunately, JJ was able to act quickly, and he called ahead to the harbor in the city of Avalon on Catalina Island and reserved two adjacent spots to anchor the boats. We were set to go. It was not the passion-finding getaway we had planned, but maybe that was a good thing. I should have called Aunt Bea to see if they were coming, but I forgot . . . or perhaps I was subconsciously avoiding being alone with Louie?

It only takes the high-speed ferry about an hour to make the trip, but both Louie and JJ had special fishing sites they wanted to try on the way over. We told both of them they could try just one apiece, so we could arrive way before dark. They grumbled but agreed.

JJ's fishing spot came first, so we followed him out of the harbor and then took a leisurely pace behind his boat. He pulled up after we had been on the ocean for about a half hour and put down his anchor. JJ and Carlos started working on the fishing poles, making sure everyone had a pole that had bait and was ready to cast. When we caught up with them, we went through the same process, with Louie and Alex getting the poles together.

Will took his pole and went around to the other side of the boat to practice in private. Alex joined him, and I heard quite a bit of laughter.

Before we started fishing, we decided we would only keep what we could eat that day, as we would want to catch fresh fish for the next day. We all cast off at the same time, after Louie gave a demonstration for our boat, and JJ gave one for his. As we waited, Alex, Louie, and I chatted about what we thought was in the letter Peter Sampson had left, and Louie told Alex about the key. Suddenly, Louie's phone rang loudly. I didn't think we would be in range of cell service, but there it was.

He saw who it was and rolled his eyes but took the call anyway. All I could hear was loud talking on the other end, with Louie offering yeses and noes and the occasional comment, all the while trying to keep a straight face. He handed the phone to me then walked to the other side of the boat then he started laughing so hard I was afraid he would drop his pole.

When I took the phone I could hear Fraley in the background saying, "I hate f---ing riddles!" He calmed down when I got on the phone and he said, "The letter in the envelope is apparently about the Carlton Richmond case. It is a confession of sorts, along with a list of places where Carlton stashed information. Some places we knew about, but others provided new information. But Sampson, like that whole case, wanted you in the middle. There is a note on the envelope that says, "The package is where Phoebe and Emma first met each other."

"OK, that's easy. It's at the Pacific View Retreat, the key is probably for one of the staff lockers."

Fraley gave me a brief sound of some sort then hung up.

"Why was he so cranky?" I asked.

Alex laughed. "I know exactly why. I think he's jealous of your and Louie's free time—I know I am!"

Just then we heard two shouts for help—one from each boat. It seemed that both Will and Colette might have some fish action. Louie ran around to guide Will, and JJ went to assist Colette. Soon there were other callouts for help on both boats, so Louie and JJ were running all over, trying to keep up. Over half of the fish got off the line easily, and others struggled on. In the end, almost everyone had a bite, but only three fish were reeled in: by Colette,

Alex, and Will. Will's fish was the largest, so we returned the other two to the water. By this time, everyone was soaked and laughing. The fish was a calico bass and weighed just under four pounds. JJ and Louie seemed happy with it, but they ribbed each other that maybe they should have kept two.

We celebrated the fish with beer and snacks after washing up. After the break, Louie rounded us all up and asked JJ to follow him out to his fishing spot. Louie went in close to the shore of Catalina Island, sharing only that there was a reef off the small island that drew in the big fish. He had a short conversation with JJ about bait, and once again, the two of them helped everyone on their boats get ready. Within minutes of casting off at the new spot, the fish were biting and everyone was struggling to bring their fish in. Over half got away, some others were obviously too small to keep (both Louie and JJ had laminated regulations about what was legal), and four were contenders. Louie and JJ looked them over and decided an eleven-pound white sea bass caught by Beatrice was best.

Together with the calico, that gave us fifteen pounds of fish to work with, but after cleaning and skinning the fish, we would have about four and a half pounds total to cook for dinner. We loaded up again, boated into Avalon, and maneuvered to our tie-up spots. As soon as we settled, Louie and JJ led a discussion of duties, and they assigned them according to our preferences. I chose to pick up the boats' cabins and lightly clean the heads for my duties. Abe, Beatrice, and Carlos chose to cook dinner.

The three cooks took their job very seriously, and in about ninety minutes we had fish stew with rice, fish tacos, and fruit salad for dinner. Louie and JJ had picked up premade foods to take the pressure off the cooks, including exotic salsa and other toppings. JJ had brought a delicious fruit cheesecake, and we all stuffed ourselves. Not too much later, due to the excitement, sun, and food, we were all just lolling around and listening to music, alternating between JJ's and Louie's selections. Around nine o'clock I saw Louie and JJ talking, and not long after, JJ got our attention and asked, "Who wants to go out fishing tomorrow at daybreak?" All the men, including Will, raised their hands. "Who wants to sleep in and go shopping and sightseeing tomorrow?" All the women raised their hands.

Louie and JJ conferred again, and Louie said, "For the sake of practicality, we suggest all the men sleep on JJ's boat, so we can slip out quietly in the morning. The women can sleep on my boat. When you are ready to leave in the morning, you can take the small boat onto shore and dock it. We will probably be back around midafternoon, and either JJ or I can take any of you who want to fish out in the late afternoon. How does that sound?"

I was so relieved to avoid a discussion about sleeping arrangements that I knew I must be turning red. Louie made sure the boat was locked down for the night, then he pulled up close to JJ's boat so the men could step over. We decided Beatrice and I would share one stateroom, and Colette and Faith would have their own cabins.

I fell right to sleep when I crawled into bed, but before I knew it, someone was gently shaking my arm to wake me up. As I started to rouse, I heard Louie whisper in my ear, "Follow me up on deck." It was dark, so he took my hand and guided me up the stairs. It was just first light when we got topside. He pulled me over to a bench and said in a low voice, "You got some mail overnight." That woke me up really fast. It meant someone had been on board, and I hadn't heard a thing.

He went on: "I came over to grab more fishing supplies and found this note and package wedged under the hatch."

I pulled out the note and did my best to read it in the low light.

> ***We didn't kill Maggie, but I think we are in danger. Here are threat letters she received in the weeks before she was killed. Her house was trashed, but she left a couple of the original envelopes with us shortly before she was killed. We will get them to you when we can. They are hidden near our home for now. We aren't stalking you; we just happened to be hiding out here on a friend's boat and we saw you come in. —Caroline and Parker***

By this time, Louie had motioned for Alex to come over, so I handed the note to them to read while I opened the large envelope.

In all, there were a dozen or so threatening letters that became more graphic and detailed as I went through them. I thought about Caroline and Parker, the mother-son duo. I didn't know them well, but I had no reason to doubt their motivations. Like us, they wanted to solve Maggie's murder.

Louie said, "Let's put this in a safe place and deal with it when we get back to Newport Beach tomorrow, OK? I don't want to ruin the party or raise suspicions." We agreed to that, and Louie put the letters in a hidden safe in the galley. Then he and Alex hustled to get back on JJ's boat before they were missed by the others.

I decided to stay up and watch the sunrise. I made coffee with a K-cup and dragged a couple of pillows out from the lounge so I could be comfortable while I waited for the others to get up.

I wondered who would join me first, and I felt confident it would be Aunt Beatrice. I heard a bit of noise and saw Faith peek her head out the door. I gave her a big smile and waved her over.

"Come join me, Faith. I've really wanted to have a moment so we could talk. But first, could I get you some tea or coffee?"

"Coffee with a bit of cream would be lovely," she said.

"Coming right up," I said, and went to make it while she got comfortable.

I came back with her coffee and then resettled myself against the pillows. "I know I said this before, but I'm so happy you came with Beatrice. I also wanted to check in and see how you're doing."

She took a moment before answering. "I'm happy that we found Nina's body and can now bury her with other family members. But the strain of answering all the questions—not only from people I know but also from strangers—is getting me down. A lot of people have theories about how and why she died, and they seem to think it's appropriate to share them with me. I am tired of being nice, like a good librarian. I just want to tell people to check their sentiments at the door.

"The constant voicing of condolences by people who either never knew Nina or knew her but were never friendly to her also wears me out. When it is really bad, I feel like I can't breathe, because no matter where I am, there are people there too. Sleeping on the boat last night was the first chance I've had to feel safe and be alone at the same time. I needed time away from it all, and I appreciate Beatrice asking me to come along. It's a welcome relief."

I felt embarrassed because I had hoped to talk about Nina too. I quashed that plan.

"What do you want out of this weekend?" I asked gently.

"I want some quiet time, where I don't have to process what people around me are saying. Also, I want a few days of not being Nina's poor sister."

"How can I help you find that?"

"I'd like a bit of time alone; also, I'd like to talk about just ordinary things."

"Of course!" I exclaimed. "How about if you go back to your cabin and I tap on your door when we decide to leave for our walk into town? If you need more time alone instead of going with us—or at any other time—just say you are feeling exhausted. OK?"

"That sounds like a plan. Thanks for the assist," she said, before getting up to leave.

After Faith retired to her cabin, I checked my voice messages and found a few new ones. Most importantly was a message addressed to both Louie and me from one of his staff persons:

"Found Clover in Lake Tahoe, we traced the money from her inheritance. Going by the name of Deni Buyers. Will tell you more tomorrow."

This was definitely something for Louie and me to talk about with Alex. Alex should be the one to chase her down and interview her, given she was a person of interest in the murders. However, I could use this quiet time to read up on anything I can find about her on the internet.

An hour or so later, I was joined by Beatrice, and we chatted about ranch business and new directions they wanted to take in sustainable agriculture. The last to join was Colette, who looked the perkiest of all of us, and she took right over in planning out the day. Suddenly, she stopped chattering and looked around. "Where's Faith?" she asked.

"Faith was up really early but went back to her cabin to rest. I told her I would tap on her door when we were about to leave to see if she felt up to joining us."

That seemed to satisfy Colette, so she bounced into the galley and started to prepare a light breakfast; she wanted to have a fancy lunch at a restaurant in the shopping district.

We made it to the dock around ten and took off walking toward the shops and restaurants. Faith had decided to join us, and the time alone seemed to have really helped. We had fun seeing all the things it was possible to buy, and at one point I bought us all inexpensive but coordinated dresses we could wear on the boat that evening.

We made it to the restaurant Colette wanted to go to and had a lengthy discussion about what to order. Everyone was trying to decide on seafood or gourmet vegetarian and what type of mixed drink they wanted. I told them we would probably have seafood again tonight, so we all chose vegetarian meals, and we soaked up every bite with the amazing homemade bread. After lunch, we spent some leisurely time doing touristy things before heading back to the boats.

We reached Louie's boat just after JJ had docked his, so we had help coming on board and tying up the skiff. Everyone was really tired and ambled off to rest for a couple of hours. I pulled Louie aside and asked if we could look at the threat letters received by Maggie before she was killed. I was too eager to see them to wait until the next day.

The letters started right after Nina's body was found and identified and continued until the day before Maggie was killed. Maggie had put a date on the back of each letter so they were in order. They started out fairly mild—"Stop trying to uncover what is better left dead"—to more overt threats: "You may not care about your own life, but you must care about the lives of Caroline and Parker." Then the last one, which said, "I am looking forward to ending your useless life."

It seemed likely that the letters pertained to information Maggie might have had about the murdered girls, so we decided to hand them over to Alex.

▲ ▲ ▲

After we emerged from our rest, we all felt a great boost in energy, and everyone except the cooks went off to explore for a couple of hours before dinner. JJ went off with Will, which made me happy. Since I had already had the opportunity to explore, I traded places with Abe in the galley, and Louie traded places with Carlos—now we just needed to think of something to cook. Louie wanted to grill the fish they'd caught, so we took them down to the beachside grills. It was our first time alone since the clan had shown up at our house, and it was nice to have that bit of time together, planning a meal rather than talking about murder.

Louie made a delicious marinade, and we had leftover salsa, so that part didn't require complex work. I wandered over to a local bakery and bought fresh bread and an assortment of chocolate desserts. Beatrice had stayed behind and made a platter of fresh fruit and a big bowl of coleslaw. We were ready for our guests. They all came back together in JJ's skiff, claiming to be famished. We all freshened up—including putting on our coordinating dresses—and had a feast. I couldn't remember being happier than I was right at that moment, with people who are connected to me and care about me. What I found so strange was that six months ago, I didn't know most of them and was only close to Will and Beatrice.

We got up around eight the next morning. Everyone was moving slowly, but in a "life is good" sort of way. We each made our own breakfast, then headed back to the mainland soon after. When we returned, we stored all the perishable food on Louie's boat and prepared JJ's boat it to be docked—he actually didn't use it but once a month or so. After making sure everything was secure, we drove back to my house to sort out our belongings. Shortly after, Alex, Carlos, Beatrice, Faith, and Will left for the farm.

It had been an unexpected weekend, but seeing the lift it had given to my friends and family, it was well worth it. Louie and I had plenty of time.

Chapter 12
Evidence

After everyone left, I decided to rest and then read some more of MG's journal. Louie decided to go over to his office, which was just three miles away, and check on how all the company's cases were going. He promised to bring back a non-fish dinner for us.

After a short nap, I brought out journal number two and continued reading. Again, there were discussions of trends for the business, who came to visit her, and how she was feeling. It was during a discussion on the effects of her drugs that MG told more of her story:

> *Daniel has slowly been increasing my drugs. He is trying to find the best balance between pain control and quality time, when I can write and sketch. My world has become very narrow but intense. My dreams are so vivid that I am often confused in the morning when I wake up, and it is hard for me to put the dreams into the categories of real or fantasy. Sometimes I feel like I have taken LSD and gone on a good trip—and I can look out the windows and see the trees dancing in time to whatever music is going through my mind. I see the colors in the paintings in my room blend together and then separate from each other. I really don't mind dreams as long as I can function during the day.*
>
> *Daniel now comes to see me every other day. Maggie has disappeared; Daniel found a nurse who comes in the afternoons so mother can still have a break. I see my condition in the reflection of my mother's eyes, and the love and appreciation I have for her is immense. Earlier in the week, I asked Daniel to call her*

into my room, and I told both of them about my dreams and the feeling of being high. I told them both I recognized their love but that when it was time to let me go, I wanted to go out floating in that dreamlike state, not asleep and not in pain. I asked them if they would help me to accomplish that last thing, and they said they would. I told them if at all possible, I would return and be there during their process of dying and death.

MG ended there but picked up her story the next day.

I got a bit off track in yesterday's writing; I had wanted to write about one particular dream I had this week. In the dream, it was the night that Nina disappeared. I was sitting in my room, watching the clock slowly tick away the seconds. For some reason, I had a feeling of doom and a sense of a coming tragedy. I strained to hear a car or see a headlight. I couldn't take waiting in my room anymore, and I pulled on my shoes and snuck out the window of my second-story room. I ran parallel with the driveway toward the road through a row of orange trees. There was a full moon, and I could see all the ruts and ridges in the field, so I wasn't afraid of falling. I heard voices, and I realized I was near the end of the orchard. As quietly as I could, I crawled under the last orange tree before the end of our property. The leaves under the tree were dry and crinkly, but the tips were sharp enough to pierce my clothes and skin. I lay on my belly and looked out through the leaves. There were rotting oranges from the season before, and I had to work hard not to sneeze or get them on my clothes. The furry oranges were shiny dark green and white with mold, and I knew if I touched one it could explode.

As I was looking down at the leaves, I heard a scream that made me shiver all over; I twisted in the leaves and had to stop myself right before I screamed back. I peeked out and saw Nina all hunched over, she was being held by Clover and a man I didn't know. A girl was leaning over her with a knife; the moonlight glinted off the blood on the knife. The girl with the knife looked like Maggie.

In my dream I blacked out just then, and when I awoke, it was cold and dewy under the orange tree. The dew accentuated the smell of the mold. I made myself look out again, but there was nothing there. I wiggled backward out of the tree and ran home. I checked my clock, and it was just seven minutes past midnight. I sensed that my clothes smelled like rotten oranges, but I got under the covers anyway. When I awoke the next day, still in my dream, it was a school day, and mother made me get ready for school and wait for the bus—just like any day in my life. In my dream, when I got to school, I looked for both Nina and Maggie, and they were gone.

I woke up just then, and I was a middle-aged cancer patient sleeping in my bed alone. I couldn't tell if the content of the dream was fantasy or memory. I felt a pull toward the orange grove. I had a desire to look under every tree, but I knew I didn't have the strength to look under even one. I realized I would die without knowing if the dream was a memory.

This passage affected me like none other in the journals. I can't remember my mother ever expressing doubt about her interpretation of reality. Not that she made me accept her own version, but she could confidently speak to the meaning of things we saw, read, or experienced. Was she trying to help me trust my instincts? I found I also didn't know if Maggie could have played a role in the murders of the girls. Why would she? She'd professed to love Nina like a sister.

I turned back to the journal. I knew it was urgent to read the rest to see if there were other clues, but I found it so emotionally draining—like when I close my eyes during really violent scenes in movies in order to protect myself from the stimuli. There were no more long essays in the rest of book two. The paragraphs and sentences had become shorter and more instructional, more like a list of what MG wanted her staff to remember to do. At one point she wrote that the instructions would stay in place until Phoebe could take over. I felt gutted, as people say, that I had not bothered to read her journals until over thirty years later. I needed to thank the people who had kept her company alive, with no help from me. As I thought about it, I wondered, She had felt too devastated to have me near her when she died, was it understandable I felt the same about reading her journals after she died? Did they cancel each other out?

I was nodding off in my chair with the journal in my lap when I heard Louie coming through the side gate and onto the patio. True to his word, he brought food: Italian main dishes from his favorite restaurant, to be followed by chocolate cannoli. Louie took the food, beer, paper plates, and utensils out of the bag. There was so much food, Louie tapped on the back door to see if Colette and Abe wanted to come over, but they didn't seem to be home.

We looked at one another and Louie said, "Food first and then we call Alex?" There was a strong agreement to follow that plan. The food was delicious and put both of us in a good mood. After I had scraped the last bit of chocolate icing from my dessert off my plate, I announced I was ready to get to business.

Louie called Alex and put him on speaker. Alex was a bit cranky when he said, "I just now got home so no report for me."

Louie said, "The only thing I have to report is that we found out more about Deni Buyers, a.k.a. Clover. Clover is a blackjack dealer at one of the casinos on the Nevada side of Lake Tahoe, and she has a small condo within walking distance of work. Her shift is Friday through Tuesday, three p.m. to eleven p.m., with a half hour break for a meal. Apparently, there is some resentment about her fixed schedule being what it is. The woman I talked with complained that the typical evening shift is four p.m. to midnight, and no one routinely gets different hours. Clover is so good and so senior, she is allowed to work when she wants. Anyway, she is scheduled to work tomorrow, and her break is mid-shift, six thirty to seven. I spoke with the company helicopter pilot, and he is prepared to take us up there and back, if anyone would like to go."

Alex said he would check with his supervisor, but yes, he wanted to go. I debated whether I should go along too, but I could not justify taking more time away from work. It was bad enough I had taken a whole weekend off without even thinking about my job; I needed to put in a long catch-up day on Monday. I told them I would have to pass, so Louie promised to call me right after they spoke with Clover.

Then it was my turn, and instead of just telling them about the sections of journal two I had read, I read the passage about the orange grove to them. When I had finished, they both sat quietly. Alex said, "I know that exact tree. We had planned to take out that row of trees and three others last year, but we didn't get around to it. It was still producing fruit, but just barely, so Carlos did not think it was an emergency. Now we will build an iron fence around it and keep it forever as 'MG's Tree.'" As for the issue of fantasy versus memory, none of us had a clue.

CHAPTER 13
Struggles at Work

I was anxious to get back to work, so I got up early and was there by seven thirty. It was quiet at that time in the morning, and I would be able to collect my thoughts and write my list of what I needed to do that day. Usually my office was my sanctuary, but I had a creepy feeling when I walked through the suite and approached my office. It looked as though I had left the blinds that covered the windows of the office wall facing into the suite closed all weekend—well, really since last Thursday. I had never done that before, and I wondered what had happened. We had just updated the office and suite security features, so I really had no thought of danger.

Keeping my curiosity tamped down, I approached my office and turned the door handle—just to see if I had forgotten to lock it. As I did pushed the door open, someone ran out the door and hit me hard. I tried to remain upright, but the force knocked me into Pauline's desk, and as I fell, I hit my head on the corner of it. Then I felt myself falling all the way to the ground next to the desk, hitting my head a second time. That was all I remembered.

The next thing I was aware of was Pauline's voice, trying to pull me back into reality. I resisted because I liked the space between consciousness and unconsciousness very much. Probably because I had been reading her journals, I saw MG walking out from under a huge orange tree that was draped over a magnificently colored palace. She came to my side and placed a cool hand positioned in a V shape on my forehead, and I felt as if I was being gently guided back to consciousness. I broke through the barrier and there was Pauline, holding my hand and peering at me. I could tell there were others gathered around me, and I could hear the paramedics rolling some kind of cart down the hall. I drifted off again.

▲ ▲ ▲

I woke up in a hospital bed, I guessed Hoag Memorial, and I could hear Louie and Alex talking about me with an older man. As I listened, I figured out it must be Fraley, and he was complaining about how I was going to get myself hurt or killed. To my surprise, both Louie and Alex defended me quite vigorously, and Alex said we wouldn't have any evidence at all if it weren't for me. At that, Fraley chuckled and told them that they were probably right about that. After Fraley left, I decided I wanted to wake up, so I struggled to open my eyes and then to sit up. Not only were Louie and Alex there, but so were JJ and Pauline.

Alex was the first to notice my movement, and he raced to my side. "Cuz, what the hell is going on?"

I had enough where-with-all to ask, "How about you, how did you get here?"

"Well, we didn't know how serious the head injury was so Louie sent the helicopter for me. I've only been here a few minutes."

Our conversation got everyone's attention, and they all hurried over. I was fully awake now, and I said, "I interrupted someone in my office. The person rushed out the door and into me so hard that I fell and hit my head on Pauline's desk and then I was out. I did not see anyone, but I was tipped off by the fact that my window shades were drawn. Did you get anything off the cameras?" They looked at one another, and then Louie was the one to speak.

"The cameras in the suite only picked up a large figure all in black, wearing a black balaclava. The person was wearing a loose-fitting outfit, like a graduation gown, so that there was no way to distinguish body type or whether it was a male or a female. The person had some kind of lock pick for the door, and the first thing they did was to lower all the blinds, making it very dark in the room. From the tape, it looked like the person was using a small pin light to look around, which was always directed away from the camera. At no point was there light on the person or what they were looking at. On the way out of your office, the person appeared to be carrying a file folder. Unfortunately, that is all we saw."

"What color was the folder?" I asked.

"Does it really matter?" Alex asked.

"Color coded," I said with effort. Then I was out again.

I awoke hours later, and it was quiet and softly lit in my room. I looked up, and Louie was dozing in the chair next to me. As soon as I saw him, I asked, "Why aren't you in Lake Tahoe?"

He laughed and took my hand. "I can go another day. I know you want to know the color of the file—it was blue."

I frowned and muttered, "Why would someone want a faculty personnel file? Do we know which one is missing?"

Louie responded, "Pauline looked through the current faculty, and all of their files are there. She did not look through the faculty who have left because she was worried that she would miss someone—she has only been on the job for a couple of years. She is going to call human resources in the morning to see if she can get a list of all the people who have left."

I took inventory of my body. My lower ribs were sore, probably from running into the intruder. My head was also sore, and feeling the side of it, I could tell that they had shaved a bit of hair and put in stitches. Otherwise, I was just achy all over from the fall. Louie was watching me do the pain inventory, then said, "No, you are not going to the office tonight. You are under observation for a concussion. If everything is OK in the morning, I will pick you up and take you by the office and then straight to the boat so you can rest."

As I worked myself up to complain, the nurse came in, gave me a stern look, and then got down to business checking my vitals. Sometime during all of this, I drifted off yet again.

▲ ▲ ▲

The doctor came by early the next morning and told me I could go home if I promised to take it easy and call in if anything changed for the worse. I agreed, and when he was gone, I crawled out of bed to get dressed, though I had no idea what condition my clothes would be in. I pulled them out of a bag and looked at each piece. I had worn a large knit sweater over a T-shirt and pants to work yesterday. There was blood on the sweater, but the T-shirt and pants looked fairly clean. I put those on, along with my underwear and the black loafers I had been wearing. I finger-combed my hair and put it in a very loose ponytail. I was ready, and I sat down to wait for Louie to pick me up.

I needed to go back to the office to prepare for my Wednesday seminar, plus I wanted a quiet place to think about who my attacker might be. Though in truth, the person did not technically attack me, just made an enthusiastic exit from my office. I couldn't say I would be in danger in the future—especially if they got away with the file they wanted.

Louie came in while I was thinking things over and sat down beside me. We both spoke at the same time: "It has to be about Maggie." This reinforced my belief that the person did not mean to hurt me intentionally—unless it was Maggie's killer. I needed to give it more thought.

After a quick breakfast, Louie drove me back to the institute and insisted on walking me up to my office. He wasn't happy I was going to work for a while, but honestly, he wasn't surprised. He'd brought me a sweater to put on over my T-shirt, a hairbrush, and toiletries. We walked upstairs and into the suite; things looked calm as usual. I thanked everyone for their concern, and Pauline handed me a list of former faculty members. I walked into my office, ready to get to work.

Louie followed me in and asked if he could help me identify the missing file. I readily accepted, appreciating his help because my head still ached. He read me the names on the list, and I searched my files. As it turned out, the files for two former employees were missing: Peter Sampson and Emma Bell. There was no connection between these people and the murdered teenagers that I could see except through Maggie.

After a bit of negotiation, Louie agreed to pick me up in four hours, which would give me enough time to prepare for my seminar and catch up on my email. I knew the material for my seminar quite well, but I liked to refresh myself on the specifics of the readings and slides, and I periodically needed to update statistics and theories. I finished up right as Louie was tapping on my door. He had picked up a picnic lunch for us to enjoy on my patio, after which I was to rest on the lounge chair for the remainder of the afternoon. A good compromise, I thought.

I couldn't remember why but I knew I wanted to talk to Colette. Right on cue, there was a tapping on the back door, then Colette poked her head through. Louie asked her to join us for lunch; she said she had already eaten but would take an iced tea. That nudged my brain enough to remember what I'd wanted to tell her.

"Colette, we'd wanted to have you and Abe over for dinner on Sunday, but you were out. I know it was last minute, but we were sorry to miss you."

"Oh, that's so nice," she said. "We were actually at a meeting with our lawyer about whether we should consider giving up the search for Angelina." Angelina was Abe and Colette's birth daughter, who had been kidnapped right after birth by an associate of Carlton Richmond. For many years, they were promised information in exchange for money and threats.

"We had decided to give up until we learned that Carlton was likely behind it all, and that something could possibly come up in his trial. Now we are confused again, so we have decided to take some time away to think it through—again. That's what I came to tell you. We are taking off for Chile this evening, then we will go on from there. You have my number, so call anytime."

After getting her news out, she took a good look at me and could see that I looked a bit rough. She said, "Oh, Phoebe—what happened to you?" Louie explained what had happened, but I interrupted before he could share whose files were taken. I didn't want her to worry about a whole new problem.

When Colette got up to leave, I stopped her and said, "Colette, of course I can't promise anything, but know that we will be keeping an eye out for Angelina as we learn more about Carlton."

She paused for a moment, then said, "Thank you, Phoebe, but please—only tell us if it is a confirmed lead. I can't take any more disappointment right now." She gave us a sad smile, then took her leave.

I couldn't imagine the devastation that Colette and Abe must be feeling. The loss of their daughter had informed their entire adult lives, and now they had again found only more lies by Carlton Richmond and his central role in the kidnapping.

Louie finally spoke. "If you feel up to it, the pilot tells me he has time to fly to Porterville to pick up Alex and then on to Lake Tahoe so we can question Deni Buyers. If we don't go today, it will have to wait until at least Friday, when she works again. Our plan would still be to catch her on her meal break, question her, then fly back afterward. I don't want to go if you feel uncomfortable being here alone, but you could stay on the boat or in one of the office suites." Then he added, "Well, you wouldn't be alone because I would have someone on staff sit outside your house and keep watch for intruders."

I thought about the three choices he had given me. I knew he was talking out of concern for my well-being, but I also knew that if we were going to have a relationship, I needed to accept the concern but also do what I needed to do.

"Those are great options, but I need to go to Lake Tahoe. I know I told you I didn't have time, but I accomplished what I needed to this morning, and since I'm taking the rest of the day off anyway, per doctor's orders, I'd like to see and talk with Clover myself. I promise I will rest or sleep during any downtime."

"Not a surprise, but we will make sure you rest," he said with a warm smile.

▲ ▲ ▲

We were settled on the helicopter by two o'clock, and I immediately fell asleep. Alex had decided to stay over for the night so we were all set to fly directly to Lake Tahoe. I awoke when we were about a half hour from our destination and stayed awake for the rest of the flight. Our conversation turned to a discussion of what we hoped to get out of the trip. Turning to Alex, I said, "Since there is no real evidence, I'm guessing you aren't hoping to arrest Clover, correct?"

"We have a lot of witness accounts and what might be called gossip, but no actual evidence of the murders. I thought we might try to shake her up and see if it pushes her to say or do anything we might use against her. Your job is to listen and see if you think she is being honest. Louie, you can help by listening for any avenues of investigation we can pursue. Also, I'd like to know if she'd been in touch with Maggie."

It wasn't long before we landed. Much to my horror, Louie and Alex ganged up on me and insisted I use a wheelchair. We negotiated that I could get out of the chair if we were able to talk with Clover.

Our goal was to be at the casino by six because we didn't know where Clover took her dinner breaks. We were a few minutes late, but when we did enter, I was overwhelmed by the lights, sounds, and smells of perspiration mixed with anxiety. As we moved through the rows of slot machines, they screamed at me to feed them money. When they rewarded those who had heeded the call, their lights circled overhead and they roared victory for the player. Between the slots and the frenetic background music, I felt disoriented and was almost grateful to be in the wheelchair. Almost.

When we'd finally moved past the slots and begun scouting the slightly quieter floor area with the card games, Alex spotted Clover at her table. He pushed me over to a drinks table, where the three of us could watch her relatively unobstructed. She looked healthier than I'd expected. I guess I had mistakenly—and stereotypically—assumed she would be a smoker and have a generally unhealthy look about her. Instead, she looked as though she took care of her health, or maybe the job was just so physically demanding it kept her in shape. A few minutes later, a manager and a replacement came to her table. After a brief discussion, she took her belongings out of a hidden space and walked toward a door labeled "staff only."

I don't know how he did it, but Alex intercepted Clover before she reached the door. He was able to lead her to a wall-less restaurant that was centered around a buffet line. The two of them went straight to the buffet, and then they grabbed a table. I had already got out of the wheelchair, and when Alex gave us a sign, we walked over to them. Alex introduced us, and we sat down. I could see then that both had only bought large soft drinks.

"Ah, the infamous Phoebe, mother's little princess!" she said in a rather mocking tone. "You took the direct flight out of Tulare County and never looked back! Sounds like we have something in common." I gave her a small smile but waited for Alex to begin his questioning. I wanted to spend my time listening and watching to see what I could learn about her.

After a few moments, Alex leaned toward her and asked, "Do you prefer we call you Clover or Deni?"

She chuckled and said, “Well, no matter where I go, the name Clover has stuck with me. It’s memorable and I don’t really mind it.”

“OK, Clover it is. I don’t know if you follow news from Tulare County, so I will summarize a case we are working on. And when I say ‘we,’ I mean me, as part of the sheriff’s office, and Phoebe and Louie, as private investigators. We also have team members from the California Bureau of Investigation. A month ago, based on an anonymous tip, we found the body of a teenage girl buried on the Canton Moon Ranch. A few days later, we found more bodies at a ranch across the street. As we investigated, witnesses described two people they saw hanging around the victims. We have evidence that suggests those two people were you and your cousin Jay.” Alex stopped there, and we were all quiet for a minute.

Clover did not say a word, just continued to look at Alex. Her face was perfectly composed, and she looked as though she could sit there listening and fielding questions all day. After a long pause, Alex asked, “Aren’t you curious about the names of the girls?”

“I was waiting for you to tell me. I was thinking that I didn’t know any girls who were missing from my high school.”

“Well, Clover, these girls were not from your high school; these girls were from other high schools in the county. What they had in common is that they were dating the boyfriends of girls you knew from study abroad.” This was a bluff on Alex’s part, but unfortunately it didn’t go anywhere, as there was no response from Clover.

“Did you know girls from other schools through some of your activities?”

“Alex, I am quite sure you know that I did know girls from other schools through study abroad, cheerleading, and the Intra-County Farm Group. None of the girls I knew went missing, except some never returned after college.”

“Ah, well the first girl to go missing was Nina Scott from Lower Sierra. Do you remember her?”

“Was she in any of the groups that I just mentioned? If not, I didn’t know her.”

Alex was starting to look slightly annoyed by Clover’s evasiveness. “No,

Clover, she wasn't in any of those groups, but we believe she got a bit too close to someone who was claimed as a boyfriend by someone you *did* know. As a matter of fact, she became pregnant by that boyfriend. We think that because of her pregnancy, she was sentenced to death. That death sentence was carried out by two people who looked a lot like you and your cousin."

This was a direct shot, but again, she had no response. "Do you have any thoughts?" Alex asked.

"That was a long time ago. I really doubt anyone can remember faces or names from then."

Alex looked thoughtful, then said, "Yes, that is true, but we have a detailed drawing of what the killers looked like, and a facial analyst has testified it is highly likely to be you and Jay. Since we believe Jay is dead, that means it would all come down on you."

At that, he pulled out copies of Amy's drawing and Clover's senior year picture and laid them in front of her. "What do you think, does this look like you?"

That did it. I saw a slight trembling in her right eyelid. Suddenly she rose from her seat and said, "I have to get ready to finish my shift."

"Please, sit back down. I have one more thing to show you."

When she'd sat down again, Alex said, "Someone has been cleaning house, so to speak." He laid two pictures of Maggie on the table—one as a teenager and one after she was murdered.

"Maybe you know this woman? She seemed to have had a role in all of this. We found her dead just a few days ago. By all accounts she was Nina's best friend. Since she retired, she has been looking full time for Nina's murderer. Do you know why her notes mention you?"

Without saying a word, Clover covered her mouth, stood, and ran toward the staff door.

Alex called after her, "That's OK, we'll be back again real soon."

After she left, we looked at each other. Alex said, I think that went rather well. Phoebe, was she lying?"

"Definitely," I said. "She kept it together until she saw the drawing and the pictures. I think she obviously had a relationship with Maggie, but did she kill her?"

Louie agreed and noted that the Maggie-Clover relationship was key.

After that, Alex said, "I'm going to get a plate of food before we go back." He went off to the buffet singing a version of "He's So Vain" about Clover. Louie joined him, but I had lost my appetite. We all knew that Clover had felt threatened by the drawing and the pictures of Maggie. We sat at the table for another half hour, but she never came back out the staff door. Wondering if there was another exit, we retreated to the blackjack area, but she hadn't yet returned to her table.

After a while, we reached a point where we were certain she wouldn't be returning to her table anytime soon, and since it was getting late, we decided to call it a day and head back to the airport. After all, I had class in the morning.

Chapter 14
A Very Long Day

I got to work a little after eight the next morning and noticed I had voicemail on my rarely used office phone. There was a message from Dean Richmond and another from Dr. Daniel Roan's administrative assistant, asking if I could attend a late lunch on Wednesday. She had called last Friday, but I had been out of the office and had not noticed the message in the brief time I was there the day before. I called her back, got her voicemail, and apologized for the late notice but said I could meet for lunch, just tell me where and when.

Then I called Dean Richmond. She wanted to know if Parker Montgomery was back in class yet.

"He was not in class last week, and I have the next class in about twenty minutes. I don't know where he is. I will ask among his peers if anyone has heard from him, but I am not hopeful." Although I was sure from our snooping how she would answer this, I asked, "Has anyone checked to see if he is attending his other classes?"

She seemed a bit surprised by the question but told me no one had checked in on him following Maggie's death, but she would have someone do it at once.

As I hung up the phone, I saw Monica tapping on my door, letting me know it was time to head to class. I gave her a big smile and a wave, gathered up my materials, and then we walked to class together.

Parker was not in class. As I did every week, I started by asking how things were going and if anyone had read any articles about poverty over the last week. Several of the students had seen articles about SNAP (food stamp) policies and the push to cut back on who was eligible. We had a spontaneous debate about the issue, during which I randomly assigned students to be pro or con on the restrictions, positions that they then had to defend. Arguing for the pro side was so difficult, we broke down in laughter. By this point in the class, no one was promoting the reduction of benefits, especially food, for the poor.

After our debate, I asked if anyone had heard from Parker. The two members of Parker's project group raised their hands and told me he was in regular contact with them and was doing his share of the work. Parker had told them his mother was ill and he needed to take care of her. One of the partner's told me he was worried he might be gone for the rest of the semester, so she was sending him her notes. He couldn't tell me his mother was sick because I knew it was a lie; instead, he got in touch by delivering the threat letters.

I had to put that all out of my mind as we officially started class, and I tried my best to engage the students in discussion.

After class, Monica and I walked back to my office, and I invited her to take a seat. When we were settled, I told her the proposal for her dissertation research was ready to go forward, and she responded with arguments about why it wasn't ready. I looked at her and wondered if I should take a hardline approach, like tell her I couldn't be her advisor any longer if she didn't trust my advice. But as I continued to watch her, I saw the perspiration beading on her forehead and how she was avoiding eye contact and knew I had to just be direct: "Monica, does thinking about your oral exam make you anxious?"

The oral defense of a dissertation proposal is a major hurdle for doctoral students. It required going before a committee of five professors, giving an oral presentation, and then answering questions. Schools differed on what the questions could be about, but as chair, I would make sure they were focused strictly on her work.

She nodded. Then I asked, "On a scale of one, where you feel perfectly normal, to ten, where you feel you are having an anxiety attack, how bad is your anxiety?"

She whispered, "A ten. When I think about doing it, I can't breathe or think. I feel faint, like I'm going to pass out."

"Can you think why you are feeling that way?'" I asked.

"I keep seeing Dr. Sampson's face and hearing him laugh at something I say. Then everyone starts laughing at me, and all I can do is run from the room."

"Monica, when I tell you it is excellent, don't you trust me?"

"No," she said, looking directly at me. "You are too nice to say it is bad."

I wanted to snort out laughing. Obviously she had not spoken to any of my former students—they knew I would never let someone go forward who wasn't ready. Instead, I quickly looked through the numbers on my phone and selected my most recently graduated doctoral student, Katrin, who was now an assistant professor at the University of Michigan. I plugged in her number and put her on speakerphone. After we chatted for a couple of minutes, I said, "Katrin, I have a student here with me who fears that I am too nice to tell her if there is something wrong with her dissertation proposal. How would you respond to that?"

Katrin started laughing hysterically. When she finally got control of herself, she said, "Everyone knew Phoebe was the toughest advisor around. She was tough so that her students would be successful and trust me—none of her students ever failed an exam. She will give it to you straight, every time." I thanked her, then hung up.

Then I said to Monica, "Can you please tell me you will think about it?" She nodded and left my office.

▲ ▲ ▲

After Monica left, I quickly checked my messages to see if Dr. Roan had gotten back to me. He had, and I was surprised to see I had only thirty minutes to meet up with him at the same restaurant where I'd met Emma Bell in July, just north of Dana Point. A coincidence? I wondered. Either way, I was happy I knew how to get there. I ran out to the parking lot and scrambled to get going.

I was only about five minutes late when I pulled into the parking lot. I ran up the path to the restaurant, gave the host Dr. Roan's name, and again, just like when I met Emma, I was taken directly to his table. Dr. Roan stood when he greeted me, and after calmly and directly surveying me, he said,

"Yes, I can still see a bit of the little girl who loved candy. How I enjoyed trying to find new kinds you had never tried. You were always so delighted." I couldn't help but smile at his obvious joy when recalling that memory. After we sat, the wait staff took our drink orders. Then we were alone.

He picked up the conversation as if we had known each other forever. "I have wanted to talk with you for so long, but I didn't know if you remembered me, or if you had read your mother's journals or talked with your mother's friends. I do want to tell you this of all things: it was a horrible experience to turn you away when your mother was dying. I imagine you may think it would have been better to be there. I can't really say. I described to your mother what her final weeks and days would be like, and she did not want you or anyone else to have that vision of her as their last memories. As she was my dearest friend, I honored her wishes."

He waited for me to respond, and I didn't know what I wanted to say . . . maybe I just wanted to sit there in the sun, looking across at the Pacific Ocean. I can't explain why, but I just grabbed his hand, and we just sat there for a long while. Out of all MG's friends I had met, including my father, I felt the strongest and most immediate attachment to Daniel. The life he'd lived during his early adulthood must have been torturous, hiding his sexuality but trying to live a life of meaning and honesty. After fifteen minutes or so, a server came by for our food orders, and we both snapped back to the present.

I knew it wasn't the best way to restart a conversation, but I had to ask: "You know, you are the second person who knew MG to lead me to this restaurant. Is that a coincidence?"

Instead of being offended, he laughed and said that no, it was not a coincidence. I must have looked confused, so he explained. "When the person we have finally identified as Carlton began blackmailing people with his hateful pictures, accusations, and messages, several of us who were in a kind of circle of trust looked for a safe place to meet and to keep valuable things. We started meeting here once a year so we could discuss the direction of the threats. When the restaurant came up for sale, on a whim we decided to look at it as a potential investment. We discovered that the restaurant dates back to before prohibition times, and as with other old buildings from that period, it was outfitted with some special features, including a secret meeting room and tunnels that lead to hard-to-find parking spots. We decided to buy it under the birth name of my mother, and we have been able to keep it a secret within the group. Your mother was actually a part owner, and I have kept your accounting separate from that of the other owners."

I was shocked upon hearing this—yet another secret I'd known nothing about. When I finally regained my composure, I asked, "Who is in the group?"

He smiled and said, "Well, now that we have found our villain, Carlton Richmond, I can tell you, but I don't think you will be surprised. You may recall that Carlton, Emma Bell, and Edward Block were in a residential childcare program together. Your mother knew that when they were younger, Carlton mistreated both Emma and Edward. Carlton tried to control every part of Emma's and Edward's lives, including beating and torturing both of them at various ages. Somehow he maintained that control over Emma in college, and MG invested a lot of effort—secretly—into helping Emma get free of him. MG made sure Emma was an owner, along with herself, JJ, and me. I know you think your mother hated Emma, but they were close—the animosity was staged to protect Emma from Carlton. She also listed several other friends, such as Sally Garrett, as having access to the two-bedroom suite hidden within the premises. This was, and still is, a place any of us can use if we need to be invisible.

"Has it been used lately?" I asked.

"Yes, but we don't share names or dates. Being a developmental psychologist, I am sure you must have thought about the most basic needs people have and how not meeting those needs can have disastrous implications for their future relationships. I met MG at a time when I was in desperate need of a person in my life who knew I was gay and would keep an emotional bond with me no matter what. Your mother gave me that well of support, which I still drink from today. I, in turn, have tried to pass that on to people I meet along the way."

I said, "I have met a variety of people since I moved back to California, and I have uncovered multiple secrets. All the while, people's underlying qualities and relationships have shifted according to whomever I'm talking to. For example, Colette might have one sense of how all these revolving people are related, and then she might be judged as clueless by others in the group. All of this shifting is confusing."

Daniel reflected as he looked at the ocean. "Do you remember in MG's journal when she talked about the dancing trees and shifting colors? Our lives were like that too; no one was as they seemed because they themselves did not know who they were. Partly it was the times we lived through. Imagine, for example, having your birth date randomly drawn as the number one date in the army draft, and suddenly you are face to face with a future you never planned for or wanted. You have to make decisions that will follow you throughout your life. Or someone hands you a hit of acid, you don't know what it is, but you take it anyway, and then the devil comes to eat you. We were innocents, and we didn't have a cadre of health educators following us around warning us to have safe sex, to not smoke, to not take drugs. We truly believed the age of Aquarius was coming, and people like us were on the cusp of cultural change. We thought we could make every aspect of life better.

"But partly it was due to our misfortune in having any contact at all with Carlton Richmond, our lives shifted. We knew about Charles Manson and how he'd hidden his innate evil within the protective folds of a counterculture identity. What we didn't know was the depth of evil that could exist in ordinary-looking students who were comfortable releasing what they felt inside. I know that evil didn't come in with or go away with our generation. But we were the Leave it to Beaver generation and we were naive. It was akin to a generational betrayal."

I realized I had little knowledge of what he was talking about or how to understand it. I had thought about boomer culture as something to joke about, not as something to understand historically as a set of events and values that converged to change personal and social senses of identity. I would have to give this more thought, but right now, I had one question I needed answered right away: "The orange-tree dream—was it real?"

His eyes reflected a depth of sorrow I had rarely seen before. "As her friend, I believe it was real," he said. "I knew your mother the year Nina disappeared, but I was already at Berkeley. Your mother called me very early in the morning after the night Nina disappeared. She told me the exact same dream then; her journal was the only other time I'd heard about it. That means that in between the two narrations of the dream was a twenty-seven-year gap. How could she retell it so vividly all those years later? Do you have a dream that you can remember in such detail? That being said, when we were younger, MG would not tolerate anyone speaking poorly of Maggie. It wasn't until she was near death that her defense of Maggie began to crack, and she let honest observations slip through.

"As a physician, I have to keep an open mind. As you can imagine, there has been a lot of research on dreams—why we have them, what they mean. Dreams may be a reaction to a traumatic event, but with new facts, people, and connections. For example, after MG heard the members of that intra-county group gossiping about Nina, she may have reassembled it in her dreams. However, she did start with a kernel of reality—that harm would come to Nina. Conversely, a dream may have been so real it created a false memory. The question is, Why was it so lifelike and believable? Again, I prefer to keep an open mind."

I gave him a surprised look as I had not expected he would take the dream so seriously or give it so much thought.

"You know how you observed that people had different views of MG? The same was true for Maggie. Maggie was jealous of all the things MG had and did. I think MG was jealous of Maggie's freedom from expectations. When people don't expect much, it's easy to look good. Maggie passed her daughter, Caroline, off as being Kent's daughter only when she was in Lower Sierra. The whole paternity charade thing led to deception, and Caroline had to go along with it. Mother and daughter were both leading a double life."

I felt like I was drowning in these memories that didn't belong to me. I took his hand and told him I needed time to process our conversation, and he promised we would meet again. As I was getting ready to leave, I noticed he was taking a small key off his key ring.

He motioned for me to stay as he removed it. "Your mother left this key with me and told me to give it to you in person. There is a built-in chest in the third-floor bedroom. During her last few months, she was preparing the chest for you. I am sorry I left you hanging for so long. I admit I just couldn't deal with the finality of letting it go."

▲ ▲ ▲

By the time I got back in my car it was three thirty. I had only picked at my lunch and that, along with the intense conversation, left me feeling dull and sluggish. Instead of heading all the way home, I pulled off at the nearest open beach. I pulled a blanket and bottle of water out of the back of my car and walked down toward the water. I texted Louie, then rolled out my towel. Maybe it was due to my injuries from Monday morning, but I was asleep as soon as I stretched out on the towel.

I awoke to the voices of childish rivalry all around me. I lifted my right eyelid and saw Louie. I lifted my left eyelid and saw Alex. These two seemed to have fallen into a kind of sparring brotherhood. Neither of them had any close guy friends, so it was probably good for them. As they continued to argue, I awoke fully, raised myself up on my elbows, and waited for them to be quiet. They finally stopped, and I asked Alex what he was doing here, which somehow started an argument about who Fraley liked the most. Just when I thought I couldn't take any more bickering, they abruptly stopped.

Alex said, "After we got back from Tahoe, I called Fraley to see what the department had discovered based on Peter Sampson's locker. He told me they were going to discuss the evidence at a team meeting this morning at ten, and I was welcome to come. My shift ended at five a.m., so I was able to make the meeting on time."

Louie continued: "After Alex told me he had been invited, I called Fraley, and he invited me too. We broke up the meeting around one and then we went to the beach. Alex had a pretty good surfing lesson. When I got your text, we thought we would stop by and share what everyone has been up to. How about if you start, Phoebe?"

I sat up fully on my blanket and took a sip of water, then filled them in on what I'd learned from Daniel.

Louie picked it up from there. "I finally found a relative of Karen Jennings, the Lindsay girl who went missing. It's a brother, living in Salinas, who said he could meet Saturday afternoon. I checked, and the helicopter is free. Does anyone want to go?" He had a strange look on his face when he said this, and I knew he was thinking that this would be two weekends in a row we had to postpone our sailing trip. I said yes, and Alex said no.

"Today is Wednesday," Alex said, "and Clover is supposed to be back at work on Friday. She has not been sighted by the agents keeping watch on her house, so we need to decide on our next move. I don't want to wait too long to see her again, as I'm afraid she might try to run.

"I was thinking that I would call on Friday to see if she is working. If she does not come back to work, I will fly up Saturday and see if we can get a welfare check. If she does go to work Friday, I will fly up Saturday and see if I can catch her during her shift or right after. So, either way, I hope to see Clover on Saturday, which means I have to say no to the trip to Salinas," Alex said, "But you'll get us a DNA sample?"

"Of course!"

"What about Fraley's case?" I asked.

Alex laughed. "Well he was a bit grouchy about it. They had to get search warrants for all the hiding spots of Carlton's documents. But it has been extremely fruitful, and not only do they have records, but they also found other assets, like jewelry, rare coins, even some gold. I think he is wondering if he has to track down every single lead. Bottom line, I don't see Carlton ever getting out of this."

We all left the beach when the sun went down, and I drove home to an empty house. I was fairly sure Louie had someone watching the house, so I wasn't truly alone, but for the first time since I'd moved in, I felt a moderate level of anxiety about being there, especially with Colette and Abe out of town. I know it sounds a bit dramatic, but I felt vulnerable on all sides.

I decided I needed to finish up with MG's cancer journals, so I took the last one upstairs to the roof deck, which allowed me to lock down the house but still get some fresh air. The deck was outfitted for electricity, so I was able to pull over a lamp with enough voltage for reading.

The third journal was not very long. Like the others, it started with a description of her disease, how she felt, and the drugs she was taking. It was close to Christmas, and all she wanted was a video of me unwrapping my presents from her. I remember that Christmas. I wanted nothing more than to be at home with MG and my grandparents. Instead, all I could do was send a gift through the mail. I spent a lot of time looking for something she would enjoy. I found a wool shawl—something warm, joyous, and colorful—in a store in Annapolis. My grandmother had sent me a picture of MG all wrapped up in it, revealing a beautiful smile that made her face glow. That was my last picture of her, and I treasured it—so much so that I had copies of it made so I would always have one with me wherever I went.

By New Year's, MG was primarily making short notations or sketching right in the journal instead of in her sketchbook. It was in this section where she started designing her cremation ceremony, who she wanted to invite, and what songs she wanted to play. She noted that she did not want me there, but she wanted the ceremony videotaped and placed in the chest she was putting together for me.

Soon after, Daniel began writing her dictations, as she had become too weak to write. She started a list of things that made her happy, but the list was interspersed with other notations. About five pages from the end, she had Daniel pen her final story while she dictated:

> *A story I have not yet told is about Sally Garrett. Sally was my roommate all through undergraduate school. And when we decided to go to graduate school, we rented an apartment together. What people did not know was that Sally was raped during our sophomore year in college. It was around Halloween, during a fraternity party she attended. Sally became pregnant from the rape, and she thought she had no options other than to have the baby. She was quite ill from the pregnancy, so she did not gain noticeable weight until around her seventh month, and then she ballooned up. I took her home with me in June, and my mother and Daniel took diligent care of her. When the time came, she decided to have the baby in a Catholic hospital, since she had grown up Catholic, and then give the baby up for adoption. A physician couple adopted her son, and they gave her permission to watch him from afar, such as attend his baptism and other*

events. After the birth, she had a few weeks to recuperate at the ranch.

When we got back to school, she had changed. She was quiet, studious, and spent her time with me and JJ or in our apartment. Because of this, the date rape planned by Maggie and the others had a profound effect on her. She never took any of the drugs because she saw what was going on. She pretended to be out of it for the duration of the "party," accentuating her ruse by urinating and defecating in her bed. I think men left her alone. To control her anxiety after her baby was born, Sally had become adept at meditation and yoga, and this helped her to convincingly pretend. And while she pretended, she heard conversations between two men and one woman. Then she heard one of the men ordering the other men around and making them help with the pictures.

When I eventually got back to the apartment, I saw that the party had pushed her way too far. Sally was having her first panic attack since after the baby. She kept saying, "Take me to the convent." We didn't know what she meant, so Jackson, Daniel, and I took her to a Catholic shelter for abused women under an assumed name. She made us swear we would never divulge the name she used, and we haven't. About five years later, I received a letter through Daniel's medical office. Sally said she was a teacher in a Catholic school and was hiding in plain sight. She was watching her son from afar and having a meaningful life.

Sally believed her old life was gone and her new life belonged to her and the people she chose to share it with. She did leave Daniel a sealed envelope that held her contact information in case there was an emergency. She updated the information periodically, but we have never opened any of the envelopes. We have tried to protect her privacy, but it has been difficult.

There were more entries from Daniel, and then the final entry about the time of her death and a notation that she had "slipped away with her eyes on the trees."

I couldn't believe all of this had happened within one day. I crawled into bed and refused to let myself think about the next twenty-four hours.

CHAPTER 15
Dead Ends

I awoke and realized it was only Thursday, but I allowed myself to expedite one of my usual Saturday rituals and pick up donuts and two large coffees on the way to work. I didn't feel bad about it because I had missed out on the rewards last weekend. When I walked into my office, my desk phone was ringing and the number showed it was my boss, Dean Richmond. I answered the phone without spilling any coffee. "Good morning, Dean Richmond," I got out before sitting down.

She rushed at me with her news. "Parker Montgomery is missing from all his classes, and I intend to have someone follow up on it later today. Do you have any insights you can offer me?"

I wanted to be honest with her without betraying Parker and his mother, Caroline. I said, "You know that his grandmother, Maggie, was recently murdered in her home. Do you think maybe he and his mother are in hiding because of that?"

"Who is in charge of that investigation?" she asked.

"It is being overseen by the Tulare County Sheriff's Office and led by Lieutenant Alex Boas," I told her as I looked longingly at my triple chocolate donut.

"Thanks! I will have the university police give him a call to see what's up." Then she signed off. I selected my triple chocolate donut and one other one from the box and took the rest into the office suite for anyone who wanted one. Then I settled in to eat both pastries and drink both coffees. I was one bite into my triple chocolate when there was a timid knock at the door. It was Monica sticking her head in to say hello. I told her to check out the donuts and then come on in.

She came in empty handed, making me feel just a bit like a glutton. "Dr.

Moon," she said, "I wasn't appreciative at the time, but now I am, for the phone call you made to your former advisee. It is hard for me to trust faculty members, but I have decided to trust you and go forward with selecting a dissertation committee. The only thing is, can we have practice sessions for my oral?"

"Absolutely we can practice. Why don't we start with you giving me a twenty-minute presentation next Wednesday after class in the conference room? It can either be just the two of us or you can invite other people." She turned pale but agreed to do it and then we talked specifics about my expectations.

Finally, I was alone with my coffee and donuts. I really did need time to think about what I learned from my conversations and readings over the past few days. I reviewed the week: Monday I interrupted an office break-in and ended up in the hospital; Tuesday I flew to Lake Tahoe for the interview of Clover; Wednesday I lunched with Daniel and learned about the ownership of the coastal restaurant.

Most importantly, we had made some progress on our goal of identifying the bodies of the murdered girls, based on a list of six missing girls from that time period. We already knew that body number one was Nina and body number two was Vickie Miller, and as for the third body, we believed it might be Karen Jennings. A brother of Karen Jennings had been located in Salinas, and we were going to meet with him on Saturday. Beyond the three bodies that had been found, three more girls had gone missing. One of those, Amy White, had been ruled out, as she had gone into hiding and was still alive. I hoped the other two were also found alive.

I stared at the work left for me in my inbox, and I started going through the folders one by one. After I had read and signed the documents in my mailbox, I went through the latest analyses of data from my studies. Then it was already one o'clock. I felt stiff, so I got up to go to the bathroom. I was washing my hands when I looked down the row of sinks and saw a large envelope with my name on it in front of the last sink in the row. I thought about where it might have come from, then remembered that someone had come in and washed their hands when I was in the stall. I grabbed a clean paper towel and picked the envelope up by the edge to take it back to my office.

Louie and I were becoming more and more in sync with each other, as he was in my office when I returned. When he saw me, he said he was wondering if I wanted lunch. Then he noticed the envelope in my hand and waved me over to the table. I put the envelope down, then flipped it over. There was a message on the back:

Sorry to have run you over on Monday, but I am not ready to share with you yet. Inside are the files I took. I had just wanted to check dates, but the files really didn't help. I am an ally, not a threat.

Parker

Louie and I exchanged a perplexed look, and I said, "I had figured that out—or at least I thought they weren't a threat because I didn't feel any intentionality in my injuries. Mostly I was surprised and clumsy." I opened the envelope and there were the files. I flipped through them but didn't spot anything unusual.

We sat down at the table, and Louie pulled out sandwiches and soup from his bag. "I thought maybe we could eat and have some quiet time. Who knows how crazy things will be tomorrow when Alex starts searching for Clover," he said.

"That sounds perfect!" I said. True, I was really hungry, but it was more than that; his presence comforted me and made me feel steadier, like I could handle anything. I took hold of his hand for a few moments, wondering if I could ever tell him how much his kindness meant to me.

After we ate, we sat at the table working; I was reading the proposals for the research papers the students in my seminar planned to write, and Louie was writing a brief for one client. After several hours of work, we decided to head for home. I packed a lot of materials so I could work at home on Friday. I was exhausted.

We started Friday morning at a glacial pace. Even trying to make breakfast was a chore. I remembered it had only been four of five days since my head injury and while the pain had dulled I just couldn't increase my energy level. Still, I couldn't give myself a grace day away from work. But Louie could. For the first time since coming to California, I took a rest day. I rested in bed all morning and when I got up for lunch I found I could now focus on reading student papers—so that is what I did.

After an hour or so of work, we got a call from Alex.

He greeted us, then said, "Clover didn't come into work today. I contacted her supervisor at the casino to see if she had called in about not making her shift. Clover's supervisor had not heard from her, and she informed me that it was the first shift she had ever missed. I'll fly to Lake Tahoe tomorrow. If she doesn't come into work, I'll ask for a welfare check. I don't expect to learn anything before tomorrow afternoon, so I've got nothing to report. Don't mean to be rude, but I am checking some things out."

Alex signed off, and Louie and I looked at each other. It had been a long week, and we still had our trip to Salinas the next day. We both needed some fresh air. We packed a picnic dinner and took off for an afternoon on the beach.

CHAPTER 16
Dead Ends

Saturday morning, we flew into Salinas to meet with the brother of Karen Jennings. He lived just outside Salinas, in the low mountains on the western edge. We had to rent a car at the airport to drive there, and as we approached the address, we saw that Robert Jennings lived on a large property covered by rows of artichoke plants, planted outdoors and in climate-controlled greenhouses. Seeing his farm brought back a vivid memory of visiting the restaurant with the giant artichoke sculpture out in front, which had to be close by, when I was a child. MG and I had eaten fried artichoke hearts, which, while delicious, made my stomach roil later.

Robert Jennings waved to us as we drove up to his house, a rustic-looking wooden structure with a large front porch, where a table had been set up with fresh lemonade and several types of dips and chips. He greeted us graciously, but I could see the caution in his eyes. I wasn't sure if he was uncertain about us or about the news we might bring. He looked as though he had worked hard in the sun all his life—different from the other members of his generation we had recently met. I wondered briefly what type of music he listened to, and I doubted it was boomer nostalgia.

We chatted briefly about the farm, and Louie was particularly interested in hearing about the process of growing artichokes and how labor intensive the cycle was. Robert offered us a tour, but Louie declined with true regret due to time. He led us up the porch stairs and over to the table, and I saw that there were several types of dips, all made with artichokes, alongside a variety of breads and chips. I was in heaven, and I hated that we had to spoil it by talking about his missing sister.

After we had filled our plates with the various options and settled in, Louie started the conversation on why we were there, explaining how the bodies had been found and that we'd learned his sister had disappeared when she was a teenager. "We were hoping you could tell us the story of how Karen came to be missing."

Robert had taken off his hat when we moved to the porch, and he now sat and rubbed his forehead where the hat had sat. He closed his eyes and spoke slowly, giving me the sense that he was trying to recapture those days.

"Karen was my little sister, behind me in school by a year. She was a pretty girl and smart as a whip. She was focused on going to college, and when she went missing, she had already sent off applications to a dozen or so schools. Our family was hardworking, and my parents made a good life for us by putting in long hours and gradually being able to build up the money to buy a small farm to supplement their income. They grew mostly vegetables, and we sold them at a stand on our property during the summer. Karen worked there, and they gave her 25 percent of the profits as payment. She spent the money on things she wanted for her senior year in high school.

"Her senior year was the first year she was in school without me. I knew that guys wanted to date her, but when I was around, they kept it to strictly formal events, like the prom. I was worried what might happen when I left, but I only went to the two-year college in Visalia, so I figured I could keep an eye on things . . . Turns out I couldn't. Once I was an outsider, people didn't seem to want to share information.

"All of a sudden she was popular, and guys started asking her out. She was dizzy with all the attention. After a couple of months, though, she changed, and started turning down dates. After she disappeared, I heard a rumor from one of the guys that she had been molested on one of her dates. I tried to find out who, but no one would say, probably because they knew I would beat the shit out of him. She grew more withdrawn around the holidays and then she just disappeared the day after Christmas. We never saw her again."

He paused for a long moment before continuing. "We went to the police to report it. They interviewed her closest friends, and that is when we found out she had been pregnant, and it was probably from being molested. None of the girls knew who had harmed her because she refused to tell them."

Louie asked, "Did anyone report seeing people around her that they didn't know?"

"She used to walk home from school with her best friend, who lived about two hundred yards from us," he replied. "She told the police that a couple of times they had seen a red car, maybe a Mustang, drive by them really slowly, with a girl and guy in the front and a girl in the back. The police tried to track that down, but they didn't get anywhere with it. I think they found only one red Mustang in the city, and it was owned by an older woman. Over time, they just gave up."

Louie asked, "Does her friend still live in Lindsay?"

Robert blushed. "No, I married her years later, and we're still together."

"If she's here right now, would she be available to talk with us?" Louie asked.

"Let me go ask her. Sonny never got over the disappearance, and it's really hard for her to talk about. She was supposed to go shopping with Karen the day after Christmas, but she had to babysit her younger brother. She's always thought she could have kept Karen safe if she had been with her. I always tell her that's nonsense; she would have just disappeared on a different day." He slowly got out of his chair and went to look for his wife.

Not long after, Sonny Jennings came out of the house, followed by her husband, and they both sat down at the table. Physically, Sonny was strong and healthy looking for her age but emotionally she looked both sorrowful and anxious. She did meet our eyes directly when we introduced ourselves. After chatting a bit and catching Sonny up on the conversation, Louie started his questions by asking Sonny about her impressions of Karen over the few weeks before her disappearance.

"Karen and I were looking forward to college, and she was focused on keeping her grades up and perfecting her applications. We mostly applied to the same schools, even though her grades were a bit better than mine. The attention she got from all the popular guys at school made her happy at first, and then she fell into a deep depression. She never would have wanted a baby at such a young age, as it would have interfered with her ability to go to college, but on one of her dates, she was raped by a boy after repeatedly telling him to stop. What's more, he didn't wear a condom.

"I had my suspicions about who the boy might have been, but I didn't say anything to Robert or anyone else because they were only suspicions, and I didn't want the boy to get into any trouble if it wasn't him."

We all sat there waiting for a name. When she didn't elaborate, I asked, "Who did you think it was?"

"I thought it was a boy she'd met at a dance after a football game. The guy was from another school, and I think he asked her out soon after they met. I never knew his name. But later, after she stopped going out, a different guy—one from Lindsay—kept trying to talk with her, though I don't think he was the one who molested her. He would approach her while she was alone, never when she was with me. But a couple of times I saw them from a distance, and she'd just walk away from him, leaving him standing there. This continued until she disappeared, but she'd never talk to me about him or her behavior towards him."

"Tell us some more about this boy from Lindsay," Louie encouraged.

"I don't remember his name because he came to the area very late in our sophomore year. His parents were doctors who opened a clinic that accepted low-income patients, including non-English-speaking farmworkers. It was a great community service, but of course people thought it just kept the 'lowlifes' in too close proximity. People viewed being poor at that time as a horrific personal failure. I know they never actually dated, but he seemed to have a crush on her."

"Is the clinic still there?" I asked.

She sat there for a moment, thinking, then pulled out her phone. She did some typing and handed it to me, saying, "This is it. I don't think the clinic name has changed, but it looks like it is now staffed by doctors your age. Maybe his parents retired."

I looked at the screen—it was the Brooks Family Care Center. I knew this was an important discovery for us.

I pulled out the pictures of Clover and Jay, both the drawings and their senior photos. I asked Sonny if either of them could have been one of the people in the red car. She studied the pictures and handed me back the photograph of Clover. "She might be the girl who sat in the front seat passenger side—she's the only one whose face was visible to us. She used to yell 'Hey, Mommy,' then they'd drive off as fast as they could. One time she yelled something like, 'We see you, Mommy.' The first couple of times it happened as we were walking home from school, but then they started showing up at other places. I know Karen was humiliated, but she kept her head up and pretended not to see or hear them."

We sat in silence for a moment, then I asked, "Was it Karen's disappearance that led you two to start dating?"

They looked at each other and then Robert said, "No, neither of us dated for a couple of years. We were both grieving and feeling guilty about leaving her alone that day. But as it turned out, we both ended up graduating from Cal Poly San Luis Obispo, and we met up at a reunion for Lindsay alumni five or so years later. By then, we could see each other as people, not as Karen's brother and Karen's best friend. We have been together ever since, and while Karen has always been in the background, we have built a life beyond our youthful dreams." He looked lovingly at Sonny, and she nodded her head in agreement.

That felt like our cue to leave, so after collecting Robert's DNA, we drove back to the airport to turn in the car. I was excited that we finally had a lead on one of the boys, and since we knew the name of the clinic his family had run, it should be relatively easy to track him down.

▲ ▲ ▲

We were just pulling up to my house when Alex called. Louie told him to hang on for a second while we quickly moved to the back patio and put him on speakerphone. Louie told him we were ready, and Alex started telling us about his day. As soon as I heard his voice, I knew something was wrong.

Alex had gone to the casino and learned that Clover had once again not checked in for her shift. "I tried to get the local police to do a welfare check, but it took some convincing because Clover is an adult and they wanted to protect her privacy. Fortunately, her supervisor was worried, so with a nudge from the casino, the police consented to go into the condo."

We both waited for him to go on. After a long pause, he spoke again: "Clover was dead; she had been hit over the head and left to bleed out, just like Maggie. The living room was a holy mess, with blood and flies and maggots. The examiner estimated she had been dead for about two to three days. Once the police found the body, they ushered me out, but I did see a couple of suitcases sitting by the door leading down to the garage. We had the right idea about her fleeing, but we got there too late. I was able to talk to the lead detective and told her I had been looking for Clover in connection to a murder that looked just like this one, so she agreed we could share information. I have a meeting with the detective this evening, then I will fly home." He sounded spent, disappointed that we'd hit a literal dead end, and regretful.

We were able to lift his spirits about the case when we reported on our trip to Salinas. He agreed it would be worthwhile to speak with the boy associated with the clinic in Lindsay, so Louie assured him his team would locate him and set something up. We also told him that the red car that had been stalking Karen had at least two people in it—a girl and a guy—and that Sonny thought the girl could have been Clover, but she hadn't gotten a good look at anyone else.

Alex signed off, so he could get ready for his meeting with the detective; Louie went to his office; and I poured myself a glass of wine and headed straight for my rooftop deck. All I can say is it's a good thing there's a railing around the deck, because I promptly fell asleep. At some point during the night, I woke up and made my way to my bed.

CHAPTER 17
Stories Begin to Be Told

I did some academic work at home on Sunday and I enjoyed it so much I decided to work from home on Monday. Just as I was getting organized, Louie called to ask if I could work at his office instead, as he thought there might be a break in the case we needed to follow. He picked me up midmorning, and we drove to his office to check for updates. On the way, we stopped by a lab that Louie often used for checking DNA, so he could give them the swab of Robert Jenning's saliva. He left directions that electronic copies be sent to Alex at the Tulare County Sheriff's Office and to him directly.

Now that we had solid information on four of the six girls, Louie had asked his staff to dig deeper into the other two. We were fervently hoping there would be at least one more girl alive and leading a satisfying life. As soon as we walked into the office, one of the identity teams called us over.

"Hey, what do you have?" Louie called out.

The team members were fidgeting in their seats, and they greeted us with huge smiles, but they let the team leader do the talking. "We solved the disappearance of girl number five, the girl from Woodlake—we, or someone had misclassified her. We sent an affiliate to the school to visually inspect the record—we had to get a court order to do so. In small letters on the back of her transcript was a notation that she had transferred to a Catholic School in Fresno County. Also on the back was the notation that she had changed her last name when her mother, a widow, remarried; she took the stepfather's last name of Winter. We pushed a bit more and found that there is a stepbrother living in Fresno, and he gave us her current phone number and address." Everyone applauded, and we joined in. Tracing down these women was grim work, and we all appreciated that another one of them had been found alive.

The team leader handed Louie all the information his team had gathered, and then I followed Louie into his office. I was exhausted from the trip and the emotionality of the interviews with Robert and Sonny Jennings, but if I was reading Louie correctly, he was eager to get in touch with Lorie Winter. I gave a slight nod, and he took out his phone.

Once he got Lorie on the line, he put it on speaker and explained why we were calling, adding that it sounded like she had not actually disappeared, and that pregnancy had not figured into her story.

After a brief pause, she said, "I want to be honest with you in case it can help you solve the disappearances of the other girls. I was pregnant, but I wasn't aware of it until right after the start of the holiday break. Of course, I was terrified to tell my mom. Before I could, I had a miscarriage right after the first of the year. It was horribly scary for all of us, but it led to a heart-to-heart discussion among me, my mom, and her fiancé about my future and how I could have the life I wanted. More than anything, I wanted to make something of my life and have a career—I certainly didn't want to be pregnant in high school.

"I didn't go right back to school after break, so I guess it raised suspicions, because I received some hang-up calls and unsigned accusatory letters. My best friend told me that kids from another school had stopped by at lunch one day to ask about me. They asked where I lived, did I walk or drive to school, was I sick, and other personal things. My friend just told them she thought I was moving but didn't know where.

"I had a creepy feeling about it because I didn't know who the kids were or who could have sent them. At a family meeting, we decided I would enroll in a Catholic school as soon as I could and change my name to Winter. My mother and stepfather's wedding was two weeks away, in mid-January, so I just stayed in the house until the wedding and then we moved into my stepfather's place in Fresno. I finished school, then went to UC Davis for a degree in finance. Did I do the right thing?"

"Yes!" Louie and I both exclaimed.

Louie continued, "We don't know all the answers yet, but we suspect the people looking for you at school were dangerous and may have harmed other pregnant girls in the county. To help us further, I need to ask you about the father of your baby; can you tell us about him?"

She hesitated as if deciding to share the information, then said, "I promised myself to never tell anyone his name because I was so stupid about the whole thing. I met him at a dance after the Exeter–Woodlake football game. He was not from my school, but he was hanging around with a group of popular boys from Woodlake, so I thought he must be OK. We started seeing each other a couple of times a week. He was handsome, smart, and rich. I was flattered that he paid attention to me—I was a junior and he was a senior—and I let him control the relationship. He never knew that I was pregnant, or at least I never told him, and he called me all throughout the break and for weeks after school started. I never took his calls, and I don't know what became of him. He told me his name was Peter Wilson. When I first met him, the guys all called him Pete."

We thanked her for her willingness to talk to us. Then, wanting to end on a positive note, I asked her how her life had turned out so far. She laughed and said, "Beyond my expectations in every way!"

▲ ▲ ▲

Right after hanging up, I turned to Louie and said, "That name, Pete Wilson, has shown up in two cases. We were thrilled by the wonderful news that girl number five was safe, but I was sure someone had been playing a game with the girls or there was a repeat offender. There was a knock on Louie's door. The same team leader who had greeted us enthusiastically when we came in was back, but this time he had a somber look. "I am sorry to report that our affiliate has now visited the school of girl number six, Sharon Lane from Exeter. Again, we have an error in reporting, on the back of her official transcript was a note that she was deceased. The affiliate poked around and found an archived story online about her death. She was in a single car crash during one of the infamous valley fog events. She was the passenger in a car in which the driver was speeding and swerved off the road and into a telephone pole. Her side of the car hit the pole, and she died instantly. The driver had only some minor injuries. Should we pursue it?"

We all quietly debated whether to use our resources to investigate further. Louie asked, "Who was driving the car? I'm thinking if it was a female friend, she might be honest with us about what was going on in Sharon's life at the time, but if it was a male friend, he might not know or be willing to share."

His staffer looked down at his notes. "It says she was with her best friend, Penny Peterson, and they were on their way to Visalia to shop for a dress to wear to the upcoming Sweethearts Dance at school."

I suggested that we ask the affiliate to try to locate the friend and do a first interview. If anything sounded suspicious, Louie and I could follow up. Everyone agreed to this, then Louie told his staffer, "How about if you notify the team and the affiliate, then send everyone home. Tell the team I appreciate them working on the weekend and searching so carefully to find these young women!" When we were alone again, Louie asked me what I thought about everything we'd learned up to this point.

"Well, it looks like Clover and Jay had a role in at least two more cases—Lindsay and Woodlake. So, there's a high likelihood of involvement in at least five of the six. We don't really know anything about the female accomplice who may have appeared after it all started. We also don't have a complete list of who the girls were dating, but it looks like the same stunt was used in at least two cases. An out-of-town boy picking up a girl at a dance. The curious thing is that the boy had friends at the girls' schools."

Just then, Alex called. He still sounded down about Clover's death—I hoped he still wasn't thinking he should have brought her in for questioning or watched her house—or worse that it was his fault. After greeting us, he said, "I have tracked down the Lindsay boy from the clinic. His name is Dr. Thomas Brooks, and he is a retired professor from UC San Diego. Looks like he lives down the highway in La Jolla. I'll text you his information. That's all I have."

I hurried to tell him the news that girl number five had survived and girl number six had been in a car crash during a deep fog. The driver had been fined for unsafe driving due to road conditions, but that was it.

We were slowly making progress, but I was looking forward to the stage where it all started to fit together. Perhaps a conversation with Dr. Brooks would get us closer.

We went to Louie's conference room and he dialed Dr. Brooks on speakerphone. After talking with first a grandson and then his wife, we got Dr. Brooks on the phone. When we told him why we were calling, we heard him suck in a deep breath, then let out a small sob.

When he could talk, he said, "You know how it was fashionable for a while to make Karen jokes about being the epitome of rudeness and stupidity? Karen Jennings was nothing like that. She was smart, kind, funny, and beautiful. When she disappeared, I was devastated."

"Were the two of you dating?" I asked.

"No, we weren't dating. Would I have wanted to date her? Maybe, but I never got the chance. Karen was my physics lab partner, and we spent regular time together, both in class and while working on our semester project."

"We heard from her friend Sonny that before she disappeared, you looked for her and tried to talk with her, but she avoided you. What was that about?"

"It wasn't about physics. My parents were both physicians, and they'd built a high-end medical practice in the bay area. Over time, they didn't feel fulfilled by the types of health problems they regularly treated and the people they had as patients. They decided they wanted to do something more meaningful in the second half of their careers, so they started a clinic in Lindsay and put it in a neighborhood of low-income homes. My dad had grown up in a similar neighborhood, and he wanted to give something back.

"My college tuition depended on my working ten hours a week at the clinic. Mostly I kept the patient rooms stocked, but when I turned eighteen, they let me escort patients to the exam rooms. One early Saturday morning, Karen was one of those patients. I took her back to the exam room, and she was distraught. I didn't ask her any questions about her visit, but she spewed it all out. She was pregnant, she didn't want a baby, and she wanted to go to college. She told me the guy was someone she had met at the dance after the Lindsay–Exeter game, and she realized now what a selfish monster he was. She asked me to stay with her until my mom came in, and of course my mom kicked me out right away.

"That night, my mom called me into her home office, and I thought she was going to yell at me. Instead, she told me that Karen wanted me to be the intermediary between her and my mother. She didn't want anyone to see her going to the clinic or anyone from the clinic calling her at home or school. My mom told me it was highly confidential, and I would need to sign a letter to that effect. After we took care of that part, she handed me a letter in a sealed envelope to give to Karen.

"Fortunately, we had physics class the next day, so I was able to give her the envelope. She tore it open and read it quickly. She scribbled a note on the letter and handed it back to me, then ran out of the room. She had written 'Yes, I want more information.' I let my youth and my curiosity take over then and saw that the letter was about how she could choose to terminate the pregnancy. I put the letter back in the envelope and taped it closed. I gave it to my mother that night.

"My mother waited and waited for Karen to contact her, but she never did. My mom had tried calling Karen at home a few times but to protect her confidentiality, she never left a message. Every once in a while, she would ask me to remind Karen to call or stop by, but she kept avoiding me. We went on Christmas break, and I tried to contact her again, as time was getting short for arranging an out-of-state abortion. I never saw or heard from Karen again. She just disappeared."

"That was before abortion was completely legal in California," I reminded him.

"Yes, but in 1967 it became legal in a California and a handful of other states for specific reasons, such as rape. My mother was part of a network of doctors and laypeople who knew how to find a way. Of course, she never advertised it, and she only took on extreme cases.

"I never guessed that Karen's life had been wasted to the point of being murdered. My mother and I never spoke of it again, so I tried to convince myself that Karen had started a new life somewhere else. Now I can mourn her and honor the life she didn't have."

When we said our goodbyes, I had nothing left to say. That certainly wasn't the phone call I had expected.

▲ ▲ ▲

Tuesday morning, I felt so stiff from all the sitting I had done over the past few days, I decided to take a run to the donut shop. Not only was I wreaking havoc with my ability to get my work done, but I was also going to be late getting to work. Two violations in one morning . . . I guess I was really getting influenced by that California culture. This thought made me giggle, and I was still smiling to myself when I ran out of the gate and ran to the donut shop.

Later, as soon as I sat down at my desk, my office phone rang. It was Dean Richmond. I picked up the phone, and she immediately started talking: "Hey, Phoebe, I have not had any luck finding Parker Montgomery; how about you?"

This question put me in a bind. I wanted to be honest, but I didn't want to betray his trust. I replied, "To my knowledge, no one has found any evidence of foul play, and it looks like he may be with his mother."

"Why is he doing that? He should be in school!"

"Well, you know his grandmother was murdered in her home, and I hate to say this, but I think he and his mom might be looking for the person who murdered her."

I heard a pencil tapping on the other end and then she said, "Ask Louie to look into it. I don't trust the police to take it seriously."

After promising her I would pass on her message to Louie, she signed off. In fact, Louie and Alex were already looking into it, but the clues had been coming directly to me.

After three hours of reading and writing, my stomach was starting to tell me it was time to eat, and as I got up to go find food, Louie and Alex poked their heads in the door. Alex shouted, "We have come to take you to lunch!"

I looked at my inbox and made a face. Louie said, "I promise you will be back in an hour and a half then you can work as late as you want. I will not say anything about it.

Louie added, "Alex met with Fraley this morning, and now he wants us to compare notes of what we know and don't know. Of course, Alex wants seafood before heading home."

I smile at my almost-cousin; we all knew food was a high priority for him. I gathered up my belongings and we left.

▲ ▲ ▲

I don't know why, but we were all in the mood to "shake our sillies out" on the way to the restaurant. We started singing or chanting ridiculous advertising songs and slogans, trying to see who could be the most annoying. It felt good to laugh after being so somber.

We ended up at a Mexican seafood restaurant. I ordered a dish of grilled shrimp and vegetables over rice, while the guys went with fish tacos. While we were sipping our beers, we looked at each other with a silent *Who wants to start?* look on our faces. No one seemed eager to spoil the mood, so I started off by telling them about my conversation with Dean Richmond. I told them I didn't think she had any idea how involved we were with searching for Parker and his mom. We decided I would just tell her that Louie would add it to his list of priorities.

Before we could start the next report, Louie's and Alex's phones pinged at the same time. Louie leaned over and shared his screen with me. The lab was verifying that Robert Jennings was related to the third body, thus identifying her as Karen Jennings from Lindsay. We had a moment of silence for Karen, reflecting on her short life. We now knew the identities of all three bodies, knew that two of the missing girls were alive and thriving, and knew that the last one had died in a car crash. We had found all the girls.

We were fairly sure that Clover and Jay, both deceased, were involved in the killings, if not the killers themselves, but we didn't know who the second girl was, and we didn't know who had killed Maggie and Clover. We were inching forward.

Our food came, and we gave our full attention to it, with no chitchat. Once my hunger was satisfied, I lifted my head and looked out at the ocean. It was one of those beautiful days when the sky and the ocean were both a brilliant shade of blue. I felt myself relaxing, and I took some cleansing breaths.

CHAPTER 18
Spinning

Wednesday was going to be a full day. I had my seminar in the morning, followed by Monica's practice presentation; a faculty meeting in the afternoon to talk about candidates; and later a conference call with Alex and Louie about the murder cases. My head was spinning, and I was having one of those days when I didn't quite feel in control of my life. I wanted to put my arms around everything going on and keep it in check, but it felt as if things were slipping through my arms and speeding off in different directions.

The morning felt like a repeat of Tuesday. As soon as I walked in the door to my office, the phone rang. Again, it was Dean Richmond, and again, she started talking as soon as I lifted the receiver.

"Phoebe, it must have gotten back to Parker Montgomery that I was looking for him. I received a lengthy email marked *Urgent* this morning. He said he was looking after his mother away from campus but that he was keeping up with his classes and was up to date on everything."

I assured her he was on top of things in my class, and she hung up the phone. A little curt, but that was OK with me. I knew she spent the day putting out fires.

There was a quiet knock on my door, and Monica stuck her head in. I smiled and nodded at her, encouraging her to come in. She stepped in, and as I gathered my materials for the seminar, she said, "We agreed last week that I would give a practice presentation on my dissertation proposal after class today, and I just wanted to say that I reserved the conference room and am ready." I tried not to show my surprise at the fact that she had actually listened to me, so I just smiled and told her that was great.

If I didn't make any more progress in the department, at least I might get Monica through the program. Her self-efficacy was inching up slowly.

When Monica and I slipped into class, I found Parker Montgomery sitting right beside my usual spot. I nodded at him, then sat down in my seat. He turned to the student next to him and started an animated conversation about their group report. After I was organized, I asked everyone how they had been doing over the past week. I don't know if it was because Parker was back or students were feeling unsure about how he would interact with me, but there was silence. The silence had met the thirty-second rule and was charging toward sixty seconds when Parker spoke up. First, he apologized for being absent, then he started telling a funny story about how his intentions to help his mother had gone horribly wrong, and he had almost burned down her house while cooking.

He had everyone laughing along, including me, and I was grateful that he had the gift to take over a crowd like that.

I announced that today's topic was on pollution and child health. I asked them to tell me which state currently had the highest levels of pollution. They had all done their readings for the day, so they knew the answer was Louisiana, but they didn't know why. Even more foreign to them was the idea that pollution contributed to an extensive list of health problems, including child neurodevelopment. I then had them work in small groups to model how poverty fits within the child health–environmental hazards relationship.

At the end of class, Parker handed me a folder and said rather loudly, "Professor Moon, here are the assignments I need to hand in. I understand if you need to take points off my grades because they are late."

I knew his assignments had all been completed on time, but I played along with him. "Thanks, Parker. I hope now that your caretaking is over, you will be able to get the rest in on time." As I turned around to put his folder with the other course materials, I saw a strange look on Monica's face. She also knew his assignments hadn't been late.

▲ ▲ ▲

I didn't want to draw attention to the folder Parker had given me, so in front of Monica, I left it on top of my desk with my other class materials, and we drifted out to the conference room. I was surprised to find close to a dozen people there, waiting for her presentation. There were students in her cohort, a couple of young faculty members, and people from outside the department. I explained to everyone that we would let Monica do her presentation straight through so I could time it, and then they could ask questions.

I didn't know what to expect, but she did an outstanding job. She was organized, detailed, and persuasive about the importance of her scientific question. Again, I thought about how much I admired her strength and ability to carry on. The talk lasted exactly twenty minutes and I saw no major flaws, so I opened things up for the audience. This led to an enthusiastic discussion of her project and ways to make it stronger. I had told her that if things were going really well, I would leave so that it was clear that she was in charge. I slipped out the back during the questioning. I wanted her to feel confident so she could respond to questions on her own. Plus, I needed to eat lunch and get ready for my faculty meeting.

▲ ▲ ▲

Right before the semester started, Dean Richmond gave me an extensive list of administrative chores she wanted completed in the department. Most important, we had to produce a plan for our scholarship and how to hire faculty in the four empty slots caused by the summer mayhem. We were making timely progress on the plan for scholarly areas, but the hiring was slower. It may have been my imagination, but it seemed as though the academic stars in our areas of study were avoiding us. I think they found the murders, arrests, and disappearances unattractive. But no matter how hard I argued that those crimes were due to external events and players, potential faculty seem unconvinced.

We were just winding up two searches, one for a senior and one for a junior faculty member. The senior faculty search had been a bust; we couldn't even find one person we wanted to invite in for an interview. As a group, we voted not to bend our standards and to try again next year, when things may have calmed down. For the junior faculty position, we had invited four people in to interview, and as we finalized the process, we decided that two of them would be good fits for our needs.

One of the weak candidates, however, had raised alarms for me, as it was brought to my attention during the faculty meeting that she had asked many of the people she spoke with if I'd had any involvement in the deaths of the girls found on or around our property. I didn't understand why she had even brought it up, because obviously I was too young to have been involved. But if it was an issue at the ranch, I wondered why Beatrice had not mentioned it to me earlier. While there were no votes among the faculty to hire her, her questions made me wonder about what rumors might be swirling around my mother's hometown.

▲ ▲ ▲

I continued to be bothered by the candidate's comments, so I texted Louie to see if one of his staff members could arrange a conference call among Alex, Aunt Beatrice, Carlos, and the two of us. He said he would get back to me after it was scheduled. True to his word, Louie scheduled a virtual group meeting for six that evening in his conference room. He picked me up at 5:40, and his assistant was just rounding everyone up when we walked in. After all forms of greetings were exchanged, I started things rolling.

"We had a job applicant who kept asking faculty members about my involvement with the bodies being found on or near the ranch. It doesn't make any sense, since I wasn't even born then, but maybe she wanted to know if the faculty members thought anyone in my family was the killer and that maybe I was covering it up. Anyway, I'm curious about what might be going on in the community."

They were all quiet for at least thirty seconds until Beatrice finally said, "We didn't want to bother you about it, but it has been all over the regional and state news. Not just the news stories but letters to the editor and calls to talk shows. There's even talk of people wanting a full search of the mysterious Canton Moon Ranch for other signs of debauchery. But I need you to know we begged Alex not to mention it until we knew what was happening."

Carlos continued, "We have tried to stay out of it, but we did have our attorney put out a statement that we welcomed a full and open search by any authorized law enforcement group. We didn't know what else to do."

Louie reminded us that sometimes it is the guilty people who are most vocal about such things. Then he asked if they were keeping a list of who was making the most outrageous statements.

Carlos said, "That is the oddest thing; they're coming from people in MG's high school class, people who live near one of our properties, and distant relatives of Maggie Stewart and her deceased husband. It is confusing and disheartening, but all we can do is keep a low profile. You know I had already put in lots of security measures due to our new crop technologies, so we know when someone enters the property. Alex has been spending his nights here as well. To be honest, we are all camping out in the study of the big house, where all the monitors are."

I gave Louie a look, then he said, "How about if I send a couple of guards who are part-time employees of my company? I have a couple in mind, and they can stay until things die down. I can have them there by ten p.m. Fair warning, though: they might be hungry when they get there."

Beatrice said, "I don't want to be paranoid, but I think it is a good idea, and I appreciate it. We can take turns sleeping and watching the property. I can't tell you how glad I am that Will is visiting the University of Florida right now. I would really be upset if he saw how the community is responding."

I gave a silent prayer of gratitude and hoped he would stay away.

"OK," Louie said, we will talk with you tomorrow, and please send us a list of who seems to be raising trouble."

CHAPTER 19
On the Edge

Thursday morning, I was feeling agitated when I got to work. There is nothing left to do, I thought, except make lists until things calmed down in my head. As I started in on my first list, it turned into a list of questions about the case we were working on. At the end of it I wrote, "No More Bodies!" This was more in the form of a prayer than a question. My second list quickly focused on work tasks I needed to finish before the winter break. These tasks were under my control, so I tended to favor them. The third list was a combination of statements and questions about my relationships. As I went over this list, one thing popped out at me: Louie and I had not yet had our weekend away.

My gaze turned to the folder Parker had given me yesterday. I didn't want to read the contents unless it was good news, and I didn't know what good news Parker could possibly have for me. It was almost time for the faculty meeting on departmental needs, and I decided to leave the folder unopened until after.

▲ ▲ ▲

When I got back to my office, Louie was there with a snack of a chocolate chip muffin and a coffee. I gave him a heartfelt smile, picked up Parker's folder, and sat down beside him at the table. I pulled the top off the muffin and ate it straightaway. I needed that burst of energy before going forward. I handed him the folder from Parker, and he asked, "What is this?"

"Well, Parker was in class yesterday, and he handed me this folder as he was leaving. I haven't looked at it, and I don't know if I can; I need good news first!"

Just then, my office phone rang. It was Alex, calling in for our conference call. After we all settled, Louie took the reins, summarizing our progress:

"We found that the girl from Exeter, Sharon Lane, died as the result of a car crash, and there was no evidence of pregnancy in her autopsy. Our totals are three murders, two survivors, and one car crash death. We also know there was evidence of Clover's and Jay's involvement in each case except the crash. We believe one or more other girls may have been involved in the murders, and Maggie is a suspect there.

"Based on tips from the interviews, my team has put together a list of likely boyfriends for each girl. We will now start to conduct background checks. My goal is to provide you with a list of men who might have information that is useful."

I said, "I have a list already started. Maybe we could add your names to it and we could take over the interviews. I have been thinking that is our next step."

"That's very astute," responded Alex, which made Louie and me chuckle. "Wait, why are you laughing?" Alex demanded.

"First off, I needed to laugh, it's been a difficult day. Second, I didn't know you knew such fancy words," I said playfully.

"I beg your pardon; I do have a master's degree from Cal Poly. However, I will take back my compliment and continue. I looked into who seems to be the most vocal regarding the bodies and your family's role in the murders. There is one particular person, Brittany Wicker, a reporter for the Fresno paper. Apparently she has a column about issues affecting the central valley, including Tulare County. OK, next?"

"Parker Montgomery was in class yesterday, and when he left, he handed me a folder and told me it was his makeup work," I said.

Alex waited for me to continue, but when I didn't, he asked, "So . . . what was in it?"

"I haven't been able to look, but I know it's not makeup work. I haven't looked because I'm dreading more negative news or phantom clues. Unless we want the family name and businesses to be forever damaged, we need to get this settled quickly."

I indicated the folder in front of Louie, and he handed it to me. "OK,

I'm opening it. First, there is a note from Parker that says, 'Before Maggie was killed, she told Mom and me where she had left a very important file in her attic. We think the materials in this envelope are what she meant. As you will see, it is in some type of code, but we think this might be what Maggie's killers were looking for.' On the first page are four columns topped by what look like identification initials. My guess is that each column represents one of our victims. Underneath each column heading are dates, amounts of money, and three letters. Column one is labeled 'OBT,' and the first entry in that column is '11/1/67—$150.' If Clover and Jay were killing pregnant girls . . ."

"Then maybe someone was paying them to do it, Louie finished. "Or multiple people." "That could be the motive behind killing Maggie and Clover."

Alex asked, "What kind of money are we talking about?"

"Totals for each victim will need to be calculated," I said as I flipped through the pages, "but it looks to be around five thousand for each girl. Oh, there's a final page here titled 'Down Payments.' There are six rows divided into three columns: initials of victim, date, and payment. The down payments for each are two hundred fifty dollars—not big money these days, but back then, it was enough for five semesters of tuition at a public university."

We were all quiet for a moment, then Louie said, "So what does all of this tell us? Let's summarize what we think we know. Number one: This group killed at least three pregnant girls and stalked at least two others. We don't know about the girl in the crash. There are four columns on what look like payment books, and if each represents a murder victim, we don't know the fourth girl. Number two: The murderers—most likely Clover and Jay and possibly a third person—were hired to kill each girl. We don't know who hired them or if it was a different person for each victim. Number three: A down payment was paid for each girl that was stalked. Right now, we are only aware of five girls being stalked. Number four: Maggie was involved somehow. We think it may have been her in a car that was seen following one of the girls. Plus, she had all this information."

We all started talking at once, but we finally decided that we would create a profile for each of the six girls, documenting what we knew so far and what questions we still needed to answer. I felt confident that we'd be able to find Clover's and Maggie's killers by looking deeper into the lives of these girls.

Chapter 20
Spite and Fire

As I walked into my office Friday morning, the phone was ringing. I hesitated for a moment, as I didn't recognize the number, but answered it anyway. A formal voice said, "This is Marcy from the *Fresno News*. One of our reporters is trying to contact Dr. Phoebe Moon for a story. Is this Dr. Moon?" After I said yes, the caller continued, "Please hold while I get our reporter on the line." Before I could object, a rather loud voice was in my ear.

"This is Brittany Wicker from the *Fresno News*; am I speaking with Phoebe Moon?"

"This is Dr. Moon."

"Phoebe, I wanted to ask you about two things. First, what is your involvement in the deaths of the women found on your family's ranch?"

"Well, the girls were murdered a decade before I was born, so I am not involved."

"That may be true, but I bet your mother couldn't have said the same thing and your aunt Beatrice knows what is going on. Can you comment on that?"

"No."

"Really? Well, let me ask you this: I have heard that a qualified job applicant was turned down by your department because she asked questions about your family's involvement in the murders. Care to comment on that?"

"Ms. Wicker, our hiring process is detailed online, and you can look it up if you have questions. Basically, the search committee considers quantifiable attributes, such as number of publications, grants applied for, teaching evaluations, and other academic tasks. Following discussion of these attributes for each candidate, the faculty make a recommendation on who is the top candidate."

"Oh, come on. I know that is bullshit. You didn't choose her because she was nosing around."

"Ms. Wicker, I am sorry you have doubts about our process. I can put you in touch with the right people to make it easier for you to voice your concerns. I'll be passing along your concerns to Dr. Ellen Robinson, the head of the search committee; my boss, Dr. Roberta Richmond; and our legal counsel, but they may want to talk with you directly." I quickly rattled off the numbers to her, then continued. "I don't know if you've spoken to Sheriff Alex Boas yet, but he's in charge of the case. I'd be happy to give you his number."

"You think you can intimidate me with all these numbers? I'll get my answers somewhere else." There was an abrupt click as she hung up.

I hated writing large group emails or texts, but as this felt urgent to me, I sent a group email to Dr. Robinson, Dean Richmond, Louie, Alex, Beatrice, Carlos, and the institute's legal team. Then I did some deep-breathing exercises. I wasn't too worried, but I didn't know anything about Ms. Wicker's journalistic ethics. What I had forgotten to tell her is that hiring committees were overseen by a member of the Workplace Equity Committee, and Ellen had reported in at each stage of our selection process.

I printed a list of meetings and tasks from my Google Calendar and settled into my job. I was curious about who would contact me first.

My first task was to edit a draft manuscript that my two new research associates had written. As I went through it, I was impressed by the professional job they had done. I had definitely hired the right people to help with my research. I used track changes on the cloud, so I could send them notifications of the edits as soon as I finished. The next task was to complete the action plan for the department that Dr. Richmond had requested. I started to pull the document up but paused when I heard a knock on my door. It was Ellen Robinson, looking a bit frazzled. I motioned her in and gave her a sympathetic look. "Did that reporter call you?"

"She did. I don't think I've ever been spoken to like that in my whole life! She was very intimidating and kept trying to put words in my mouth."

"I forgot to tell her about the equity officer who was informed of our decision-making every step of the way. Regardless, I don't want you worrying about anything. From now on, we should both refer her to Dean Richmond or the legal team, so we are not tempted to give her a newsworthy quote."

She gave me a sly look. "I got your warning right before she called, and I accidently recorded the conversation."

"I would love to accidentally hear that sometime," I said.

She left my office looking brighter than when she came in.

An hour later, there was a second knock on my door. Louie poked his head in, then dangled a large bag in front of me. "Lunch?" he asked.

I waved him in, and we converged at the round table. I knew this was going to be a serious talk judging by the sheer amount of food he pulled from the bag. The two types of dessert really gave it away.

We sat down at the table and both started in on the delicious tortilla soup. I could tell he was avoiding making eye contact, so I left him to tell me whatever it was in his own time. We then moved on to fajita salads—still without any meaningful conversation. After we had each chosen a dessert, he looked me in the eye and said, "There is a commotion at the ranch. A group of fifty or so people are across the road from the entrance and are trying to block access. They are also chanting and waving signs. There are TV cameras there, along with a news van from the Fresno News and a reporter with a microphone trying to interview the protesters. The primary chant is 'Lock up the baby killers.' Fortunately, Alex put sheriff cars at the entrance, and they are trying to keep the calm."

A bristle of anger and disappointment rushed over me. I thought about why I was feeling so distressed; the murders took place well before my birth, and Beatrice was only fourteen when they occurred, so neither of us could be associated with them. I think I was angry on behalf of my relatives, and maybe I was feeling some genetic shame. How could a crowd turn on a family that had always supported the community? I knew part of the answer. People were scared; they didn't trust the experiments going on at the farm, which were strictly agricultural, and someone was rousing them. I thought back to the killer. Is this something the killer might do to shift attention from themselves?

All of this was going through my mind as Louie sat there, waiting for my response. I told him what I was thinking, then asked, "Do Alex, Beatrice, or Carlos recognize any of the people? I wonder if Carlos could have someone take pictures and try to attach names to them. If we had good data, we could construct a social network of who is involved and see if that fits the names of the dumped girlfriends and the fathers of the babies. We would need someone familiar with the families to help put it together. Maybe Nina Scott's younger sister, Faith would be willing to help?"

Louie thought it over, then said, "How astute, Dr. Moon." His attempt to raise my mood was very kind, and it freed us up to think about how to address both the immediate problem and the identity of the murderers.

We decided to try to get Alex on the line. As we waited, I told Louie about the calls from Brittany Wicker and the threats she had made. As I described her level of anger, Louie just shook his head. We decided that no one in the family should get caught up in a conversation with her. I also wanted to ask Alex about Brittany's family and their role in the community, assuming they'd been in the area for a while. If we could build a network, we could see who had the densest network of relationships and who was off to the sidelines. We also wondered if Alex should hold a press conference and try to clear up their questions.

After about a half hour, Alex called us back and told us he was parked across the street from the protesters. I asked him to describe what he saw.

"It is actually pretty interesting. People are hanging out in clusters, and it is just an impression, but I wonder if some of the people are being paid to be there. Groups seem to show up in packed cars, wave signs around in front of the cameras, then leave. Then new groups come. There is a more central group, and all those people seem to know each other. They have lawn chairs and coolers with food. One group tried to start a campfire, but we called the fire department, and a crew put the fire out right in front of the chanting crowd. It was good theatrics for the cameras, but the crew told the group that next time, they would arrest them. No one wants a fire in these dry hills.

"Also, there are a couple of people who seem to have come just to spark the crowd, and a handful have wanted to search the property themselves. Unfortunately, it is a big property, and there are no visible fences. There are cameras scattered around, lights throughout, and closer to the structures there are sirens that sound when movement is detected. I don't really know how safe the property is, and at this time we are taking a defensive stance. If someone or something gets hurt, we may have to change our minds."

There was a lull in the conversation, so we told Alex our ideas about taking pictures, asking Faith and Beatrice to work on putting people into related groups, and holding a news conference to talk in vague terms about the direction of the investigation. He liked the first two ideas but was reluctant to attempt a live news conference. Apparently he'd already tried it once, but the protesters drowned him out. He said he was willing to give the press a fact sheet, but he asked if we would draft it. Louie and I agreed to do so.

There was another lull, and this time I got the sense that Alex wanted to say something but didn't quite know how. We waited. Finally, Alex said, "There is a complicating factor that you should know. Brittany Wicker's maternal side of the family owns the Valley Farmers' Bank. In fact, they have owned it since its inception in the mid-1800s. The grandfather, Miles Curtis, married into the family. His wife is Deborah Sutton Curtis. I think they were high school sweethearts, and when they got married, they merged their families' business interests. His dowry, of sorts, was partial ownership of the Curtis Automotive Group. They have a half dozen car dealerships scattered around the county. Rumor has it that after the merger, the family could both sell and finance the cars.

"Anyway, the members of the Curtis family are conservative Republicans, and Miles Curtis is running for Congress in the district that overlaps with Tulare County. His Democratic opponent is a Hispanic incumbent who has been heavily supported by the Boas family. It isn't clear if this case will be taken away from me. We have always centralized family giving, so all the donations are in Carlos's name. I am living day to day with the case because it could be grabbed from me any day."

"Wait a minute!" I said. "Deborah Sutton was mentioned in MG's journal. This circle is getting smaller, as it seems like her granddaughter has decided I am her enemy. It's like a multigenerational feud I knew nothing about."

We called Carlos after we had spoken to Alex. He told us he was in the monitoring room, and everyone was focused on one or more cameras. I could tell he was feeling anxious. Louie looked at me, then said, "We will come right away, and I will send two more bodyguards. Is there a back way into the ranch, so we don't have to go past the protesters?"

Carlos told us that we could go through the adjacent orchard and end up at the back of the ranch property. He would meet us there and guide us to the house. We called Alex back, and he said he would send a car to pick us up at the airport. Then Louie placed the order to have the helicopter pick us up at the closest landing spot.

One of the ways Louie was affecting my daily life is that I now kept a go bag in my car, something I would never have dreamed of doing six months ago. On the trip over to the valley, I thought about all the other ways I had changed over the past six months. One way I didn't like is that I had gained a fuller appreciation of how evil people could be to the innocents around them. Other ways were positive because I now felt more connected to what I could loosely call my family. It was comforting to care about others and to know they cared about me. Sometimes, though, I wasn't sure in which direction I had changed the most.

▲ ▲ ▲

It didn't take long to get to Porterville Municipal Airport. The car Alex had sent drove right up to the helicopter; we quickly got in and were whisked off. The guards Louie had hired had to drive up from Orange County, so they were still a couple of hours away. I didn't know what we could do to help, but at the very least, we could help with the monitors. Carlos met us at the agreed-upon spot; he was riding one of the ranch horses. He asked us to turn off the headlights and follow him slowly through the property, as he didn't want the car to be seen heading back to the ranch. The night was clear, and the moon was bright, but the trip still seemed to take forever. I didn't fully breathe until we pulled up to the barn. At that point, we all got out of the car and waited for Carlos to take care of the horse.

We were walking from the barn to the house when I heard a low hum in the distance. It became louder and louder until it seemed to be right overhead. We stopped and looked all around us. After thirty seconds or so we saw a glint in the sky; the moonlight was illuminating something shiny. Then we all got it; it was a drone circling the buildings of the ranch. There seemed to be a specific target.

Louie guessed that it had a camera attached, and whoever was flying it was searching for something. I felt uneasy as it flew over my head. Were we the targets? By now, the house was empty, and we were all just standing around, all eyes on the sky.

The drone continued to circle all the buildings, and at some point, the operator turned on a spotlight. We were all pointing, shouting, and trying to guess in which direction it would go. Suddenly I heard gunshots. Carlos was frantically trying to shoot the drone out of the sky. After each of his shots, the crowd seemed to grow angrier and louder. The operator reacted quickly, and the spotlight was abruptly turned off. We were back to following the drone by the maniacal sound it made.

And then, it simply fell from the sky. We watched with gaping mouths as the drone fell like a stone into the experimental agriculture building. It fell to earth and there was a massive explosion, which shook all the buildings and cars, and shattered some windows. Immediately there was another type of explosion: a noise explosion. The crowd was cheering and stomping their feet like they were witnessing a touchdown or a home run. The aftermath was a massive fire burning out of control and a crowd chanting "Burn it down!" The smoke had a strong chemical smell, and every breath seemed to make my throat and lungs burn.

"The workers, the workers!" Carlos cried out as he ran toward the building. We ran after him. Sickeningly, we could still hear the crowd cheering from the other side of the orchard. Alex must have seen the fire because he came flying down the driveway with his sirens calling out. It was chaos at the buildings. Louie got the fire extinguishers, I went for the hose, and Carlos was frantically looking for the two workers who monitored the water and temperature of the plants overnight. I trained the feeble flow of water where I thought Carlos had entered the building. Alex was on the phone calling for a fire truck and an ambulance, and I could only hope they'd arrive in time to save the men.

Suddenly I realized I did not know where anyone was. The smoke was so thick I could not see anyone around me. I was standing too close to the hottest part of the fire, and I could feel intense heat on the front side of my body. I started to back up, but I still felt too hot. I looked down and there were sparks on my pants. I turned the water on myself, and the sparks sizzled out. I felt sick that the small level of fire I had experienced could feel so painful.

I backed up all the way and focused on containing the fire. I realized the best I could do was to put out sparks touching down near the other structures. There was something flitting through my brain, but I couldn't quite grab hold of it. Then it hit me: I remembered my grandad showing me how to turn on the watering system for the orchard, and I ran there now to turn it on. The valves were hard to work, but then I heard it: the sprinklers were throwing out a small amount of water on the trees.

I ran back to my hose and continued to work on the embers, running back and forth between buildings. The smoke and heat were wearing me down, but I had to keep going. Then I heard the first notes of a distant firetruck. The crowd was still cheering as the firetruck and then the ambulance tore down the driveway. Soon I heard someone yelling, "I've got it from here, ma'am!" I continued to wave the hose, but the water had been cut off already. In a daze, I let them pull me back closer to the house, where Beatrice and others were watching the fire. A second firefighter pulled Louie back toward the waiting area, but he was sent directly to the ambulance to be checked out. Then people were pointing at me, and I was led to the ambulance too.

A minute or so later, a second fire truck and ambulance pulled up; that is when I realized things may be worse than I thought. As my head cleared, I noticed there was no more cheering. All I heard were sirens and loudspeakers telling people to stay where they were.

The medics wanted to take Louie and me to the emergency room, but we both insisted that they wait for the missing men. When they balked at that, we simply refused treatment; I couldn't leave without knowing what had happened to Alex, Carlos, and the two workers. They compromised by placing oxygen masks on us and telling us that they would be taking us to the hospital shortly.

As we stood by helplessly, putting our faith in the firefighters, we heard a great commotion from where the protesters were being kept back. We heard someone on the loudspeaker yelling, "Sit down on the ground with your hands behind your back. You are being taken in for questioning on the charges of arson and attempted murder. If you try to run, you will be tasered. Participants have been photographed. We do, or soon will, know your identity." I didn't realize it the first time through, but the message was a recording, and it played over and over.

I stopped hearing the words and could only focus on what was going on as people hurried in and out of the greenhouse. Louie stood beside me with his hand on my shoulder. When I looked up at him, under the filth of the fire, I saw tears and pain. Surely it was taking too long.

Within minutes I heard one of the firefighters call a paramedic over. He ran back to the other medics; they scrambled into their units and then ran back to the firefighter carrying two stretchers and a body bag. We all caught the meaning of that at the same time, and there was a collective cry of grief. We asked ourselves only one question: Who had died?

On top of the noise caused by the confusion and wailing cries, we heard a helicopter circling to find a place to land. The medevac team ran to where the firefighters were standing, loaded two bodies on stretchers, and ran back to the chopper. They took off in a whoosh in what seemed to be mere seconds. Slowly the local paramedics came back carrying the body bag; they loaded it into one of the trucks and took off. The other paramedics then came looking for Louie and me, and they loaded us up. Just as we were readying to leave, Alex came stumbling out of the building. The paramedics ran to him and helped him into the ambulance. They put Alex on oxygen and made him lie down on the gurney. Louie and I were allowed to sit on the bench seat. After we were strapped in, we took off.

More than anything, we wanted to know who had been killed, but one of the paramedics was working nonstop on Alex, so we just kept quiet and still.

▲ ▲ ▲

We must have all dozed off on the way to the hospital because the next thing I knew someone was transferring me to a wheelchair and wheeling me into an emergency room. Louie was in a chair next to me, but I think Alex had been taken straight back to a bed. Louie and I were loosely holding hands, but staff took us to adjacent emergency bays. I managed to clumsily remove my clothes and put on a gown. When I looked down at my legs, I saw small burns from my midthighs to my calves. The more I looked at them, the more they seemed to hurt, so I focused instead on trying to get information. I learned we were in a Level 3 trauma center in Visalia, but the helicopter had taken the others to a Level 1 trauma center in Fresno. There was no one there for me—we were all on our own for now.

After I had been cleaned up and treated for smoke inhalation and given pain meds for the burns, I was allowed to go next door to Louie's room. I had to take my drip with me, so it was slow going. When I got there, Louie was asleep. He was also hooked up to a drip, but he had some other machines too. I couldn't think of what to do for him, so I slowly walked back to my room and got in bed.

I awoke the next morning with a nurse hovering over me, taking my vitals and drawing blood. Besides a headache, a sore throat, and the pain from the burns, I felt much better. I walked with my drip into Louie's room, but he was still asleep, so I returned to my room.

As I sat down on my bed, my room phone rang. I was afraid to answer it, afraid to find out who had died, but I pushed down the trepidation and answered it.

It was Beatrice. I could hear her crying softly, then she spoke and asked how I was doing. I told her I had mild injuries, Louie was still sleeping, and I had no information about Alex or anyone else. She sighed and said, "Carlos is alive and in the Fresno trauma center. I am here with him because they told me his injuries were more severe than yours. He, too, is asleep. He has lung injuries and second-degree burns on his arms and hands. He is on a ventilator, but overall, they think he will pull through. One of the workers, a former student apprentice named Miguel Sanchez, did not make it. He was directly underneath the blast, and Carlos couldn't get to him. The other worker, also a former student apprentice, was closer to the entrance, so Carlos was able to pull him out. Had Carlos stopped then, his injuries would be less severe, but he kept going back inside to grab things—his research logs, plants, and equipment. I called about Alex; he sustained a variety of injuries and burns. Most serious is that one of the beams fell across his leg, and it was several intense minutes before he was able to get it off. He had his gloves on, so his hands are OK, but the burn on his leg is nasty.

"I'm sorry to tell you all of this on the phone, but I knew you would be going crazy with not knowing about Carlos, Alex, and the workers. I will be at your hospital in about an hour and a half, and we can figure out what to do next."

I leaned back on my bed and cried with grief. The loss of Miguel, a young student trying to make his life and the world better, hit me hard. Miguel believed in what he was doing, as he served the greater social good. And he died for what? So that a horrendous crime that had nothing to do with him could be covered up for a few more days or a few more weeks?

CHAPTER 21
Keep Going

I lay in bed waiting for Aunt Beatrice to arrive. I was in that state between asleep and awake, and it was starting to mess with my mind. I began to imagine that I'd be stuck there forever, and it was extremely unpleasant. After a couple of hours, Beatrice stepped into the room. She told me she had been sitting with Carlos, getting ready to leave, when the other patient had a medical crisis. She had waited until he was stable.

I asked, "What's going on at the ranch?"

She closed her eyes as she thought about what to tell me. "First, the experimental greenhouse is demolished. It is a charred, empty space. Second, the other structures are fine, but the animals are still distraught from the smoke, fire, and noise. We have a vet there now, looking them over and treating those who need it. It will be a while before they fully settle down. Third, based on the videos of the crowds and witness statements, the person working the drone was identified, and a lengthy list of charges was filed against him. He is in his mid-twenties, so he will stand trial as an adult. Fourth, the tide seems to have turned with the newspapers, and they are digging a bit deeper into the murders, who was involved, and how the bodies were discovered. Of course, they don't mention their role in causing the frenzied activities of the crowd."

"Who's in charge now?" I asked.

"Stay calm, OK? In the past, the California Bureau of Investigations was consulting with the Sherriff but now the investigation has been handed over to them. Now, Alex will be a consultant. That is the best they could do because of the nature of the crimes and Alex's role as a victim."

I had reached information overload, and not long after, I fell into a deep sleep.

When I awoke, I heard low conversation coming from Louie's room. One of the voices was Beatrice's, but I didn't recognize the other male and female voices. I got out of bed and pulled my line after me as I limped into Louie's room. The conversation stopped, and everyone turned to look at me. Everyone except Louie; he was still sleeping.

Beatrice hurried over and lowered me to a chair. She made sure my gown was closed in the back, then she introduced me to Louie's aunt and uncle, and we exchanged greetings. Then I asked, "Has he been awake?"

Beatrice reassured me that he'd had short periods when he was awake, but they had not matched the periods when I was awake.

"Alex?"

"He is the same, Phoebe. When he is awake, he asks about what is going on and your and Louie's status. He keeps saying that the three of you need to talk. I told him that as soon as you are all awake at the same time, I will get you together."

"OK," I muttered and stood up to go back to my room. Beatrice followed behind me with one hand under my elbow and the other keeping the back of my gown closed.

▲ ▲ ▲

The miracle finally happened on Sunday, two days after the fire. I was sitting up in bed sipping juice when Beatrice came in pushing Louie in a wheelchair, followed by a deputy pushing Alex. We looked at each other carefully, verifying for ourselves that we were all alive. We sat quietly waiting for Beatrice and the deputy to leave, and after a while they got the hint.

We all sighed at the same time, and then the guys rolled over to my bed and held my hands. We had all been traumatized. Not just by the fire and loss from it but by the circumstances. Someone had purposefully launched a firebomb that had the potential to destroy our ranch and kill all its occupants. We weren't in a war. We weren't in a fight. We were just trying to protect ourselves. How did this mayhem break out?

Alex was the first to speak as he let go of my hand and backed away from the bed. His voice was low and rough as he said, "The man who flew the drone was from out of state. He was hired to fly the drone into the greenhouse. He claimed that no one involved knew there would be people inside. Basically, that is all he is saying."

I said, "It sounds like we are making someone very nervous that the murderers will be found."

Louie finally spoke, and his voice sounded about like Alex's. "That sounds right to me. You may not remember, Phoebe, but you met my aunt and uncle. My uncle is my dad's brother, and they have always been in business together. My uncle knows Curtis—the boomer version. He said Curtis has a reputation for being competitive to the core. Allegations have been made about his tactics, but nothing has ever been proven. My uncle did reassure me that he and his friends would make maximum contributions to his opponent's election fund, and he would quietly spread the word about what is happening."

That made me smile.

"Beatrice told me the CBI is taking over the case. I was actually glad to hear it because we had no idea what we were getting into," I said.

Alex looked at me with sorrowful eyes. "Does that mean you are backing out of the investigation?"

"No. It means I am happy to be in the background, doing the analysis we have been doing and putting things together in our own way. Maybe it will draw attention away from our families."

He smiled at me. "Good. I didn't want to think my kick-ass cuz was going soft on me!" Then he grew serious and asked, "When is everyone getting out of here?"

Louie and I shouted, "Tomorrow!" at the same time.

"How about you?" I asked.

"I was told I can have my computer back tomorrow, and if I am really doing well, I can meet with the CBI too. But I need to stay at least until Wednesday. They want to make sure my lungs are healing and that my leg doesn't get infected. I may have to use a cane for three to four weeks as my leg heals."

We looked around, avoiding each other's eyes, until Louie said, "Hey, it's Sunday! Any football games on?"

We were all happy to discover there was a San Francisco 49ers football game on TV. We tried to join in with the crowd and the shouts coming from other rooms, but we didn't last through the first quarter. We were all asleep within minutes. When I awoke, I was in my room alone and dinner was being served. Just as I was peeking under the lid of my food, which was a soft diet of sorts, Louie wheeled himself in, trying to balance his tray on his lap. He pulled up to the side of my bed and placed his tray on my bedside table. He looked at his food and sighed. We both went for the chocolate pudding, then for the red gelatin. It wasn't much, but I was full.

We just sat and held hands after that. It wasn't that we were uncomfortable, but if Louie was feeling anything like I was, he was trying to adapt cognitively and emotionally to this new reality. Who had we frightened so badly that they would risk life in prison to send us a message?

Finally, I broke the silence. "I want to see all the relevant high school yearbooks. I want to map out the social networks of the girls who went on the study abroad trips from each school attended by the six known girls. I also want to map the networks of Clover and Maggie to see if they overlap in any way. Then we can look at their social media posts to see if they were still connected at this stage of their lives. I think I will try it out first on Nina's school, Lower Sierra, because we have Beatrice and Faith to help.

"My number one priority is to speak with the boyfriends. We are sure that Miles Curtis was somehow involved. How many more guys do you think there were? Let's get going on that."

Louie's face lit up, and he asked, "When do you need to be back at work?"

"You probably remember that Dean Richmond stayed at our ranch last summer for a couple of weeks, and she and Beatrice became good friends. The dean told Beatrice she absolutely does not want me back before a week from tomorrow."

Louie tilted his head and asked, "Did she know how much sick leave you used before they hired you?"

That made me laugh, which promptly turned into a coughing fit. When my breathing was back to normal, I said, "I used to never take sick leave. I used to get awards for attendance in school."

"I'm sure you did," Louie said and smiled. Quickly, though, he turned the subject back to work: "How would you feel about staying in the office suites for two or three days when we get back? That way we won't have to worry about security or food. Beatrice wants to come back with us, so she could have the third suite and help with tracing the social networks. If Beatrice is there, my aunt won't demand to move in. Plus, Carlos's daughter wants to take care of him, and Beatrice doesn't want to be in the way."

He was very persuasive, and I told him it was a great plan. He squeezed my hand, then rolled back to his own room, his parting comment being, "Wheels up at eight thirty. Don't oversleep!"

CHAPTER 22
Let's Dig Some More

Aunt Beatrice came to my room at 8 a.m.; I was dressed and ready to leave. Before she rolled me out through the front of the hospital, she said there was something she needed to tell me. "I can't go back to the ranch for a while, and I am not sure I can ever go back permanently. I just can't understand how the people I have known all my life could turn on us. Even when the case is completed, will people ever welcome us back?"

I wanted to tell her that I felt the same way, but I couldn't bring myself to do it. The same community that had created the protesters also created her best friend, Faith. And it created Daniel, who had devoted his life to understanding the causes of and treatments for cancer. It is not really the place that is at fault; it is the people who control the place that define its nature.

I gave her a big hug and said, "Beatrice, you always have a home with me. We will go to Louie's office and then when we are ready, we will go to my house. You can stay there as long as you want or need." The look of relief on her face was unmistakable.

She pushed me out of my room and through the hospital, and as we exited the building, we saw there was a car waiting for us. Louie was standing there, talking to the driver, and as soon as they saw us, they loaded everything, including us, into the car. The helicopter was parked at a nearby airport, and then it was just a short flight to our landing spot.

A car was there to meet us and take us to Louie's office building. On the way we had a call from Louie's security company, telling us there was a problem at Louie's family home. We detoured directly there, and we could see security police roaming the property. We got out of the car, and one of the security team members came over to greet us.

"The alarm went off about ten minutes ago. When we couldn't get you on the phone, we decided we had better check it out. There is nothing obvious out here, but maybe we should go inside and look at the monitors?"

Louie agreed, and we trooped inside. It was my first time inside the house, and it looked nothing like I had imagined. It was bright and airy, with streaming sunlight and minimal furnishings. What furnishings I could see were modern and unadorned. I could tell Beatrice was taking it all in as well, and she gave me a bemused look. Louie led us to the study and set the monitors back twenty minutes. We spotted them at the back door minutes later. Two men dressed in black, including black gloves and masks, came into view. One tried the back door, and when it didn't open, he tapped a pane of glass with his gun. The glass broke, and the alarm started to scream. Fortunately, the security company left the alarm on until they reached the property. It looked like the two men had hesitated a moment and then ran around to the side of the house closest to their car. There was no sign they had stayed behind. The security camera that was focused on the entrance to the property showed two men in a generic black SUV tearing out of the driveway.

Just then, my cell phone rang. This time it was my security company. I could see my monitors on my cell phone, and it looked as though the same two men were now at my back door, trying to get in. I told the security company to call the police right away but to turn off the alarm. The manager did so but stayed on the phone with the dispatcher to guide their response.

I was watching the intruders on my monitor. After using the same technique of breaking a glass pane but the alarm sounding only briefly, their courage or stupidity took over. They slipped inside, but within minutes the house was being surrounded by what looked like a SWAT team.

Louie led us back to the car, and we took off toward my house. I was watching the situation as it unfolded. The police were waiting for the men to exit on their own. We rolled up on the side street and parked a hundred yards or so behind the police. We all waited. After another ten minutes, the first intruder stuck his head out the door. He edged out, and then his partner followed. I couldn't see anything in their hands—what had they been looking to find?

They stepped off the back step and were immediately surrounded by the police, who had been positioned on the other side of the fence with the door and on both sides of the house. They had their riot gear on, and their guns were pointed at the intruders, who had no viable choice but to surrender. Louie eased out of the car and slowly walked toward the commander, keeping his hands above his head. When Louie got to him, he pointed at the car, and he and the commander walked over to us.

Louie introduced Beatrice and me and explained that it was my house and that we had been watching the cameras on my phone. He also explained that we'd had a call about his parents' home because he was the responding person while they were traveling. The intruders had tried there first, but they were scared off by the continuous alarm. I emailed the file from my monitors to the commander, and Louie gave him the contact information for his security company. We promised to be available should they need us.

I turned to Beatrice and said, "I know it looks bad, but you will be safe soon. I promise."

Louie drove us the few miles to his offices and parked right next to the door. The door had a double lock, requiring both a key card and biometric data. We also needed the key card for the elevator and the office suite. Finally, Louie gave each of us a key card for our individual suites. When Beatrice used the final key card to get into her hidden suite, I thought she would cry with relief.

Beatrice's reaction to her suite was the same as mine when I first saw it: 100 percent amazement at the view and the level of comfort. She turned to Louie, "Can I move in here permanently?"

Louie said, "Trust me, it is a good place to hide out for a little while, but you will be ready to get out within a few days."

▲ ▲ ▲

It was just minutes past noon by the time we had settled into our rooms. While we were busy doing that, Louie had asked the catering staff to set up lunch in the main room. When Beatrice and I walked out, there was a crowd around the lunch buffet table, and we joined them, making sandwiches and spooning salads onto our plates. As soon as we were seated, Louie introduced Beatrice and then he managed to give a humorous account of his stay in the hospital and his relative level of energy. There was visible camaraderie, and the teams wanted to report on the progress they had made. The food was great and the conversation stimulating, but I was falling asleep at the table. Louie, Beatrice, and I decided we would take a two-hour break and then discuss our next steps.

I went back to my suite, set my alarm, and fell asleep. When my alarm rang, I had no memories of dreams or even moving; I had found I always slept soundly in this building, and I was thankful to have it as a resource.

I washed my face, grabbed a bottle of water, and went out to meet the others. Beatrice was already sitting at a big table with the yearbooks of our first victim, Nina Scott, scattered around her. She was going through them slowly, looking at all the group and individual pictures. She looked up when I sat down, and she said, "I had forgotten how small the school was and the high percentage of the people I would be able to name. The difficult part might be if local kids attend an event with someone from a different school. But overall, I feel comfortable identifying everyone. Faith is at work, but she has the same set of yearbooks with her and is standing by if I get stuck. She has kept up with everyone unless they moved away. Now, exactly what do you want me to do?"

"Basically, I want you to make a big drawing of what will essentially look like a spiderweb for each of the primary characters in our story, using lines and arrows to indicate connections between people and the primary character. We want each class year plotted with a different color of ink, so that we'll be able to see if and when links are formed, maintained, or broken. Start with Nina in her first year of high school; she will be person zero. Write her name in the center of the paper, then go through the yearbook and record direct connections between Nina and the people she shows up with in pictures."

I flipped through the yearbook till I came to a picture of Nina and Maggie sitting on a bench eating lunch. "So here you would draw a direct line between Nina and Maggie. Then if you saw a picture of Maggie playing volleyball with a different girl, you would write down that girl's name and draw a line between the two. After you are finished, we will go through them again to see if we can figure out the possible directions of the lines. For example, Maggie and Nina's line would have an arrowhead on both ends, since they shared information with each other. For weaker relationships, we will just have to guess, but I hope it will be enough to give us a big picture of the relationships. Nina will be our test case because we have Faith to back it up with more details. Second, we will do these networks for the girls who went on the study abroad trip and, if needed, their boyfriends at the end of their junior years. As soon as we can figure out how they are all connected, we can stop."

She gave me a weak smile; it was all new to her, and I could feel her anxiety. "Once you feel confident in what you are doing, Louie said he would appoint a couple of interns to help you out." That made her brighten up.

I waited, but Beatrice didn't seem to have any more questions, so I left her to it. I moved over to a nearby desk and pulled up the set of files we had received from Parker. We had managed to fax the files to the company's main computer, then transform them into documents we could manipulate. I started opening the documents one by one. The files looked like copies of handwritten tables that someone had transferred to an Excel file. There were initials in codes and dollar amounts.

There was a set of text files that also appeared to be in code. Each brief file had an identifying number as the title. The documents were in narrative form—were they questions and answers? Were they a list of meetings or interactions and what transpired? I sent copies of the text files to Louie and asked if anyone on staff was good at breaking codes.

Then I went back to the spreadsheets. I came to realize that none of the initials for the cases matched the initials of our known victims. But because I knew the real initials, I was confident I could figure this one out.

I made a table of the alphabet and the numbers of the letters. As I examined the original documents, I noticed that one of the pages had scribbles at the bottom. After staring at them for a while, I realized they were rudimentary algebraic statements. I thought about Clover, the girl who may have developed this scheme. I imagined her studying for her SATs and reviewing her algebra notes. Would she have made a code of the alphabet using a simple algebraic statement? The first statement on the page was $L = (2x + 1)$. I immediately saw the problem with this, as it went beyond twenty-six and some letters had the same code. The next two I tried did not work either. The last statement on the page was L = (2x / 2 + 1). Was it that simple? When I changed Nina's initials (NAS) to the code, they were OBT. I looked at the list and saw that OBT was the first case listed. I quickly filled in the rest of the targeted girls, based on what we knew. When I got to the initials for the fourth murdered girl, I translated the initials but didn't know what to expect. The initials TCM translated to SBL—Sharon B. Lane, the girl killed in the car crash.

I sat there in shock. How had this murder happened? Who paid for it? And why had we so easily accepted the "accident" explanation?

▲ ▲ ▲

Louie had been holding meetings with his teams since we'd arrived. When he walked out of his office around four, he looked exhausted. He came over to where I was sitting and tried to give me a smile.

"Everybody on track?" I asked.

"Yes, everything is running smoothly. I don't know if that means I'm superfluous or the greatest boss ever. It could go either way," he answered.

I gave him a sympathetic smile and a brief hand squeeze. We had agreed we needed to keep our relationship at work collegial and nothing more.

After a moment, I told him that according to the records from Parker, the car crash had not been an accident. "Someone started paying for it, but payments stopped abruptly after about ten years. Not huge amounts: it looks like between two and three hundred dollars a year. Odd, right? That would barely seem worth the effort."

"How did you figure this out?" he asked me.

I told him about the algebraic statements written on the original document and how the one that fit was simple. "When I translated the last victim's initials, they matched the girl who was killed in the crash. So, in the versions of the tables Parker gave us, there were four completed cases and two that were started and then dropped. Fortunately, the names of the victims in the records match what we have, so there are no unknown girls out there, just the change of status from accident to murder.

"I was thinking about our car crash victim, Sharon. Are we certain she wasn't pregnant? If not, it certainly breaks the pattern."

Louie thought for a moment, then said he'd have someone look into it. He then said he'd had a brief talk with Alex, and they had scheduled a conference call for 4:15 p.m. I went over and asked Beatrice to join us in Louie's conference room. When we got there, the room was set up for a video conference, and Alex was just joining from his hospital bed. Greetings were exchanged all around, and we all checked in on everyone's health.

Alex started the conversation. "Well, the CBI are a little upset that we did not invite them in earlier. I was told the proper time would have been when we first found the three burial sites. At any rate, they are deciding whether they want a multiagency task force or just a small team of a few CBI agents and a couple people from the sheriff's office. I reminded them that the case also had a link to Lake Tahoe and possibly to Orange County. By my counting, there have been six deaths: three girls, Maggie, Clover, and the ranch employee. I am guessing there were multiple murderers."

"Alex," I interrupted, "there are indications that four girls were murdered. We found a listing and payments for the girl killed in the car crash, Sharon Lane. Payments seem to have been made for about ten years."

"Add one more, then," he said wearily. "Let's piece together our theory. It seems to have started with Nina. She was pregnant, presumably dating a popular football player. Clover found out and started a murder-for-hire business with her cousin Jay. The purpose seems to have been to get rid of pregnancies that would have "inconvenienced" other people. This went on throughout the 1967–68 school year. Clover and Jay extorted someone associated with each murder for as long as they could. Searching for a body on your land, based on an unfounded tip that a friend of your mother's was buried on the ranch, yielded one body and led to two more. In searching, we found a total of three bodies on or near your land, and a fourth girl's death had been ruled an accident. When we initially found the bodies, someone grew nervous and killed Maggie and then Clover. Fearful the truth would come out, someone organized protests at the ranch. They went so far as to pay out-of-town aggressors to attach an incendiary device to a drone and burn down the experimental greenhouse."

Louie broke in then. "We haven't had a chance to tell you that both our houses were broken into this morning. A SWAT team caught the invaders at Phoebe's house. They were also from out of state and had criminal records. As far as we can tell, nothing was stolen, but we didn't go inside to look around. The thieves are claiming it was a job arranged on the dark web, and they have no idea who hired them. I think the basic theory is solid, though. They refused to say anything else—such as what they were sent to look for. Someone with something to lose, or something to hide at least, is afraid a secret will be revealed, and they will do anything to protect it."

"OK, thanks for filling that in," Alex said. "If Jay and Clover committed the actual murders, we don't know who paid for them or who committed or paid for the current murders. The most visible suspect is Brittany Wicker's grandfather, Miles Curtis, because he is running for Congress. But as Phoebe said, there are likely to be multiple people involved with each murder. I think that one urgent line of investigation is to identify and interview the men involved."

Louie asked, "OK, how can we handle talking with Miles Curtis? I don't think he would bother talking with Phoebe or me. Phoebe because she is the 'enemy,' and me because my family's political views are known to him. Can you do it, Alex?"

Alex looked as though he was warring within himself. "If I wanted to make a point, I probably could, but I have heard he is quite racist, and my family is backing his competitor. So, I don't know how successful I would be. How about if we ask the senior CBI detective to do it but also to record it for us. It's not ideal, but maybe it's OK as a first pass?"

We all agreed with his logic and told him to go for it. "Maybe two agents should go," Louie added. "One can take notes if Miles won't let them tape it."

I spoke up then. "I hate to mention this, but I don't think we can rule out revenge as a motive for Maggie's and Clover's murders. It is even possible that one of the survivors or a family member of any of the girls wanted retribution for a murder. We need to pick up the links among the people and see if the networks lead to a trail. One thing we do know is that all the roads lead back to Clover and Jay. I think the vehicle for connection for the girls was the Intra-County Farm Group. Are we able to glean any more information from this circle?"

We were all thinking this over, and Louie said, "I think this would be a better task for the CBI than us. The more we dig into them, the more we will become an object of their wrath. The families who still live in the county pretty much consider themselves to be the elite strata, and they will likely fight back. I think we should continue looking at the social networks and doing background checks. We have both the staff and the capabilities for that."

Alex looked exhausted, but he managed to make a summary. "OK, we give the CBI the information we have on each of the victims and the list of the girls from each of the target schools who went on the study abroad trip. We also share our file on Clover—but let's hold off on sharing anything about Maggie for now. The CBI will also have the paid criminals to track down as they try to find the source of hire." We all nodded yes, and then we made plans for our next conference call.

Chapter 23
What Am I Doing?

I awoke the next morning feeling disoriented. I had fragments of a dream in my mind. It had been the kind of night that took me through cycles of dreaming, waking up, then falling back to sleep and into the same dream again. In the dream I was trying to hide, but I never felt safe enough.

Now, for whatever reason, it had left me with a question: *What the hell am I doing?* I'm a professor, not an investigator. By trying to chase down these murderers, I was neglecting my responsibilities. Dean Richmond had not told me I needed to focus on my job, but I felt I was taking advantage of her. The case last summer was justifiable because the department couldn't go on being at the center of Carlton Richmond's craziness. But the overlap between this case and my department was much more tenuous.

I took an inventory of how I was feeling. Physically I was tired and achy, and my chest felt tight. Psychologically I was overwhelmed and unsure. Overall, I guess the word I would use is bruised. I didn't have a tolerance for the level of violence I had experienced.

Just as I was about to get out of bed, my phone rang. The screen said "dad." Even though I'd known about JJ for a few months, I kept forgetting I had a dad in my life now, my biological father. He hadn't abandoned me; he had just stayed in the background for my own safety. I answered the phone, and before I knew it, I was telling him everything. He was an excellent listener.

After a while, our conversation turned to the secret refuge at the restaurant. The way it had been described to me, I thought it was just a single room, but as it turns out, it was a large enough space for a person to live in for a while, with two bedrooms, a sitting room, a bathroom, and a kitchen. He told me I could use it and that I could bring Beatrice if she wanted to come. I told him I'd talk it over with Beatrice and Louie. Having another option made me energized enough to get out of bed and get ready for the day.

Breakfast was still spread out on the table when I went out to the workspace. Just about half of the employees were there, so I didn't feel too lazy about the time I'd spent in bed. I looked around and saw that Beatrice was back at her table drawing networks, and Louie was engaged in a conversation with one of his teams. I got a cup of coffee and a chocolate donut and went to my workstation, then tried to figure out where I had left off.

Ah yes, I was deciphering the letters that appeared next to each payment. I suspected these were the initials of the payers. Unfortunately, they used a different code—or at least I thought they did. When I tried the code I'd used for the targeted girls, the initials didn't match anyone on my list. Either there was a different code, or there were people involved we didn't yet know about.

I remembered what I had read in MG's journal. For her school, only three of the study abroad attendees were invited to join the Intra-County Farm Group. Because they wanted the members to take part in pageants, the girls would probably be the cool/pretty girls. A very sexist notion. If I looked at the girls' pictures, I might be able to put them into likely and unlikely categories. The network analysis might also show that the girls were in different social circles.

I wandered over to Beatrice's table and asked if I could see the picture of the study abroad group for Nina's school. The editors of the yearbook had graciously separated the seniors and the juniors. I looked at the pictures of the seniors, and it was obvious to me which girls had pageant-level looks. In addition to MG, there were Brittany Wicker's grandmother, Deborah Sutton, who was now Deborah Curtis, and a girl named Pricilla Lyles. I didn't know if Pricilla had married and stayed in the area. I recognized the girls' names from MG's journal but I hadn't connected everything before. I would look into both of them, especially Deborah Curtis due to her relationship with Brittany Wicker.

The CBI would interview all the girls who went on the study abroad trip, and Beatrice would work on the networks. I had an idea. Maybe the girls from Nina's school who went on the trip but were not invited into the Intra-County Farm Group would be willing to speak with me. I would track them down. My funk started to lift.

I walked over to one of the teams Louie had working on the case; this team was trying to locate key people we might want to interview. Because we had all agreed to start with Nina's case, it would make sense for them to have already collected information about the study abroad group. It turned out they had, and they handed over a document to me. For now, I only wanted to talk to the three senior girls who were not invited into Clover's club.

All three were still alive, but only one had remained in Tulare County: Millie, a retired pharmacist. The other two women lived on the California coast: Rachel in Santa Cruz, and Constance just north of San Francisco. I looked up to see that Louie had just ended his meeting with his team and was walking toward me. He sat down at my table, and I told him what I was thinking: that it might be less disruptive to start by talking to the women who were not invited to join the farm group. We talked it over and decided to take a risk. We would try to arrange a group interview and see where it took us. Just to be safe, Louie went over and tasked one of his employees with seeing if the women had a social media presence and if so, if there were any indications that they were estranged from each other.

My other topics of concern were the coding of the payers' initials and the narrative pieces. I had asked Louie for staff help with decoding the narratives, but I hadn't been given any results yet. Waiting was hard for me. In the meantime, I could continue to try to understand the codes for the payers.

Louie wandered back over, was quiet for a moment, and then let out a big sigh.

"We need a break," he said. "Is there anything you would like to do?"

"Yes. I would like to have lunch at the Pacific View Retreat and see if JJ could join us. I'd like to see if he has any thoughts on the situation, and I want to see the guest lodgings at the restaurant."

"We can do that, but is there a reason you want to see the lodgings?" he asked.

"I'm feeling like I need a backup plan, especially because I feel responsible for Beatrice being here. I don't know where she will feel comfortable and safe until all of this is over. I'm not sure she will ever go back to the ranch. Maybe that was all a long staycation for her. I guess she'll tell us when she's ready. I'll call JJ and see if we can meet him around one. If nothing else, we can at least sit outside and feel the ocean breeze."

"OK," Louie said, "I'll arrange the transportation. Let's surprise Beatrice with the location." He started to walk away but then stopped. "There's something else," he said. "I've had a staff member drive around your neighborhood a couple of times a day, to make sure no one tries to break in again. He just told me there were some large brown boxes on your doorstep this morning. Are they important?"

I started to say I had no idea what they were, but then I remembered. Right after Daniel Rowan had given me the key to my mother's trunk, I had sent the key to Beatrice. She had promised to box up the contents of the trunk and send them to my house. They must have been in route since before the fire.

"Yes! They're my mother's belongings that she had set aside for me. Maybe we have one more chance to find something helpful to this case."

"Great. I'll send someone to pick them up while we're at lunch."

▲ ▲ ▲

The car picked us up at 12:40. I could tell Beatrice was worried about safety, but she was also excited to see where we were taking her. As we drove down the coast toward the restaurant, she became engaged with the view and seemed to relax a bit. The car let us out right in front of the entrance, and JJ was waiting in the foyer to greet us. A server took us to a quiet patio table with a full view of the Pacific. Two bottles of wine, one white and one red, were already breathing and were ready to pour. I heard a quiet sigh from Beatrice. She was trusting that we would take her someplace safe, and this seemed OK with her.

Because I had reassured JJ that I was on the mend, after we got settled, I asked Louie to fill him in on everything that had been happening.

The more Louie told him, the more visibly upset he became. When he'd finished, he asked JJ if he had any thoughts on the people involved or any sources of information we may have overlooked.

JJ took a long pause, then asked, "Would it be all right if we have lunch before I try to answer that question? In the meantime, I'm going to make a phone call after we order to see if I can get some outside help. I do have ideas and ways to guide you, but I want to get an outside opinion." The server was just walking up to pour our wine and hand us menus. He paused when he got to JJ, who gave him his lunch order, then excused himself from the table.

The rest of us were having a hard time deciding what we wanted to eat, as JJ had gotten permission from the chefs that we could order off the lunch or dinner menus. There were multiple seafood options, including every type of shellfish, as well as Latin American traditional, European, and California vegetarian dishes. We finally placed our orders, then sat enjoying the view and sipping our wine. Just as our food was being delivered, JJ came back to the table. As a not-too-subtle cue that he was not yet ready to talk, he took over the conversation with a colorful description of the restaurant's past, complete with prohibition pirates and bootlegged booze. JJ kept us entertained all through lunch and dessert, and we were able to put aside everything we'd been through, at least for a little while. At about 2:30 a server came to the table and handed JJ a note, after which JJ announced that he wanted to give us a tour and show us all the influences of the past.

▲ ▲ ▲

JJ walked us through the kitchen and into a more corporate-looking hall. He told us that before we had our tour, he wanted to talk about the murders, so he guided us into a conference room. We sat around an oval table, and when I looked at the computer screen, I was pleasantly surprised to see Daniel Roan looking back at me. JJ introduced everyone, then said, "I didn't grow up near the ranch, so I called in Daniel to see if he could help us out. Daniel doesn't know much because he graduated a couple of years before MG. Phoebe, from reading MG's journal, you know about her dream and what she thought had happened. Daniel told me he had a bit more to add."

"I think you all know that MG was my cover girlfriend for many years. People thought we were secretly married and that Phoebe was my daughter. Of course, I knew I was gay since around my sophomore year, but there were heavy expectations that I should date and go to formal dances. When I came back to Porterville after my oncology residence, there would be galas a couple of times a year that I had to attend—you know, for causes like funding a cancer wing in the hospital. MG came with me whenever she could arrange it.

"One year, Phoebe, when you were three or four years old, I asked MG to come down for a charity auction and dinner-dance. Your grandparents were happy to have you for an evening, so there was nothing standing in the way. At one point, while we were dancing, a group of women came up beside us and tried to guide MG away from me. One of them even offered to dance with me instead. So as not to be rude, I released MG and started dancing with the other woman. The women led MG away from me, and I could see them having a heated discussion in the corner. At one point, one woman—I think it was Deborah Sutton Curtis—laid a hand on your mother's arm, and I thought your mother was going to punch her. Instead, she wrenched herself away and came back to resume dancing with me. I asked her what was wrong, and she told me the women were truly evil, and she did not want to be around them.

"I noticed that they kept giving her threatening looks throughout the evening, but she wouldn't say anything. When we were on our way home, she told me that the women had taken part in the most horrible crime she could imagine, and they were afraid she would tell someone. She said they'd threatened the safety of everyone who was important to her if she ever said anything.

"Besides Deborah and her posse, there was a tall blond woman who kept trying to get MG's attention, but MG ignored her. I don't know who she was, and MG refused to tell me anything about her. I continued to see the women around town, but they never acknowledged me. When Deborah's husband, Miles Curtis, decided to run for a state congressional seat, I was invited to a fundraising event for him. It would have been good for my practice and for cancer care to donate, but I just couldn't do it. I wondered if other people had been snubbed by his family. Besides, by this time, about twenty years ago, he was becoming known as a rather slimy businessperson. There were concerns about the solvency of his bank and his use of preferential loan practices and possible redlining. I guess his campaign team got the hint then, or maybe they looked at the voter registration rolls and saw I was listed as a Democrat, but they never asked me to contribute again.

The closest that I came to the group after that was when I treated one of the women for breast cancer. A couple of times it seemed as though she wanted to tell me something, but she never did. The last time I saw her for a follow-up, she told me she had grieved MG's death and regretted how she had treated her at the auction when she was with Deborah Sutton Curtis and the other women. Then, as she was walking out the door, she said, 'We should have chosen MG over Deborah.' I never saw her again after that. Maybe she felt she had said too much. Maybe she was afraid she had incriminated herself. I really don't know."

Daniel fell silent then, and we all just sat there, coming up with our own interpretations of what this all meant. To me, it made it clear that there were things MG did not disclose in her journals. Maybe she didn't feel safe enough to put them in writing. I also wondered why Daniel didn't bring this story up when we had lunch. Then I remembered that I had asked him about the restaurant, MG's treatment and decline, and the dream she'd recorded in her journal, so he'd been sticking with what I wanted to know at the time. It then occurred to me that MG may have kept her secrets in the locked chest in her room.

▲ ▲ ▲

When we were out in the hall again, JJ asked if we wanted to start the tour. I wanted to see the historical section of the restaurant, as did Beatrice and Louie. So far, what I had seen looked like any other modern Southern California beach-themed restaurant, and I was curious to see beyond the visible walls. JJ led us back to the kitchen, where he picked up two bottles of wine that were waiting for him. We walked through the sleekly outfitted room to a locked pantry in the back. One feature of the pantry is that it held a row of lockers, each with a label and a built in lock. There didn't appear to be any doors within the pantry, but JJ held his finger up to a sensor on a side panel of a cabinet. The cabinet moved, revealing a hallway that looked as if it had been preserved from the 1920s.

The hallway was dark, with dim lighting running along the top. As we made our way down the hall, lights turned off behind us and turned on in front of us. The hallway emptied out into a lounge, still in 1920s decor, which featured red velvet couches and chairs. There was a polished wooden bar along one side, a small stage, and scattered cocktail and card tables. JJ put the wine down on the bar and pulled some glasses off a shelf. He opened the wine and filled a glass for each of us while he explained that at one point, this was the club within the restaurant. He pointed out one hidden door and told us it led to a number of underground passages that were connected to disguised parking spaces from prohibition times. For example, one path led to an old barnlike structure that used to be customer parking.

There was a second hidden doorway, and we went through it. A short hallway that looked like the one leading out of the pantry met us, though it was a bit darker than the first. At the end of it, JJ typed in a code on a keypad, and the door slid open to reveal the guest suite. The suite was not only gorgeous but also invisible when looking in from the outside. What must have been the front of the building had only a row of small windows toward the ceiling. Two of the walls had no windows at all. The fourth wall was glass, and it looked out on a private garden that included a fountain and a few benches scattered among various flower beds. We walked out of the living area and saw that there were two bedrooms with glass walls facing the garden. Across the hall from the bedrooms were the kitchen and two bathrooms. JJ told us that covering the garden were fake solar panels that looked dark gray from the outside but only slightly tinted from the inside.

There was a doorway along one wall that led to a set of stairs. At the top of the stairs was a deck with slatted wooden walls. From that vantage, looking out you could see the ocean, but looking in, from the parking lot, it looked like a place to hide the air conditioner or other apparatus.

JJ was right; you would have to know what you were looking for to find the suite, and even then you would have to be willing to destroy walls to get to the occupant. The inside of the suite was modern, bright, and inviting.

I looked at Beatrice and told her that anytime she wanted to get away, this was hers to use. I could tell she was interested.

We made our way back down to the lounge, and I squeezed in beside JJ on one of the red velvet couches. As the others finished their drinks, JJ answered questions about the history of the place. At some point I asked JJ if any of the lockers we had passed belonged to him, and if so, what had he saved over his life?

JJ just gave me a look, put down his empty glass, and asked everyone to come with him back to the pantry. We walked down the passage and entered the room. JJ got out his card to find his combination for the door to locker three. I was not prepared for what I might see inside, and I was wishing I had never asked. But then the door was open, and I was looking at a collage of pictures of me and MG stuck to the inside of the door. Five boxes were neatly labeled: "MG and Jackson at college"; "MG, Jackson, and Phoebe"; "Phoebe at school"; "Phoebe and family"; and "Professional Phoebe." I turned away—and walked straight into JJ's outstretched arms. I knew intellectually it was normal for parents to display signs of love for their children. But until that moment, I had never suspected such love being directed toward me.

CHAPTER 24
Lost and Found

It was late afternoon when we left the restaurant. Louie had slipped away from the rest of us and had ordered a picnic dinner with a couple of bottles of wine to take with us. He had driven his truck to the restaurant, so we all piled in with the food on our laps. He surprised me by turning south as we drove out of the restaurant instead of north toward his offices. About five miles later, he turned onto a dirt road parallel to the ocean. There was a small parking lot at the end, with only a few cars parked there. Following his lead, we got out of the truck and walked down towards the beach.

As we sat down, Louie explained that the beach was so hidden away that it was often passed over by everyone except locals. He told us that sometimes he would stop by and see kids surfing, but overall, it was a peaceful getaway. He opened both bottles of wine. I chose white, and then I sat there, watching the late afternoon sun. We were all quiet, trying to process what we had seen and learned that afternoon. Seeing that we were lost in thought, Louie announced that he was going to take a quick run on the beach, and then he was gone.

After a while, I asked Aunt Bea what she was thinking about.

"I was thinking about how memories get distorted over time. Sometimes we remember things as worse than they were, and sometimes we remember them as better. I believe I'd romanticized the idea of home and forgot why I left. Coming to terms with that now is overwhelming." I gave her a hug, and said I knew what she meant.

About that time, Louie came jogging up from the beach. He looked much calmer and more peaceful than when he'd left.

The sun was beginning to slip away, so we opened the food containers and had ourselves a gourmet picnic. We sampled everything and drank the rest of the wine, then topped it all off with a chocolate dessert.

We all stretched out on the blanket and watched the last rays of the sun disappeared. Still, we lingered, relishing the fresh air and the sound of the waves. A chilly wind slapped us back to reality, and we knew we needed to return to our everyday lives.

▲ ▲ ▲

The boxes of my mother's belongings were stacked in my suite. I wanted to open them that night, so I went next door and asked Beatrice to join me, then we both sat on the floor, staring at them. Where should we start and what would find? I knew I needed to make the first move, so I retrieved a sharp knife from the kitchen and started cutting the packing tape. The first big box contained five smaller boxes and the shawl I gave MG for her last Christmas.

Curious about the general contents of each of the boxes, I opened them all one by one. The first box was made of intricately carved wood, and it was filled with random pieces of jewelry. Box two contained MG's sketchbooks, and box three looked to be letters from her friends and family. Box four was mostly legal documents, and box five were personal mementos, including a few items of clothing. I looked at each of the boxes for a moment, then put them back on the floor in the same order.

I knew I couldn't go through them all tonight, so I grabbed the wooden box and the shawl. I wrapped the shawl around myself and took off the lid to the wooden box. I turned the box upside down and emptied it onto the floor, holding my breath as I did so.

Dozens of pieces of jewelry tumbled out. I laughed at how eclectic the collection was. Jewelry had always been a fundamental part of MG's persona. Seeing the collection of bright colors and impossible shapes brought back fond memories of the sights and sounds she created when she moved. The image was powerful as I remembered the look of bliss on her face as she swayed to the music she loved. I looked over and saw a soft glow in Beatrice's eyes. She was remembering it too.

One by one, I examined each piece of jewelry, then passed it over to Beatrice. Each piece she had saved had a story. I knew this because each had a small tag attached to it with a piece of red string. On each was the date and place of acquisition, and the reason she had kept it. Most had sentimental reasons, and most were costume jewelry. Included in this category was a long necklace of shiny wooden beads. The note read that I had given it to her for her birthday when I was five. There were pieces that I know must have been expensive, including family heirlooms and gifts from JJ and Daniel.

Toward the bottom of the pile was something that didn't fit in with the other pieces. It was a beaded bracelet. The small beads alternated silver, turquoise, and lapis. In the middle of the beads was a silver heart. The bracelet was definitely for a thin wrist, probably for a teenager. It was curious because it was stylish in an understated way and probably a bit expensive if everything used to make it was real. The tag read: *Found at edge of orchard, spring 1968. Kept so as to give back to owner. Too nice to throw away.*

I passed it on to Beatrice, and she had a strange look on her face. "I was with MG when she found this. We were riding horses together on the ranch, and we drifted too far away. If we went back the way we came, we would have been late for dinner, so we came down the edge of the road on the side opposite to our land. I remember that because the edge between the trees and the road was wider, so it was safer for the horses. As we neared our driveway, she spotted something shining in the sun in between the rows of trees. I remember I got really mad at her for stopping and making us even later, so I rode on without her. She came in minutes behind me and showed me the bracelet. It wasn't big or bold enough for her liking, but she said she would keep it because it might belong to someone who missed it."

She still had a strange look of intense concentration on her face, so I asked, "Is there something else?"

She took a moment and said, "I have a sense that I have seen that bracelet before . . . recently. Maybe in a yearbook?"

"That doesn't sound like MG to wear someone else's jewelry, unless she wanted to find the owner."

"Not on MG," she said quietly. "On someone else."

▲ ▲ ▲

I slept reasonably well that night, no dreams about looking for a place to be safe or about the fire. I awoke feeling the best I had since before the firebomb, and I thought maybe I was beginning to heal both physically and emotionally. I had been given some emotional gifts yesterday, and I intended to appreciate the love shown by JJ, Daniel, and MG. I had also been given a possible clue to the murders. Who knows if it will be important?

After breakfast with the staff, I sat down at a table with Beatrice to go through the yearbooks. While it was most obvious to go through the book for her alma mater, it was at least possible that she had seen the bracelet someplace else. I picked up the Porterville book and started to go through pictures of clubs and teams, thinking it might be part of a group identification. About ten minutes in, Beatrice and I both shouted, "I have it!"

Then we looked at each other and said, "What?" at the same time.

I looked at her page and saw the cheerleaders all wearing the same bracelet that had been in the box. She looked at my page and saw the same. I groaned to myself, thinking this probably wasn't the best clue. But Beatrice wasn't deterred. She said, "Maybe toward the middle to end of the year, someone stopped wearing their bracelet." After a few minutes of scrutinizing the pictures from the two schools, she exclaimed, "They're not all the same! Look, the bracelets from Porterville seem to have silver, pearl, and another color bead. Damn these black-and-white photos!"

We hurried to look at the bracelets from all the schools. Each seemed to be just a bit different from the others. Each school had a silver heart, a peace sign, or a cross as part of their bracelet design. All we needed to do was figure out which bracelet matched our school. Only two of the schools had hearts: Lower Sierra and Exeter. The Exeter car crash happened later in the school year, after MG found the bracelet. Our school, Lower Sierra, seemed to be a match on the surface, but we didn't yet know the colors.

"OK, now we look to see if any bracelets are missing," I said.

As we were looking, Louie came up and told me that the video conference call with the senior girls who went to study abroad but were not in the Intra-County Farm Group was in five minutes. I was so excited about the bracelet that I had forgotten. I picked up my notes and ran to the conference room.

I pulled out my notebook and wrote the women's names down: Millie, Rachel, and Constance. I knew I couldn't trust myself to remember their names, especially when I got excited. I had drafted out a script for the questioning, but I would stray if needed.

The women popped on the screen one at a time, and within thirty seconds, the level of noise arced up substantially. I gave them a good five minutes to catch up, then tried to call them to order, gently at first and then a bit more demanding. Eventually everyone was focused, and I introduced myself and explained what had been happening. Then we spent another five minutes talking about MG, her success, her family, and her death. I finally got them to settle down when I told them they could stay online and talk for as long as they wanted after we finished the meeting.

I picked up my script. "The period of your lives I want to talk with you about includes the summer abroad trip before your senior year and the rest of your senior year until graduation. Let's first talk about study abroad. How did the girls relate to each other on that trip?" Again, the women started answering all at once, and I had to remind them to speak one at a time. I got the sense that it might not be a straight line to get our answers, but that we would get there eventually.

They verified what we'd suspected, except we learned that MG hung out more with their group than she did with Deborah and Pricilla. "Sometimes, especially when the blond girl was with us. They pestered MG to do things with them, but she never asked them to do things with her," Millie said. "In fact, the blond girl, who they all called Clover, was always asking who the virgins were in our class and who was having sex. No one in our group admitted to having sex, but I wasn't convinced. Clover particularly pestered MG about Daniel, asking how she could possibly not be having sex with such a good-looking guy."

"Did you ever hear Clover's real name?" I asked.

Millie said, "I thought it was her real name, and I was too scared to ask her anything. I mean, she was so aggressive and loud, she was scary." They all nodded in agreement.

Millie continued: "Sometime during the middle of the summer, Deborah and Pricilla both changed. They became ruder than they normally were, and they were always whispering by themselves. They started complaining about every little aspect of the trip and counting the days until we went home."

"What happened when school started?" I asked.

This time, Constance picked up the story. "We were all in the same classes, except for electives. There were basically three cliques: Deborah, Pricilla, and the other cheerleaders and dancers; our group plus a few more girls; and then the poorer students who happened to be smart. MG kind of floated among the groups, but she also spent a lot of time in the art studio. MG started teaching crafts at some children's program that had just been set up.

"A couple of months into the fall semester, one of the girls in the lower-income group disappeared and things became intense. There was gossip and speculation, but nobody in our group knew the full story. MG became even more absent after that. Basically, she went to class, ate lunch in the art studio, then taught crafts. Her mom volunteered with the same program, and she often picked her up from school. When she went to social events, like the prom, she was with Daniel."

Now curious, I asked, "Did she hang out with Maggie too?"

This time, Rachel responded. "Not so much. They had been good friends, but that seemed to have cooled. Maggie hung out with Nina, the girl who went missing. After that, she hung out with other girls in that group until she went away to college."

I held up the bracelet and asked, "Does this bracelet look familiar?"

Again, they all started speaking at once, so I turned back to Rachel, trying to keep their speaking time equal. "That school year, the cheer squads in the county decided they all wanted to get along, so they encouraged each school to get a unifying bracelet. Our school colors were white and blue, so each girl got a basic bracelet of silver and blue, then they chose an additional color of their own. Each school also chose a silver charm; our school's was a heart."

"Do you know who had this particular color combination?" Louie asked.

They all laughed and shook their heads no; obviously, it was a minor detail from way too long ago.

Millie said, "I do remember they only wore them during football season, and then I guess they switched to something else."

"Can any of you give us the names of the most popular boys?" Louie asked. Again, they started talking among themselves, but this was an instance of friendly arguing. It was starting to get a little loud, so Louie asked if they could give a few names off the top of their heads.

Millie started: "I think Tony Farr is at the top of the list. He had everything, including being a good guy. He didn't really date much our senior year, but he was friends with everyone. Miles Curtis was a good athlete but he thought too much of himself. He and Deborah were the school's power couple, and they could make a person's life miserable if you crossed them. Deborah made Nina's life unbearable until she disappeared." She seemed to have realized what she'd said, and she halfheartedly threw a hand over her mouth, clearly not sorry for the implication.

"Hey! Don't forget about all the visitors!" Millie said.

This was the first time I had heard of any visitors. "What do you mean?"

Millie explained, "Some of the boys were in this Intra-County Leadership Group, whose members acted like ambassadors among the schools, meaning they had permission to attend any school event within the county. They had these special identification cards saying they were above the rules."

"What do you recall, Rachel?" I asked.

"I remember one of them—he got drunk and hit on all of the cutest girls. Curtis was even asked to take him out of there one time. I don't remember his name, but somehow it reminded me of the Beach Boys—I mean his name did. Tell me the names of the Beach Boys," she said laughingly.

I pulled out my phone, not knowing if she was serious or not. "OK, we have Brian, Dennis, and Carl Wilson; their cousin Mike Love; and Al Jardine."

I looked at her with raised eyebrows.

"That's it! Wilson."

The name Wilson had come up before. Then I remembered two of the girls had mentioned Pete Wilson as a person of interest. Was Wilson a first name too?

As soon as we hung up our end, I asked Louie if he could assign someone to track down Tony Farr's current phone number. As I waited for the number, I kept glancing at the phone, and it looked like the women stayed on for about an hour. I wished I had a recording of that conversation.

▲ ▲ ▲

The researcher came back about an hour later with Tony Farr's work and home phone numbers. Tony lived in a small town outside Denver and owned a chain of sporting goods stores, each with different sport specializations. Given its rise in popularity, he even owned a lacrosse store in downtown Denver.

We decided to try him at home first. An older man with a crisp businesslike voice answered the phone on the second ring. We explained who we were and why we were calling. There was a long pause on his end that ended with what sounded like a sob. When he came back on the phone, his whole demeanor had changed; he sounded much older and sadder when he spoke.

"Nina was the love of my life, but I will never know if it would have been a lasting love. She was taken away from me too soon to know for sure. My greatest regret in life is that I drove her away during our senior year. When I found out her body had been recovered, along with that of a fetus, I felt like my life would just melt away to nothing. In some ways I wanted to join her, but I can't walk away from my children and grandchildren."

"Mr. Farr, can you tell us what happened with Nina over the course of your senior year?" I asked.

"My football coach was also my math teacher. He was worried about me getting behind in my precalculus class, so he asked me to get a tutor over the summer and to master the material in the first third of the book. Nina had taken the course the year before, so he suggested that I ask her to tutor me about four hours a week. We had two sessions of two hours a week, starting in June.

"I don't know what happened, but I fell hard for her. I knew my family would give me grief, so I started dating her in secret. She told everyone she was dating someone from work, letting people think it was someone from the nursery.

"I had dated Pricilla my junior year. She was pretty, but we didn't share goals or values. When Pricilla came back at the end of the summer, things went crazy. I tried to avoid her at school, but she followed me around, hanging on my arm. My parents kept asking me to have her over, to take her here or there, and at first I gave in to their harping. I hated every minute of it, but they threatened not to pay my college tuition. I think everyone in both families, except me, thought I would marry her.

"Nina saw all of this and stopped talking to me, focusing instead on her friends. Then she just disappeared. I had the feeling that Pricilla knew something about it because she had a secret language she used with Deborah. When I asked her about it, she would giggle and say it was nothing. Finally, I had a big blowup with my parents, and I told them I wanted to focus on sports and classes and that was it. If I didn't date at all, they left me alone.

"When I left for college, I didn't know anything about where Nina was or what she was doing. I dated a few people, but I didn't marry until my mid-thirties. My wife died several years ago from early onset Alzheimer's, and I've been single since."

"How did you learn about Nina's death?" I asked.

"My older brother, Clark, still lives in Lower Sierra. In fact, his grandson is engaged to Deborah's granddaughter. Well, I guess she could be considered her daughter as well because Deborah and Miles adopted her.

"Clark told me about the baby, and the grief was unbearable, made all the worse because I had no one to talk it over with.

"Recently I've begun to believe that Nina had been killed by Pricilla and the gang of people she hung out with. After I heard about the trouble they all caused at your ranch, I was confident they were trying to erase the past."

"Tony, what would have happened if you dated Nina out in the open?" I asked.

"My parents would have forbidden it, and my guess is that they would have taken everything away—one at a time—until I stopped. By everything I mean my car, allowance, and college tuition. Now I can see it was partly because they wanted to protect the generational wealth and partly due to their view that poor people were dirty and ignorant."

"How about Miles Curtis—did your parents like him?" I asked, just to tie things up.

"Oh yeah, I was expected to be his best buddy, and because he was dating Deborah, it was natural for me to date Deborah's best friend. What my parents didn't know is that Miles chased girls, and then women, relentlessly. I don't think Deborah liked it, but she put up with it because she felt she and Miles were destined to be together."

"One more thing," I said. "When you decided to focus on getting into college, who did Miles hang out with?"

"Well, Miles had people lined up to go carousing with him. I think one of them was from the leadership group, Wilson Peterson. It turns out he married Pricilla after college."

At that moment, Louie and I looked at each other that silently screamed that it was all fitting together. Of course, I couldn't verify that we also thought Pricilla, Debra, and Miles had a role in the murders. I reassured Tony that we were close to a solution, and I would put him on my list of people to call. With each passing day, the number of people who had been affected by the actions of a half dozen grew.

CHAPTER 25
Decision Time

I woke up on Wednesday morning feeling off kilter. The dean had told me I absolutely could not go to work—even to teach my class—for an entire week. Monica was excited to take the class and it would give her some good teaching experience. We had discussed her plans by phone last night so I felt assured she would do a fantastic job.

The rest of us had a conference call coming up with Alex. I was having a hard time curbing my anxiety because I wanted to know what the CBI had found out from Miles Curtis. I tried to relax and let my mind wander about the bracelet.

There was something wrong about where MG had found it. Nina had been buried on our property, but the bracelet was found across the street on a neighboring ranch. Why would it have been there? Most obvious, it could have been left when Vickie or Karen were killed. But why would MG not know who owned the bracelet? Was MG's note just a ploy to account for why she kept the bracelet? Was it insurance to make sure our family was never extorted?

Most believable to me was that the bracelet was associated with one of the other murderers and that MG knew exactly to whom it belonged. Maybe the badgering by the other girls when she was out with Daniel was over getting it back. Maybe the break-in at my house was as well. But why burn down the greenhouse? The greenhouse was the least likely place MG would have hidden the bracelet, and they would have wanted to find it or make sure it had been destroyed, neither of which would have been accomplished by bombing the greenhouse. No, that was more to get our attention and serve as a warning.

There was another thing that bothered me, though. Someone knew they had lost a bracelet, but how did they know MG had it? I thought about it for a while, then decided to ask Beatrice to help me brainstorm. When she came over to my table, she was carrying rolled-up sheets of paper. Before she could say anything, I asked, "When did you learn MG had kept the bracelet?"

"I think I first saw it when MG did. Let me try to remember the day. Because we were late, we hurried through caring for the horses and ran in for dinner. I don't recall any conversation. Our dinners were cold, and Mama made us clean the kitchen before homework. That was it. I didn't know she had kept it until we saw it in the box. I thought she meant to give it back."

I told Beatrice my theory about MG keeping the bracelet for protection and that she covered her motivation with the innocuous note. I also told her that I thought the bracelet was connected to all the other troubles the family was having, but I couldn't see how anyone had found out about it.

Then it hit me: JJ said the boxes MG had left for me were in her room while she was being treated for cancer. Maggie had a lot of time in the room during periods when MG was asleep. Maggie could have gone through her jewelry and found it. Maybe she could have used her imagination and her knowledge of the situation to threaten someone. But then why did the women bother MG when she was out with Daniel? They knew the bracelet was missing, so did they just assume MG had it?

I then told Beatrice what the conference call had revealed about each school having its own colors; she assured me she didn't know about this because she didn't go to any football games until the following year. But when I told her about the nature of the cliques, she said, "That sounds like the makeup of my class too. I didn't know it at the time, but later, according to Queen Bees and Wannabees, I would have been called a 'floater.' I followed my own interests and had friends across groups. I was always busy, and I never felt left out, even though the girls in the popular group would stop talking when I walked by. It really didn't bother me, but on the other hand, I was ready to leave after graduation."

I tried to imagine what life was like in the late 1960s. Research shows that methods of shutting people out have changed over the years, but the process is the same. I thought about the concepts of shunning and malicious gossip. In the sixties, this shunning was physically turning one's body or face away when someone walked by or, even less subtle, acting as if the person were invisible. Gossip was transmitted by word of mouth through communication networks. Ghosting was accomplished by not answering letters, or even sending them back to sender, and not answering phone calls. Today those processes are easier to implement but no less hurtful. We can shun people by taking them off our friends lists, blocking them, and spreading false pictures or stories. We can ghost in much the same way, revoking or hiding any mode of communication. The rate of ghosting has seen a sharp rise over the past generation. These behaviors, almost understandable among teenagers, are bizarre when adults engage in them. It is harder to tell someone face to face your friendship is over than to let it play out on the internet, which almost makes it unreal and blameless.

It was my impression that the murdered girls had been both shunned by the popular kids and found guilty of breaking the social rule of dating above their status.

I tore myself away from these thoughts and back to work. I asked Beatrice about the rolled-up papers, was it her network analysis? She told me it was but that there was something else she wanted to show me first.

"Faith reminded me that each yearbook had a summer supplement that was handed out in the fall. She sent me copies of the supplements for the summers before and after Nina's senior year. You know there are events in late spring, like prom, and in the summer, like the Fourth of July swimming party, that don't get into the regular yearbook. Check out this picture from the swim party the summer before senior year."

It was a picture of a laughing Maggie, Nina, and Tony Farr sitting on the edge of a pool. Nina and Tony looked to have eyes only for each other. This could have been what caused the disruption in the study abroad group. I turned back to earlier pictures until I got to the section on the group's junior prom. There were candid shots of kids sitting around tables. One picture was of two couples and the caption read: *Deborah, Miles, Pricilla, and Tony, relaxing after dinner.*

I flipped back to the swimming pool picture. When I folded the two pictures so that they were side by side, I felt a shiver. The primary physical characteristics of Maggie and Pricilla were similar: long curly dark hair, tall, and slender. It would be easy to confuse the two in the darkness. Was it Pricilla that MG saw in her memory/dream, not Maggie?

It was then that I felt, maybe for the first time, that we would find the killers. It struck me that if you dug deep enough, secrets long buried began to reveal themselves.

"Can we look at your network analysis?" I asked.

"Yes, I've made a lot of progress, especially with Nina and Lower Sierra but with the other victims too. Fortunately, Faith helped with everything, because she has access to county resources that I don't have access to. Is it about time for the call with Alex?" I looked at my watch and saw that time had indeed gotten away from me—our meeting was in two minutes.

"It is! Let's take all of this into the conference room," I said, and helped gather everything up.

▲ ▲ ▲

Alex and Louie were already chatting when we arrived. I could tell by the background scene that Alex was in his home office. He looked better than before, but he still sounded raspy. Once Beatrice and I were settled, I said, "It's good to see you back at home, Alex."

"Thanks, Phoebe. It's good to be out of the hospital, though they did take really good care of me." He paused for a moment, then said, "But can we maybe not do that drone bomb thing again?" We all quietly nodded, making that silent promise to each other.

Alex then said, "All right, so the good thing about working with the CBI, in addition to their ability to make people do things, is their level of resources. Right before our meeting today, they sent me a recording of their conversation with Miles Curtis. I have already queued the tape to start at the first question by the agent, Darby Lambert. Here we go."

Darby: Mr. Curtis, I would like to ask you about the summer before your senior year of high school. I know that your girlfriend at the time, Deborah, who is now your wife, was out of town doing study abroad; what did you do that summer?

Miles: My dad worked me really hard that summer. He made up a rotating schedule for me so that I could experience different parts of both the farming and the car businesses. I figured he was trying to decide if he wanted to spend his money on sending me to college by seeing if I could do more than play football. Most of it was hot, dirty work. In the first half of the summer, I worked in the fields pulling sprinklers, replacing trees, and hauling brush. In the second half, I washed cars and kept the lots clean. I even helped with the Labor Day sale preparation. I was madder than hell with him, but I didn't dare ease off or disobey him. He was a "big man," and damn did he have a temper. More than once that summer, he lashed out at me both in words and physically. I was so happy when school started.

Darby: What was your social life like?

Miles: Well, that was a bit different too. All of a sudden Tony Farr, up until then my best friend, ghosted me without ever telling me why. I started hanging out with a friend from another school, but he was kind of a womanizer.

Darby: What do you mean?

Miles: He started chasing after every girl he met, and not in a good way. He seemed angry and cruel about it. He would lie about who he was and what he felt for a girl, and then he would drop her and move on to the next one. I felt embarrassed, and I was glad when he went back to his own friends at the end of the summer. In the time Deborah was away, I only dated two girls. They were both nice, but I knew in the end that Deborah and I had an "arranged marriage." All our parents knew it, and I accepted it because it benefited everyone. I never had any ill feelings about her; she took care of me then, and she has continued to do it.

Darby: What did she do when she found out you went out on her?

Miles: She gave me her chicken look. Not like she was afraid of me. She kind of clucked her mouth and bobbled her head. She still does that sometimes. But I have told her all along that the only way a marriage could work is if it was open. But anyway, I got all of that out of my system in my late twenties. Since then, I have only cared about politics.

Darby: One last thing, Mr. Curtis. Did you father any children that summer?

Miles: Of course not! But hell, I was only seventeen then, and to tell the truth, I never had sex before that summer, and I was still learning the ropes, so to speak. Anyway, my daddy taught me to own up and take responsibility for my actions. And I would have if anyone had told me I had gotten them pregnant.

Alex reached over and clicked the tape off. "There was a bit more on the tape but nothing pertaining to the murders of the girls. What do you guys think?"

"I think Deborah was already cleaning up his messes," I said.

Louie asked, "Was she cleaning them up or making them up? We don't know who is telling the truth. Maybe Clover told her Miles was responsible so she could extort money from Deborah."

We all thought about that for a moment. Then Alex asked, "You have anything to report, cuz?"

I wasn't sure how to tell my story succinctly, but for my part of the findings, the bracelet was the key. So that is where I started. I explained as best I could, then said we needed to look at the inter-school relationships.

Beatrice took over then. "I worked on the networks for all the murdered girls, and an interesting pattern emerged. We know that the popular girls had intersecting networks through study abroad, cheerleading camp, and the Intra-County Farm Group. The popular boys also had intersecting networks through sports camps; the all-star football, basketball, and baseball games; and something called the Intra-County Leadership Group. This is something Faith helped me with by finding news articles in each school's local community newspaper. Funny thing, there was very little overlap between the boys in the private club and those selected for the traditional Boys State high school leadership experience. The two intra-county groups basically served as private fraternity and sorority clubs for high school seniors. For the most part, people stayed in their lanes, and they dated people from the corresponding club.

"But for every murdered girl, there was a documented transgression. The summer before senior year, when the Intra-County Farm Group girls were away, the boys found other people to date. As I coded the networks for all the victims, I found very few instances of overlap. The murdered girls often served as tutors for their classmates, mostly male athletes. I found a picture of Nina sitting on a bench by Tony, who was in his football uniform, studying for a math test. So, if you were a pretty, intelligent, poor girl who caught the attention of one of the Leadership Group boys, you were very vulnerable—especially if you got pregnant. The two intra-county groups seemed to line up marriages that would protect the existing social order and power structure. In Lower Sierra, both Pricilla and Deborah eventually married boys from the Leadership Group pool. Tony, however, married a woman later in life.

"There is something else both Faith and I observed. While we don't know all the names yet, it seemed like the same faces showed up at social events across the schools. For example, a boy from School A shows up at dances at Schools C and D. It's like cross-pollination of a social kind."

Although I had suspected something like this, it made me feel disgusted, dirty, and cheap. I was proud of MG for having nothing to do with it but angry that she didn't take steps to get justice sooner. Maybe the girls had applied too much pressure on her.

After speaking with Tony Farr, I didn't think he had any involvement. On the contrary, he had taken some socially brave steps to distance himself. I had doubts about the innocence of Miles, but it was hard for me to believe he was responsible for getting all the other girls pregnant. Could it be someone like Miles but from a different school?

"I think it's important to name the boys who were cross-pollinating. Rachel mentioned a boy named Wilson, and Miles said he'd been hanging out with a Wilson Peterson. Can you check that out, Bea?"

Next, we turned to Louie.

"Well, I didn't find anything as horrible as all that, but I did find some financial pieces. Here is my key point: At the time of the murders, the ranch across from Canton Moon was owned by the Sutton family. This was before they bought their own land through the agricultural corporation. By the way, they gave themselves a very nice price for the land. Like Phoebe's family, the Suttons had pieces of land throughout the county, and this was what formed the basis for their corporate empire. They sold each piece to the corporation for more than the property values estimated by outside banks. Then they started a war to buy property next to or near theirs for lower than the valued prices. I found efforts to buy pieces of Canton Moon, but Phoebe's grandfather wouldn't sell. Now that Phoebe has resurfaced, the pressure will be on her and Beatrice to sell to the corporation."

"Have there been other holdouts?" I asked.

Louie sighed and said, "Yes. Some owners have had unexpected losses through tree viruses, poisoning, lack of water, and bank recalls. One family they have pressured for years is the Roan family. Now that Daniel is in charge, he has vowed not to sell, and he is looking into land trusts. That would allow the land to remain deeded to the county and used only as designated. It is something you might think of doing with Canton Moon if you ever want to go in that direction. One way to do that would be to clear the land and let it return to its natural state, or you could designate it as a park or a wildlife camp."

Beatrice and I exchanged a look. Our lease with Carlos was coming due, and maybe there were pieces we could think about putting into a land trust.

Alex must have seen our look because he said, "I don't know if Carlos has the will to go back to ranching after the fire, but a trust for something like an experiential farm might be attractive to him. It's definitely something to think about." He paused for a moment, then started his report.

"OK. As you know, I have been working with the CBI, primarily on the recent events surrounding the murders of Maggie and Clover, the firebombing, and the break-in at your houses. They believe several things.

"First, Maggie and Clover died in the same manner, and the killer searched both of their homes for something specific. Both crimes left little evidence except for a couple of stray fibers and unidentified hairs. The CBI believes the same person killed both of them.

"Second, the fire bomber and the burglars who were caught at Phoebe's house all tell the same story. They were hired via the dark web to do a specific job. You know, bombs or break-ins of some sort. They were paid half of the negotiated price up front via cash delivery. The second half was to be paid pending successful completion of the task, and only the fire bomber received the second installment. The money for the job was on him when he was arrested.

"Third, the CBI is looking into the finances of local people who have the means to draw on that kind of money but keep it quiet. The Curtis family has funding sources that are kept private, and they have been building this secret wealth for quite some time. They have their personal accounts, their corporation accounts, and their political accounts. The CBI forensic accountants are finding the work tedious and difficult.

"Finally, CBI staff seem to have bought into the theory that if they find the people committing the current crimes, they will make headway into the old murders." He took a raspy breath, then continued. "I know this may be a touchy subject, but I suggest we turn the bracelet over to them for full analysis in case there is evidence we can't see visually."

"Do they know we have touched it?" I asked.

"Yes, but maybe there are skin cells in-between the beads," said Alex.

If the bracelet was the reason for the break-ins, then that was a good idea. I said, "I would only do that if they would guarantee safekeeping of the bracelet and the findings. Do you think they can do that?"

"Truthfully, I don't know," Alex responded. "But I worry that someone is going to be seriously hurt if we don't get rid of it. It's probably safe there, but who knows what they will do?"

Suddenly I felt a powerful sense of dread and of being overwhelmed. Alex was right; how could we justify putting everyone in danger? "OK, how do we go about turning it in?"

Alex said, "I will put it in the gun safe in my truck and drive it over to the CBI. We can take pictures from every angle first, and we can keep trying to identify the owner."

Reluctantly, I agreed. "When will you pick it up?" I realized that now that we had made the decision, I wanted it out of our possession.

"Soon as I can get over there," Alex said.

After the call, Beatrice left the conference room, and Louie and I finally had a minute alone. He came up behind me and wrapped his arms around my shoulders for a hug, then sat down next to me.

We just sat there enjoying the quiet moment. It was soothing to just sit with someone who was not judging me. Then he said, "We still haven't had our alone time. I spoke with your aunt, and she would like to visit with

Carlos. She thinks it is time for the two of them to discuss what they want to do with the ranch and the other properties. I was thinking maybe we could send her and an escort to the hospital, and we could take the boat out. Maybe to be extra-cautious, we could take JJ's boat instead."

Somehow it didn't feel right taking my father's boat for a romantic getaway. I said, "Yes to the trip, no to taking JJ's boat. Let's just be prepared for violent actions. Can we do that?"

He thought a minute, then agreed. "I can have Klaus at the marina get my boat ready and spread the word around the marina he is taking his family for the weekend." He gave me a quick kiss, then we went to join the others for a group dinner.

CHAPTER 26
Out of Hiding

The next morning we drove by my house so I could pick up a few things for our get away. Most important were a swimsuit and a nice little black dress—just in case. We entered the backyard and I could hear some forlorn music coming from Colette's backyard. I went to knock on the big door but she beat me to it. She took a look at me and hugged me until I couldn't breathe. Finally I was able to pull away.

"I asked Abe to stay in Chile—away from me at any rate, while I thought about his omission of facts about Angela's kidnapping. He kept his memories about how my nursing uniform disappeared and who had been wearing if from me for what, forty years? I know we were apart for most of that time but he did know how to reach me."

She hugged me yet again and I asked her to sit with me and have a cup of tea. In true Colette fashion, she stiffened her shoulders and gave me an *are you kidding* look.

"I've got a party to plan. James Taylor is coming to town and I am planning an adventure. That is all I will say for now, but be on notice." With that, she glided back through the door, head high and back straight.

I couldn't have imagined her acting any other way. She was ready to go forward regardless. Louie and I just gave each other a shrug and went into the house.

After packing a few items, we drove to the marina, and Louie parked his truck as close to the guard's station as possible. There was a smallish clubhouse just outside the gates going down to the docks, and we stopped by there first. He needed to tip Klaus, the employee who had done the prep work, and ask how things had gone. We caught up with him in the supply room.

Louie handed Klaus an envelope and asked about the preparations. "Well, I ordered your supplies and put them away. I made sure everything was tied down and where it was supposed to be. Strange thing, a couple of muscled guys dressed in dark clothes came by while I was up on deck, and they wanted to know where you were. They said they were from your office and had papers you needed to sign. I told them you were out of town, and you had loaned me the boat for the weekend. Hope that was OK; they caught me off guard."

Just as Louie was answering Klaus, his phone rang. He showed me his screen: it was his security company telling him he had a breach on his boat. He took a second to text a yes back to the company, indicating that he wanted them to send the police. Then we all started running out the door and toward the dock where Louie had his boat slip. As we ran, we could hear the alarm sounding and we could see owners streaming from their boats to see whose boat was at risk.

As we neared the boat, one of the beefy guys appeared, looking as though he intended to jump back on the dock. Instead, he ran back the other way, and we heard a splash and then a second splash. This was followed by the sound of a small motorboat. Everyone ran to the end of the dock, but by the time we got there, the getaway boat was fifty yards ahead of us and moving out of the harbor.

We were learning something interesting about these thieves: they had amazing resources and surveillance knowledge. Both of the attacks today had been well planned. It made me wonder if these guys came from a different source of hire.

Louie thanked everyone for their help in chasing the thieves off his boat. As we turned to go aboard, Klaus called out, "Hey, Louie, there is a small-craft warning for the next twenty-four hours. You might want to think about staying put for a while."

We looked at each other and laughed. But our laughter didn't last long because the police showed up, and they definitely weren't laughing. They spotted Klaus first, and because they knew him, they asked what was going on. He explained all that had gone on that day, ending with how the boat owners had chased the guys off. Louie told them the one guy we saw was wearing gloves, so there was no use looking for forensics unless there were shoe prints or drops of blood from a cut or scrape.

The police took a careful look around, but they didn't find anything. What Louie did not mention is that he had hidden security cameras.

After everyone left, we went below to the galley. Louie started opening the shutters on the windows, so we'd have some natural light. When he was done, he pulled out his laptop to examine the security footage. The men had covered most of their faces with black cloth masks, with holes for their eyes. I was really over these guys. Yes, I felt some fear, but this was overshadowed by my anger over this invasion into my life. I didn't want to be hiding in an ever-decreasing number of safe places.

Louie closed the laptop and set it aside. He sat down beside me and took my hand. After a while, he said, "What would you like to do about our trip? We have options, including staying here. We know the alarm system works."

I tried to explain what I was thinking. "We have been at this crossroads for quite some time now. We keep waiting for the perfect romantic setting and something always comes up. It makes me wonder if the perfect moment is a fairy tale we tell ourselves because we don't want to move forward. And if we don't want to move forward, maybe we need to accept that we are just good friends."

"Is that what you want?" he asked.

"Sometimes it is," I admitted. "Sometimes I feel so overwhelmed by my life and how out of control it has become. You know, for example, I haven't fulfilled my weekend rituals in weeks. I know they are trivial acts, but they keep me focused on what I need to be taking care of. Now, I feel like I am scattered, unfocused, and doing a lousy job at everything. I worry that a relationship would be just one more thing I would fail at."

"Are you concerned that by being more spontaneous you won't be able to keep going? Or is it more that you can't take on another possible source of stress?" he asked.

"Maybe both."

"Would it help if I told you Klaus got your favorite donuts? Sometimes two people can take care of each other better when they are a couple rather than when they are two singles."

His act of caring made me a bit blurry eyed. Plus, it made good sense. Being together offered the possibility that life would be easier if we shared it, not harder. There was no reason to stand alone in stubborn resistance. And what was I resisting? The loss of my routine or my happiness?

Louie looked me straight in the eyes and said, "It may be a fairy tale we are imagining, but I know what I want to do. There is no doubt in my mind."

He looked at me with loving eyes, and I knew I felt the same. I had no doubts. I realized I had been manufacturing excuses, and there were several reasons why: I didn't want to feel disloyal to my dead husband. I wanted to be a positive role model to my female students. I didn't want to be a source of gossip for my colleagues or rivals. On the other hand, I couldn't imagine a steadier relationship to take a chance on. The beefy guys could come back or there could be some other obstacle. But these were our lives, and we needed to grab hold and take them where we wanted them to go. I pulled Louie up, and we walked back to his stateroom.

▲ ▲ ▲

Hours later we were catnapping in bed, and both of our stomachs started to growl. I realized I was hungry, happy, and tired, but I had enough energy to make a light supper. In all the excitement, we had forgotten to eat lunch, and we had gone straight to bed instead. When we got to the galley, Louie stopped me from looking around and instead poured me a glass of wine and told me he would take care of things. That was fine with me.

We turned our attention to the dinner Louie had put together—a boxed supper from our favorite Italian restaurant.

As we were lounging around drinking more wine, we felt the wind picking up and the boat starting to rock. Louie was deep in thought, so I asked him about it. "I am trying to decide if beefy guys will come back in this weather. And if so, how do we want to deal with it?"

"What do you mean?" I asked.

"If I set the alarm for a loud response, it will probably scare them away again. If I set it on silent, they may be emboldened to make a greater effort to get in. Then there is the issue of whether we want an automatic call to the police or if we want to do that after we assess the danger."

Moments later, his phone rang with what I recognized as his emergency ring. He listened to the person on the other end and said a very sincere "Thanks!" and hung up.

"That was the security company for my office building. What beefy guys didn't know is that there are motion detectors after dark, each with a camera. Before they tried to open the door using a stolen key card and a copy of my fingerprint attached to one of their hands, the police were already rolling up and surrounding them. They were taken in to join the two we caught at your house."

"Does that mean we are OK for tonight?" I asked.

"It depends on how strategic we think these guys are. Trying to get into the offices of a detective agency specializing in high-tech crimes is not very smart. On the other hand, if it is a diversionary tactic, it's brilliant. They may be hoping we let down our guard while another team tackles the boat again."

"I vote to assume they are brilliant," I said. "I think we should lure them in with a silent alarm that actually calls the police. Do you need to do anything to increase our security other than set the alarm?"

"It's always good to check things out. We do have blackout shades, so we can keep a low-level light on. How about you go get dressed in the darkest clothes you have, and I'll make one more round of checks, then get dressed. Let's meet in the lounge when we're finished."

▲ ▲ ▲

We sat in the lounge in the near dark. Louie had his gun on the table in front of him, and I had a baseball bat and other heavy items. Mostly I was to stay out of the way; we didn't know if the intruders would be armed. Unless group two had been watching the office building, they wouldn't know their colleagues had been arrested. I wondered if it had been part of their original plan to come here while they thought we were sleeping.

We sat that way for an hour or more. And then we both heard scratching around one of the windows. The scratching then moved all the way around the outside of the boat as they discovered they could not get in through any of the windows. The windows were bulletproof and too small for beefy men. The men must have decided to work on the hatch, as we heard scratching there, followed by a series of key entries that didn't work.

Then there was silence. The silence was eerie, and I had trouble breathing normally. Louie must have found it uncomfortable too because he sprang from the couch, grabbed his gun, and walked outside as quietly as possible. As he did, I heard a loud, "Oh, shit!" and scrambling around the deck. The next thing I heard was a splash followed by a muffled explosion. It hit me then. We were dealing with people who would go to any means to win, including a direct attempt on our lives. This brought a whole new sense of urgency. The people we were dealing with, across generations, gave little thought to killing as a way to protect their interests.

I was also grateful for Louie's way of thinking. He had obviously been rolling over the risks in his mind and chose that moment to make an actual assessment of what was going on outside.

As I sat waiting on the couch, I heard voices. I took a deep breath and willed myself to walk out on the deck, where I found two police officers talking to Louie. In between them was a handcuffed man I had never seen before. This one wasn't beefy but a regular-sized man in his early twenties. He had a vague resemblance to someone I knew, but I couldn't place him.

Louie turned to me and said, "The officers spotted two men running away from the boat as they walked down to the marina. They were able to stop this one. I would guess they were running because they didn't want to be caught up in the boat blast."

"Who is he?" I asked.

One of the officers responded: "He won't tell us, but hopefully we will know soon." With that, they turned and led him back up the dock.

It was getting late, but I was wired. Louie and I decided to go straight to bed. I wasn't sure we would make it through the night without more break-ins, but I was too exhausted to worry. Maybe if I slept on it, I could reason why the latest thug looked familiar.

Chapter 27
Identity Issues

When I awoke the next morning, I found Louie eating French toast covered with blueberries and a drizzle of chocolate. I must have been looking at it longingly because he jumped up and grabbed my plate and a cup of coffee. I found myself wondering if life with Louie would always be so sweet. I decided not to ask.

He looked at me and smiled, and I melted. I wasn't sure if waiting so long to be intimate had been the only way to go, but at this point I was happy with the results. In some ways, it felt as if we had been a couple for a very long time.

"So what's going on?" I asked.

He scrunched his eyes in thought, then used his fingers to count out our updated information. "You know about beefy guys one through three, so I will start with the two from last night. When they saw beefy guys four and five—that is, the guys who tried to enter my office building—they gave no signs of recognition or knowledge that they were being arrested as part of the same case. So it seems likely that there were three different hires so far. Second, the skinny guy from the boat invasion is not in the system, and he did not have any identifying information on him. Third, Alex is coming for the weekend—now that the excitement is over. At least I hope it is over."

I thought for a moment, then suddenly it came back to me. After being insulted by Brittany Wicker I had looked her up on social media. I said, "Can you get on Brittany Wicker's social media account? I thought maybe I saw a family resemblance with skinny guy, but I'm not sure."

After a bit of typing, he pulled up her account. Right off there was a hint: she listed herself as having two brothers. We scrolled through her pictures, and we found a group photo of her engagement party. The "brothers" were biologically her cousins, suspected by us to be skinny guys one and two, known to everyone else as Brett and Hamilton.

"The captured cousin must be Hamilton," I said. Do you think the one that got away was Brett?"

Louie sent a text to the officers who had caught the intruder with his name and where we'd found his picture online. He received a return text from one of the officers, and I heard him mumble, "That is really good work."

After he finished texting, he said, "The coast guard got the other one. He won't give his name either, but I think it's probably Brett."

I continued to think it through. "So someone spent enough time and money to seek out five paid guys and then they turned to family members. What next? Maybe they were so arrogant they thought they could do a better job than the paid help? Whatever their reasons, they must have something big at stake . . . Can we make a list of all the information we are waiting on?" I asked.

Louie said, "Sure. Most important to me is to find out who, if not Miles Curtis, was dating the murdered girls. It would also be great to find out who is paying for all the hired help."

I added, "Most important to me are the translations of the documents Parker found in Maggie's attic."

We both thought for a while, then I said, "I would like to have the completed network analysis to see if there is any pathway, either direct or indirect, that would link all the victims."

"Is that it?" Louie asked.

"For the most part," I said.

Louie said, "It is Thursday morning, but Alex won't be here until dinnertime. I know we have spent a lot of time in the office, but do you mind if we go in and see if anyone has uncovered anything? We can check in with Beatrice too. If we find nothing is moving yet on what we want to know, we can skip out and spend time outside."

"Hmm, why do I think that last part is unlikely? But yeah, sounds like a plan."

We both sat there, neither of us wanting to make the first move back to reality. I broke first, letting out a huge sigh; then I got ready to go to the office.

▲ ▲ ▲

After the jam-packed twenty-four hours we had just had, the office seemed tame. People were in small groups talking or sitting at their computers. Everyone was engaged in tasks. Louie led me over to the person who was working on the translations of the files Parker had left for us and asked how it was going.

"Great! There were maybe a dozen small files of text, ranging between a hundred and a hundred fifty words each. They were not in sequential order, so I had to put them together in my own order after I translated them. Clover had used a simple alphanumeric code. Here is a version that seems to make sense chronologically," she said as she handed Louie a thumb drive.

I took the thumb drive from Louie and walked over to one of the tables that had a desktop computer. Louie left me to it and went to check in with all the teams to see what they had found out or if they needed any help.

The code breaker had pulled the small files together after translating them. The combined file was named "Clover's Confession." That made me pause. Was this a tell-all that would name names, or was she playing more games with us?

If you are reading this, it is highly likely that I am dead. Probably the person I gave it to for safekeeping is dead too. We had a system of how to protect this file. I gave it to Maggie to keep, and she would pass it on to a friend should she ever feel threatened or just want it out of her possession. I understand; it is a dark story.

When I was ending my junior year of high school, my parents out of the blue told me they didn't have the money to send me to college. They said the dairy had taken losses and they were barely scraping by. All of my life I'd thought that my family was not just solvent but well-off. We had the appearance of wealth, just not wealth. The joke was on me!

The dairy was a family business, so it meant my cousin Jay was also not in good shape financially. He had put off the inevitable by going to community college, and he was hoping for a wrestling scholarship somewhere nearby. But even if he received one, it wouldn't pay for the lifestyle he thought he was entitled to. So we began to plan.

We asked ourselves, "What are we good at that will make us college money?" Jay said the only thing he was really good at was wrestling, which could probably be extended to hurting people. I told him that what I seemed to be best at was getting people to do what I wanted them to do. The thought of actually getting a real job never occurred to us.

I begged my parents to at least send me to summer school through study abroad. I had been bragging that it was my plan to go since the ninth grade, and I knew I'd be humiliated if I didn't get to go.

I was really close to my grandmother, and that saved me. As I was growing up, she and my grandpa lived on the dairy farm, too, but in their own house. My parents agreed to go to my grandparents to see if they would pay for study abroad, and they did. Actually, they seemed happy to be able to do something for me.

The girls that I went to summer school with were the wealthiest and most popular girls in their schools. Around midsummer, the girls started getting letters from friends telling them that their boyfriends were having "summer flings." Not only that, but they also heard rumors that guys were cheating on them with girls from the other side of the tracks—or, using the language of the day, "white trash."

I must say that at that time of my life I was a snob, and it infuriated me that what I saw as trashy, filthy girls had the nerve to date above their station. What if the girls got pregnant? Would the boys be made to marry them? Thus, an idea for a business for Jay and me was born. If any of these relationships ended in a pregnancy, we could sell our services to help with the problem. At this time and in this place, birth control was hard to come by and abortion was illegal. Of course, we didn't run around telling girls we could take care of their problems; we approached them after the rumors had started.

The test case was a girl named Nina Scott from Lower Sierra High School. The girlfriend, Pricilla—a member of the Intra-County Farm Group—got the news over the summer that her boyfriend, Tony Farr, had been seeing Nina behind her back. Pricilla had had it in her mind since middle school that she was going to marry Tony, who was rich, good-looking, and smart.

When I heard about the problem, I offered her our services. But I told her there were rules. It had to be confidential to the point of death, there would be fees, and she had to play some part in the process. I am not sure if she understood at the time that we meant murder. We arranged to meet on land belonging to MG's family. We thought it would be the last place anyone would look for a body.

It was easy for us to pluck Nina away from her house. We watched her house all evening and eventually her friend Maggie dropped her off. All we had to do was snatch her in the brief instant between Maggie leaving and Nina making it to her door. Jay had been hiding in the shadows and he was able to cover her mouth and carry her to my car. Jay pushed her into the back seat and I drove away down a dark side street. Jay was a little too interested in the murder part, so by the time Pricilla arrived, he had already strangled Nina. Pricilla was either too nervous or too naive to realize Nina was dead. We told her Jay had drugged Nina, and she had to help with the kill by plunging a knife into Nina's womb. I guess she didn't notice that very little blood came out. Jay then forced her to watch as he cut out the baby. Having worked around birthing calves, Jay was familiar with C-sections. Did Pricilla enjoy the experience? No, but she still wanted a shot at snagging Tony.

The baby wasn't really recognizable as a person, but we wanted to place it with its mother. I stole crocheted bags from my grandma's sewing basket, and we used them as tiny caskets. At the time, Grandma was crocheting dozens of bags to hold wedding favors for my cousin's ceremony. She never noticed a few were missing.

As it turned out, Pricilla was just plain stupid. She didn't get it that Tony didn't like her, was never going to marry her. After Nina died, he basically didn't date the rest of his senior year. When it came time for the prom, he asked Nina's best friend Maggie to go with him. My guess is that they spent the evening pining over Nina. He left for college in the fall and never looked back. I have always wondered if he thought it was suspicious that Nina disappeared when she did. I also wondered if Nina was the love of his life.

Deborah was "luckier" than Pricilla in the end. She did finally marry Miles Curtis, but it took her nomination of two different girls to be taken care of. Additionally, she contacted us during college about someone else, but we told her no. We didn't need the money, and we didn't want to take the chance. We killed Karen because we believed he was the father of her baby. There must have been very little trust in that relationship because Deborah never doubted that Miles was the father, and she paid generously to get rid of Karen.

As it turned out, Miles and Deborah were made for each other. They became well known among their ex-friends and associates as people who would do anything to win a contract, an office, or whatever furthered their goals. At least for Deborah, that included bribery, extortion, lying, and pulling in "favors."

Penny Peterson was also in the Intra-County group. She contacted us about a "friend" who was competing for the same scholarship she was. Jay drove the girl's car into a tree. To reduce suspicion, Penny and Jay claimed that Penny had been driving and Jay was a passenger.

Miles and Wilson were extremely careless as they made up names to give to girls. Anyone who spent a few minutes thinking about it could have figured it out. Vickie was due to the stupidity of Penny's brother, Wilson, who was extremely aggressive. Two other girls, Amy who was attributed to Miles and Lori to Wilson, were nominated, but they slipped through our hands. I was glad, but Jay was disappointed.

Now, what did we get out of this? I am sorry to say that Jay enjoyed the process way too much. He may have gone on to commit other unrelated murders, I never asked. However, each murdered girl paid for a full year of college for Jay and me. It is not that we charged so much, but tuition at Cal Poly was only $50 a semester! Then we turned to extortion, with good success.

I have lived my life knowing my role in all this. I tell myself that Jay did the actual murders and I just set things up. The girls who hired us thought they had killed someone, but Jay had taken care of the four murders himself. Standing behind Jay, I fake screamed each time one of the clients plunged a knife into a victim.

When I graduated from college, I had the skills for a middle-class job, but that was boring to me. After I started working at the casinos, life became more interesting. As part of my job, I was around people of all social classes, and my hatred started to thaw. I began to regret what I'd done, and now I feel horrible about the lives taken. Plus, the death of the babies makes the guilt almost unbearable.

After MG died and Maggie found a way to dig through MG's

secrets, Maggie put together some evidence and tracked me down. She was missing a lot of the details and she didn't have enough for a conviction. To keep her quiet, I made a deal with her: I would write a confession, but she would not read or release it until I died. In my confession I would fill in the blanks and name names.

Mostly I've spent the rest of my life urging people to bet money they don't have, so I'm still ruining lives. And I do feel bad about that—all of the ruined lives I have contributed to causing.

You might ask about levels of guilt. Jay and I are of course guilty of murder. But what about the people who paid us and then kept on paying? I have mostly told the truth in this letter, but it will be up to the reader to discover what I left out.

Deni (Clover)

Now that I had read the confession that Maggie never saw, I didn't know what to think, but I knew I wasn't ready to talk about it yet. I needed time to process everything, as while it contained a lot of information, it raised questions about who exactly was guilty and who would go to such extremes to keep it all quiet.

It sounded like Pricilla, Deborah, and Penny had been willing to pay and kill, but if Miles and Tony were not involved, was there anyone else? Of course, Miles may not be lying, he may not know he had gotten someone pregnant. Instead of talking to anyone about it, I emailed copies to Beatrice, Louie, and Alex and asked them to read the attachment before we had our conference call. Louie was still collaborating with his teams, so I went to my suite for a nap.

▲ ▲ ▲

I was in a heavy sleep, but I roused to consciousness as I felt someone stroking my hair. I opened my eyes, and there was Louie leaning over me with a big smile. He said, "You gave me a moment of panic! I was knocking on your door, but when you didn't answer, I came in to see what was going on. Everyone is here; Beatrice decided to come home from the hospital, and Alex has arrived hungry. They both want to go out to dinner. Are you up for that?"

"No, let's order in," I said decisively. We've got things we need to discuss, and it's better if we do it in private."

Louie asked for our dinner to be delivered to my house so we could get away from the office for a while. We decided to go back to my house and have our meeting there on my patio.

We chose to order from a seafood restaurant because Alex would complain if we didn't.

When we got to my house we walked directly into the backyard. I immediately asked if they had read Clover's confession. Amazingly, they all said no. They gave their excuses, but in reality I think they were hoping for some escape from the misery we were all feeling. I watched their faces as they stopped to read it, and their expressions noticeably darkened as they went through it.

"So, this clears some things up," Alex started. "Also, I'm sorry for being so childish about going out to dinner. I didn't know you had such news, and I was hoping for a night off. But I am in serious cop mode now."

"This is what I see," I said. "We have been close but slightly off this whole time. Jay murdered all the girls, but then died in a prison fire. Clover facilitated all the murders but didn't actually do the killing. Pricilla paid for Nina to be taken care of, and then, as far as she knows, was the one to kill her. Deborah paid for Karen, Penny paid for Sharon, and Wilson paid for Vickie. Then we are down to the two girls who escaped. I think Amy was nominated by Deborah and Lori by Wilson. What we don't know is who paid to have Clover and Maggie killed."

Louie said, "So what do we know about our suspects? Pricilla and Deborah are still around creating mayhem and likely at least partially responsible for the death of Carlos's student in the fire. We have no idea what happened to Penny. What do we know about Wilson other than him being Penny's brother?"

Alex looked at his phone like he was waiting to call someone, probably his CBI colleagues. He said, "I don't have enough to arrest them, but I will ask CBI to put all of them under surveillance for a few days. They have more resources than the sheriff's office."

CHAPTER 28
Tired of It

Early the next morning, we sat down at the patio table, all of us looking grim. It was clear we all felt that this gruesome case had taken too much energy and caused too much sorrow. But I also knew we would stay with it until it was finished. As we looked around the table, it was obvious no one wanted to start. Finally, Alex said, "OK, let's begin."

"Let's talk about Clover's confession and I'll start," I said. "The one thing that struck me about Clover's confession was the language about Miles Curtis. She claims he didn't do any of the killing but would do anything to succeed. It sounds like he shared that trait with Deborah, and she cleaned up his messes and kept him on track to be a US congressman. We need to take a closer look at her activities, to see if there are other, related crimes."

"Anything else, Phoebe?" Alex asked.

"No . . . I feel like some thought is trying to come to mind, but I can't seem to grab on to it."

"OK, we'll move on for now, but let us know when it comes to you." Alex turned to his left and said, "Beatrice?"

"I've been working on the rest of the social networks, and I found a curious thing. Based on our initial theory, we thought the murdered girls had been dating the boyfriends of girls who both studied abroad and joined the Intra-County Farm Group. All of these girls, except MG, were cheerleaders or dancers and wore those silver beaded bracelets. We also suspected that all the men were members of the Intra-County Leadership Group, and that Miles Curtis was the president during the 1967–68 school year. Thus, there were two tight network circles, and the circles were joined together. Because the circles cut across schools, it would have been difficult to form a link. Oh, and Wilson Peterson—the brother of the girl from Exeter, Penny Peterson—was also a member of the leadership group.

"Then I looked up the campaign committee for Miles Curtis's bid for the US House of Representatives. All the inner-circle members were in the Leadership Group or the Farm Group. The only exceptions are family members, including Brittany Wicker."

As I listened to this, I remembered what I wanted to bring up. "Beatrice," I asked, "did you find out the professions of the men who overlap with the campaign committee?"

With a big smile, she said, "I did. Wilson Peterson is a financial planner with a master's degree from Stanford. He came back to the county and opened his own business. His name comes up when you google 'financial planners in Tulare County.'"

"Hmm. Do you know if his sister Penny won the scholarship, the one she had her friend killed over?"

"She did not win it. It seems to have been won by an 'outsider.' By that, I mean the winner was far outside the network of popular kids. Her activities were chorus and the home economics club. The pictures I saw of her made me think she sewed her own clothes. I wondered where she'd ended up, so I asked Faith, who said she's a high-powered San Francisco defense attorney, who gives money to support the opera. I would call that scholarship a worthwhile investment."

It struck me just how tight this circle was. I could believe Miles did not pay for or commit any of the murders, but I couldn't believe he didn't know what was going on. I also began to wonder if the Exeter girl was really killed over the scholarship—Penny obviously didn't need it—or if there was some other transgression. Then I asked, "Louie, are we certain that Penny Peterson was the only person in the car with Sharon Lane when they ran into the telephone pole?"

"You're thinking about Clover's claim that Jay was driving the car. I don't know. Our associate only provided the names of the victim and the driver. Why, what are you thinking?" he asked.

"Well, we don't know how much credibility can be given to Clover's confession. She claimed Jay was driving but Penny was in the car, which seems like a pretty dangerous situation to be in if you know you're in a car that is about to crash." I paused for a moment, then said, "I don't know if I believe Clover, but I'm wondering if the case we thought was the simplest is really the most complex. I wish we could get ahold of the full police report on it."

Alex said eagerly, "I can do that. I'll text a request right now. It may take a day or two, since the crash was so long ago." He paused, then said, "Is it my turn to report?" We all nodded, and he began.

"As you know, we have five known criminals and two family members of Brittany Wicker under arrest for crimes related to arson plus murder and break-ins. The drone bomber, to the best of our knowledge, was working alone, while the others were in two-person teams. Each crime was solicited on the dark web—on the same site. We tend to believe them because they all independently named the same site. The posts they responded to have since been taken down, but the CBI is looking for a way to reconstruct them. Brittany Wicker's cousins are not saying a thing beyond their official statements. Unlucky for them they are all technically of adult age. They claim that a friend of their grandfather has a boat at the marina, and they were trying to find his boat when they were accosted by the police. So that is at a standstill for the moment. The CBI is trying to confirm whether the drone bomb at the ranch and the bomb at the marina were made by the same person, but it is a bit complicated unless the farm drone bomber made more than one bomb in the beginning. He claims that he made three and left two of them at a designated spot at the farm across the street. When I followed up, they weren't there."

I was spinning ideas in my head. "How about if we create a situation where they all either cooperate with us or their grandkids are blamed for everything recent. And if they don't cooperate, we tell them they will be arrested or at least brought in for formal questioning?"

"How would that work?" asked Bea.

"Well, we have Brett and Hamilton in custody. Alex could ask, or order, Deborah and Miles to come to the sheriff's office to discuss not only the consequences of the kids' actions but also their own actions regarding the fire and subsequent murder. We can add Pricilla and Wilson to the list by telling them we have heard from several people that one or more of them paid the arsonist for the bombs, and so someone is guilty of murder for hire. Just that much might bring them in and get them to turn on each other or at least get one of them talking."

Louie was nodding his head along with me and asked, "Exactly who would you bring in?"

"I don't think that Tony Farr is guilty; he cut ties with the group as soon as he could. Miles is around and has plenty of motive, but Clover swore he was innocent. I do think it would be good to see if we could make him nervous enough to tell on someone. So Miles, Deborah, Pricilla, Wilson and Brittany—I think she is the one who stirred everyone up about the ranch. I think we should try to track down Penny Peterson, as we have no reason to think she's dead."

Louie was looking doubtful. "That's a lot of people to bring in at one time. Also, what about the grandkids' parents?"

Bea said, "I can see why Brett and Hamilton's parents would come in but what about the other parents?"

I groaned, "Good point, guess they have no incentive."

"I'll see if I can get approval from the prosecutor and find out what we need to make it happen," Alex grumbled.

I raised my eyebrows questioningly.

He said, "Don't get your hopes up. It's a big ask. To keep the grandkids, we might have to go ahead and charge them in Orange County. Can we get Fraley to help us out?"

"I'll give it my best," Louie promised.

We finished our meeting rather abruptly. Alex went off to confer with his partners at CBI and the sheriff's office. Louie rushed out to hunt for Fraley and to start a national search for Penny Peterson. Bea went back to work on the network. I had work to do as well. I could feel the end was near, and I was desperate to find out the truth.

Finally, the house was quiet, but I still felt uneasy being there alone. To help quiet my mind, I picked up the Lower Sierra yearbook for 1967–68 and started casually flipping through it. Toward the back there was a two-page spread about the yearbook staff. All at once, I felt both stupid and humbled. MG was the art editor for the yearbook, meaning she reviewed the layout for each page, but more relevant than that, the chief and assistant photographers were also listed. Maybe there were some color pictures out there somewhere, which could help us identify who the lost bracelet belonged to. After all, it was the reason for all the recent chaos.

As I sat thinking about the importance of the bracelet to the case, Louie called. "Hey. I'm searching online for Penny Peterson, and I am running out of energy. Alex is here with me—he's been calling in favors nonstop. Do you mind if we spend the night here? If you feel cautious about being alone, I can come there or you can come here."

Upon hearing about Louie's fatigue, I started feeling it too. "Well, here's another option. How about if I spend the night at Colette's? That way we can get started on the yearbook pictures sooner." I was hoping Colette and Bea were tired too, as I was in no mood for a slumber party.

CHAPTER 29
The Search for Color

Beatrice, Colette, and I had planned to get an early start on the yearbooks the next morning, and we were going full speed by eight o'clock. Once we had assembled in Colette's backyard, I showed Beatrice the two-page spread in the back of the yearbook and asked if she knew any of the photographers.

"I know the junior editor, Joyce Hough, because I worked on the activities pages the following year. I'll start by calling Faith and see if she will call Joyce—an out of the blue call from Faith would work better than one from me. What are you looking for?"

"Any color pictures she might have on file." At this I realized I was shouting because Colette had turned up the music and all I could hear was James Taylor singing "Carolina in My Mind." I feared this would go on as prep work for the concert, which was still two weeks away. Personally, I had always preferred the Carly Simon music in the couple's repertoire. Give me "You're So Vain" over "Carolina in My Mind" any day of the week. But what could I say? Beatrice looked happy, and that was what mattered. Still, I had to tell them no music while we were working. I did, and they both pouted.

Beatrice recovered first, and she dialed Faith at home. Faith picked up after several rings, and Beatrice apologized for calling so early. "Faith, we have an urgent question to investigate. Joyce Hough was the yearbook photographer our sophomore year. Do you have any idea if she kept extra yearbook pictures?"

"Yeah, funny you should bring that up. She came into the library a couple of days ago to put up a sign for an estate sale. She's cleaning out her house so she can sell it and move to the Oregon coast for retirement. She was telling me I wouldn't believe all the high school history she'd accumulated, and she wanted to know if the library wanted any of it."

Beatrice asked, "Could you look through it to see if there are any pictures from the year Nina went missing? If so, could you have a courier drive them to Phoebe's house? I'll give you a credit card to cover the charge."

She sounded surprised by the request but said she'd be happy to do it. Then I asked how she was doing.

"I think people have completely forgotten that Nina was my sister. Or maybe they don't even care. They ask me if I've heard any gossip—not news, mind you, but gossip. I guess they think I'm not enough of an insider to be informed about any actual progress in the case. Deborah is the worst; she finds a reason to come into the library almost every day. She'll casually ask if anything is new because she knows people like to confide in me. One day I told her that I was just a librarian, not a priest. That kept her away for a few days!"

We all laughed at that, and then, before we could sign off, Colette asked Faith if she wanted to come to Newport Beach and go to the James Taylor concert. Faith of course said yes, and the three of them started making plans for a sleepover at Colette's. Before they could get too far into it, I told Faith I looked forward to seeing her but that we had a lot of work we needed to get to. Before signing off, I thanked her again for her help in getting us the pictures.

Around noon, JJ showed up with a bag of sandwiches and salads. He had come through my property and knocked on the door in the wall. When I saw him, I realized I had not heard him walking through my yard or across my patio. That made me nervous as the purpose of working at Colette's was to feel safer.

After greeting us, he said, "I brought lunch. But first I need to talk to you about personal safety. I came through your yard and knocked on your back door. I tried it, and it was unlocked. I hope you don't mind, but I locked it and set the alarm."

I smiled. He was really mastering this whole protective dad thing. I was grateful, though.

Colette busied herself with bringing out drinks and setting the table. Beatrice took the food into Colette's kitchen and put it on serving dishes. I turned to JJ and said, "Thanks for looking out for us." As independent as I am, I found I really meant it.

We went back to working on the yearbooks and the networks. Then I had an idea that was so mundane I was embarrassed I hadn't thought of it before. I grabbed Wilson Peterson's senior yearbook, then took a picture of his senior portrait with my phone, then I did the same for Miles Curtis. I created a new file on my computer, then sent the pictures to it. I asked Beatrice and Colette to help me find six more senior pictures that looked similar in terms of photography style and basic physical characteristics in all the high school yearbooks except Porterville and Woodlake. After we had gathered an array, I emailed a set to Amy White and Lorie Winter, the surviving victims from Porterville and Woodlake, and asked them to take a look and let me know if any of them looked familiar.

Both of the women got back to me right away. Amy positively identified Miles Curtis; Lorie was less certain but thought Wilson Peterson looked familiar. Of course, this wasn't enough to include or rule out anyone, but it was a bit strange that Wilson Peterson thought that just switching his first and last names would keep him safe. I thanked them for being so helpful.

▲ ▲ ▲

Colette had everyone over for dinner that night, and we spent some time filling Louie and Alex in on what we had found that afternoon. While not official, the identification of Miles by a survivor would help in getting him into the sheriff's office for questioning.

During a lull in the conversation, we heard what sounded like a potted plant being knocked over on my back steps. We all jumped up at once and got ready to barge through the door. Alex led the way, keeping his hand on his gun as he did so. By the time I got through the door and into the backyard, Louie was completing a running tackle and had a young man pinned to the ground; he had the man's right wrist in a death grip. Alex ran to the back step, but I couldn't see what he was doing. As he drew away, I could see a bomb on the top step of the porch. Our luck was high this evening because we'd walked in right before the detonation.

I stopped in my tracks and stared at what was going on. A bomb in my yard?

As I slowly was able to focus again, I saw that JJ was looking through a wallet. This made me think that the man wasn't very experienced. JJ said, "The intruder is Evan Peterson, a senior at UCLA. Another relative, this time a grandson of Pricilla. He is not saying a word except that he wants to call his parents. What do you want to do?"

After a brief discussion, we decided we wanted to turn him over to the same detective who had come out about the boat bombing. In the meantime, Alex said he would call the CBI and ask if they wanted to question him.

This left me wondering about how someone could let their grandkids get involved in all of this, especially planting a bomb. Was somebody willing to save themselves at this late stage of their lives in exchange for the whole lives of their grandkids? I went inside to grab a glass of water; this was really all too much. On the dark but bright side, maybe Priscilla and Wilson would show up at the family meeting.

I heard a commotion, so I ran back outside to investigate. The intensity of voices and movements grew increasingly louder, and soon I discovered that Beatrice and Colette were right beside me. The voices were coming from Colette's patio, where Alex had put the would-be bomber to wait for the police, who had just arrived. The door in the wall was open, so I had an unobstructed view. Evan Peterson was having a complete meltdown. He was refusing to let the police touch him and kept yelling, "I can't go to prison."

After a moment, Alex very calmly looked around and said, "Let's all take a step back. Evan, is there something you want to tell us before we arrest you?"

By this time Evan was sobbing, and he couldn't get any words out. Everyone waited a moment for him to get himself together. Finally, he gasped out, "I never wanted to do this. I don't know who lives there or why they wanted me to plant that fake bomb. I just got a package yesterday afternoon with instructions to take the bomb to that address and put it on the back porch. I was to push a button and leave right away. I just thought it was a prank that my dad wanted to play on an old fraternity friend. They are always doing stuff like that to each other."

Alex stepped closer to Evan and said, "First of all, Evan, it's a real bomb, and we have called the bomb squad to remove it. Second, if Louie hadn't stopped you from pushing the button, as you say, you might have been blown up with it. Third, that is the home of Dr. Phoebe Moon, who has already had two other bombs detonated where she was staying. Why did you assume the note was from your dad? Was it signed by your dad, or was it in your dad's handwriting?"

Evan looked down at his feet, not saying anything. Not only did he look scared to death, but he also seemed to have realized the bigger picture. We waited for him to speak again, but he remained silent. Louie nodded at the officer to take him away.

CHAPTER 30
Picture This

Early the next morning, I was eating breakfast with everyone and I heard my front doorbell ringing. I walked through the house and found a courier putting a large box on my front porch. The box was from Faith so I signed for it and then Louie and I staggered back to the patio and put it on a table. I opened it, and saw that it was the box of photographs and negatives we had been waiting for. We took it upstairs to my office so that nothing would be ruined. Alex took pictures as we opened it. Fortunately for us, the box was full of large brown envelopes, each labeled with the date and contents. After looking over all the labels, we each selected an envelope to start with. Beatrice took "Cheerleader candid," Colette took "Pep rallies," and I took "Lower Sierra versus Exeter games."

In truth, we all wanted to see everything, so we started with Beatrice's packet. Each of us had a magnifying glass at the ready, to help with any details. Fortunately—or unfortunately, depending on how you looked at it—there were very few color pictures. There were substantially more negatives in color. We put aside the negatives that we couldn't see well enough to judge relevancy—the rest we put back into the envelopes.

We didn't find anything in Beatrice's envelope, so we moved on to Colette's. The pep rallies envelope, which included pictures throughout the year of cheerleaders and the pep squad dancers. They appeared to have had different uniforms for winter and spring, but more importantly, the dancers also wore school bracelets. Using my magnifying glass, I looked carefully at both groups' bracelets and noticed an important difference: the cheerleader bracelets had two charms on them—one a heart, the other the school mascot—while the pep squad bracelets had only one charm. From what I could tell by the shades of gray in the black-and-white pictures, it looked like all the school bracelets were the same except for that extra charm. When we finally found a color picture of the Lower Sierra dancers, we could clearly see that all the bracelets had lapis and coral beads. Nothing else was useful in envelope two.

The third envelope had categories of pictures clipped together. There were pregame pictures of the rallies, action and human-interest shots of the players and coaches, crowd reactions, cheerleaders, the band, and something called a dance-off. According to Beatrice, the dance-off—a friendly competition between the two squads—happened during halftime. Each school's band would play a song, and both pep squads would dance to it. Among the stack of dance-off photos was a colored picture. Using our magnifying glasses, we concluded that the Exeter bracelets had turquoise and lapis beads, just like the one MG found. We would need to check the photos for the other schools, but it looked like our theory about the bracelet belonging to someone at Lower Sierra had been wrong. Our next step was to check the Exeter yearbook to see if we could make an identification. In my mind, however, it could only be one person: Penny Peterson. But if so, would that mean she was involved with other deaths besides the car crash? If not, then how did her bracelet end up by the trees near the ranch?

▲ ▲ ▲

After going through the box, I had a new appreciation for high school photographers. These students spent endless hours going to events, taking pictures, developing pictures, and offering ideas on layouts. And for all their trouble, they mostly got complaints from kids who either didn't like their pictures or thought they weren't in enough photos.

Of course, as I went through the box, I came across pictures of a young MG and a younger Beatrice; there was even one picture of them together, which I slipped out and put aside. Otherwise, I wasn't finding anything that would give us more evidence or understanding than we already had. When I got to the bottom of the box, there was a thin envelope labeled "Coming home." I had already gone through the homecoming file, complete with the king and queen dance, so I didn't know what to expect. Inside the envelope were pictures taken at an airport, the ones on top showing various people walking through the gate of an Air France flight. This was back in the old days, when people could meet friends at the terminal gates. All at once I realized that these photos must be of the kids who had participated in the study abroad trip, all returning home together.

The photographer had followed the kids through the airport as they got their bags and found their family and friends. It looked like they were even followed out to the front of the airport, where they climbed into their transportation. When I got to the last picture, I froze. I studied it, then turned it over to see the caption. For the first time, I was sure of what had happened.

The picture was of Jay Schmidt and Wilson Peterson picking up four girls at the airport: Clover, Deborah, Pricilla, and Penny. Jay had his arms around Clover and Penny, while Wilson had his arms around both Deborah and Pricilla. On the back of the picture was written "Reunion of the dirty half dozen."

It looked like this particular group of kids had an ongoing relationship that did not include Miles or Tony Farr. What had brought these kids together?

Suddenly I realized that what we had been looking for all this time had been found at the bottom of a box of old school pictures—which was, in my book, a good reason for never getting rid of anything.

CHAPTER 31
Ups and Downs

I called Louie to tell him about the picture I'd found. Louie said he was flying up to Porterville to help Alex set the meeting with the parents and grandparents. Everyone involved thought there was enough evidence to convict Deborah, Pricilla, Penny, and Wilson. While some murders had been on Mile's behalf, he apparently was not knowingly involved. If he had a good lawyer, he could probably slip by. The grandkids were waiting in jail and could be brought north anytime. I declined to go with him because I really did want to go back to work the next day. My week of recovery time was over, and I missed the solitude of my office and the slow rhythms of academic life. I asked him if I could check with Beatrice to see if she wanted to go.

I found Beatrice and Colette on the back porch engaged in serious conversation. I sat down quietly beside them, not wanting to disturb them. I heard Colette mention Abe's name a few times so I could imagine what they were talking about.

I told both of them about the picture of "the dirty half dozen" I had found. Then I told them that Alex, Louie, and the CBI agent were taking the helicopter to Porterville to set up the meeting with the parents and grandparents at the sheriff's office. I asked Beatrice if she wanted to go with them. She smiled and said, "I told Colette I would stay here for a while and keep her company, and she promised she would not play 'Hey Jude' again." I smiled at that and said I would pass the information on to Louie.

I waited all night for a call from Louie, but none came. The next morning, as I got ready for work, I felt a strange combination of excitement and anxiety. The two emotions together made me lose my coffee.

I got to work by eight and found the outer suite empty. As soon as I walked through my office door, I felt calmer. I knew what to do in this office. I knew how to be a successful professor, and I was learning how to be a chair.

I looked around and noticed that all my moving boxes were gone—they had been emptied. The books were on the shelves, the artwork was on the wall, and as I looked around, I saw that there were flowers on my table along with a platter of my favorite donuts. Just as I went to grab one, a dozen people barged into my office and yelled, "Welcome back!"

I snatched my hand back from the platter of donuts and everyone laughed. Pauline was the first to respond, and she said, "Go ahead, Professor, you deserve your donut!" The next thing I knew, they were surrounding me and hugging me. Instead of feeling my usual discomfort, I felt myself embracing the warmth. They seemed genuinely happy to see me, and I was happy to see them too.

After we chatted for a while and I assured everyone I was fully recovered from the fire, people started to drift out of the office. I only had a few minutes to myself, as Pauline had scheduled back-to-back meetings for the day, starting with my research associates. The day flew by, and by five o'clock, I was exhausted. After the last person left, I did something I rarely do. I turned my chair so I could stare out the window at the ocean view. I found myself thinking about the babies who never grew to be children and the mothers who never grew to be adults. I thought about Maggie, whose death was the result of trying to understand Nina's murder.

Before long, it was beginning to get dark, and I realized I didn't want to go home to an empty house. JJ immediately sprang to mind, so I called and asked him if he could meet me at my house. When I hung up, I realized that it wasn't just because I didn't want to be alone—I actually wanted his company.

▲ ▲ ▲

When I got home, I could see that the patio lights were on, so I entered through the side gate. I shouldn't have worried about being alone because Beatrice and Colette were already there having a glass of wine. By the time I put my things away and sat down at the table, JJ was walking through the gate carrying a big bag of Chinese takeout. We busied ourselves with grabbing things from the kitchen and setting the table. The last thing I did before going out to the patio was to turn on a playlist. The first notes of a song started just as I sat down. Colette raised her head in a pose that reminded me more of a person sniffing the air than listening to a song. Then she demanded, "Who is this?"

"Amber Run," I told her. She didn't say anything, but I could tell that she was enjoying it. Then I announced, "Let's talk about anything but murder until Louie calls," followed by murmured approval all around.

Then Colette said, through a mouthful of fried rice, "Hey, JJ, want to see James Taylor with us?"

"Colette," I gasped. "How many tickets did you buy?"

She and Beatrice started to giggle—to tell the truth, I hadn't even known older women still did that. "I bought a whole box, which I believe holds up to ten people." Seeing the look on my face, she said, "It's for a good cause; you can come too if you like."

Our evening continued this way, with the good-natured banter flowing. It was getting late for a work night, and I was torn between going to bed or staying up to wait for a call from Louie. Around eleven my phone rang. It was Louie, so I put him on speakerphone.

"I can't begin to tell you how hard it's been to arrange this meeting," he began. "Even though the grandkids are all young adults, we told the parents they had to be at the meeting too if they wanted any kind of alternative sentencing for their kids. The parents they didn't give us any trouble. The grandparents fought us every inch of the way. Finally, we told them they either came on their own or there would be two armed deputies coming to get them. They didn't want that, especially Miles, so they agreed to be there at nine tomorrow morning. Phoebe, could you please come too? You know the evidence better than anyone, and I think you can present a coherent story."

Reluctantly I agreed to be picked up by helicopter at 7 a.m.

Chapter 32
The Circle Is Broken

The helicopter flew me to Visalia, the location of the meeting, early the next morning. This case had taken so much out of me I needed to see it through. All night I had dreamed about whether the grandparents would take responsibility for the murders and lighten the load for their grandkids.

Louie met me at the airport, and we stopped at a café near the sheriff's office to pick up coffee and pastries. Then we went to the sheriff's office, met up with Alex, and followed him to the meeting room, where we set ourselves up to wait for all the groups to show up. The kids, looking worse for wear, were led in early. We were meeting in a large conference room, and the kids were on one side of the room, handcuffed to their chairs. Next to the conference room was a smaller room with a one-way window. The parents were led into that room and told not to make noise or to try to communicate with their children. Then we waited. After an hour or so, it seemed clear the grandparents were not coming. Because the whole point of the meeting was to attempt to get a confession from the grandparents, it was futile to hold a meeting without them. The parents were released, and the kids were led back to the holding cell.

We all felt a sense of letdown, but we knew we needed to confront the grandparents. "Follow me," Alex said gruffly under his breath. He led us to the parking area and said, "I can't let you ride with me, but I think we need to do a welfare call. This doesn't feel right." We decided to check Deborah and Miles's house first because it was the closest. Alex flew out of the parking lot with his siren blaring, and we tried to keep up in Louie's rental car.

It took us forty minutes of mostly driving country roads to get to the couple's ranch. We pulled into their driveway, a half mile-long gravel road lined with palm trees. It was quiet and looked undisturbed. Three cars were parked in front of the garage. No people or animals were milling about, and there were no indications of a political campaign being waged.

Alex decided to go in without backup. He must have been thinking an older upper class couple couldn't be that dangerous. The front door was unlocked, and it pushed in with a light nudge. Looking down, we saw bloody footprints pointed toward the front door. It looked like someone had fled the house wearing coverings over their shoes or something similar. There were places on the carpet and tile where we saw indications of someone sliding across the floor, making long bloody marks. There were no identifiable shoe prints.

Alex led us into the kitchen where we discovered a scene of devastation. Two bodies were falling out of chairs around a breakfast table, and both had been shot in the head. There was blood and spatter everywhere. The same bloody footprints were all over the kitchen, but this time they were joined by smaller prints going out the patio door.

Even through all the blood, we could tell that the victims were Deborah and Brittany. In addition to being shot, Brittany had been brutally stabbed, and the knife was still sticking out of her abdomen. Miles was sitting upright in a chair, tied tightly with nylon rope and wearing a blindfold. He was alive, but a strange noise, somewhere between a cry and a whimper, was coming from his mouth.

A bit too late, Alex told us not to touch or step on anything. As we backed out of the kitchen, I looked up at an interior wall. Someone had written in blood, "It has to be this way." I was mesmerized by the message and felt like I couldn't keep moving. Then I felt Alex's hand on the back of my shirt pushing me toward the door. As soon as we were outside, Alex radioed for backup. We were all confused about Miles and why he had been left alive.

Alex went back inside the house and took dozens of pictures of Miles and the ties binding him. Then he cut the rope, leaving the knots intact, and gently led Miles through the back door in the kitchen. He left the blindfold on until he got Miles to the front of the house, then turned him over to the paramedics, who had just arrived. When the blindfold came off, Miles just stared ahead, saying nothing. I wasn't sure how long it would take for him to come back from where he'd gone, if he ever did.

Abruptly, Alex gave some directions to the officers on scene and said he was moving on to Pricilla's ranch.

We were filled with dread as we climbed back into our cars and drove a mile to the other house. Again, we found the place to be vacant and still. Alex quickly went to the front door. This time the door was closed but not locked. There were very faint footprints with touches of blood across the living room going toward the kitchen. At this point, Alex told us to wait outside. Ten seconds later, we heard a loud curse, and we imagined that the scene looked much like the first one.

After about five minutes, Alex came back out. He told us there were two bodies, Pricilla and Wilson. Then he showed us a picture of a kitchen with a second message written in blood. It read, "And now it is done."

"It looks like the suspect went out through the kitchen door this time," Alex said.

I thought about why that might be. "Maybe they feared slipping and falling on the tile or carpet? The grass would give them more traction."

Alex looked even sicker than he had at Deborah's place. Again, he called for backup, and soon he was trying to supervise two murder sites. After making sure procedures were being followed at both places, he led us around back to a patio table by the pool.

We took a seat and just looked at each other. I tried to think who could have committed the murders. It seemed like the messages had a dual meaning. Message one could have been written by anyone, possibly one of the original killers. Message two conveyed a final act, like the third act in a play. I briefly wondered who the message was meant for. Were they all equally guilty?

Tears fell down my face. What no one had ever told Pricilla and Deborah is that they didn't actually kill anyone, as presumably only Clover and Jay knew that fact. Pricilla and Deborah died thinking the knife they wielded had killed one or more girls and their babies. Blame is such a slippery concept. Where did the blame lie in this case? With Deborah's parents, who talked of nothing but hate for people who were different from them? With Clover and Jay, who dreamed up a scheme to make money off the lives of the poor and to trade those lives for their financial well-being? Or did the blame lie with Pricilla and all the members of the dirty half dozen? Even though only Jay actually killed anyone, they all went along with the plan—with the exception of Brittany —and they all kept silent for over fifty years.

I was particularly confused about the death of Brittany and the mercy shown to Miles. Brittany was essentially double killed by being shot and stabbed. Did the killers despise the spread of hatred to a new generation? Or did they see her as being more dangerous? From what I had learned about her, she seemed to be an idealogue; was there a special benefit of her death for anyone?

And Miles, was he being acknowledged as innocent in all of this?

I didn't understand the behavior that caused this situation. I had never felt that level of hate. I could not understand the lack of value given to the lives of people who were different. What I *did* know was that it was hate and devaluation that allowed for wars, prejudice, and policies that kept people down. But that was all theoretical. Up close and in a way that affected my own life, no, I couldn't understand it.

As we waited for permission to leave, Louie and I talked about who might be responsible. We did not know the location of Penny Peterson—she hadn't been seen in years. I couldn't see how she would benefit from the deaths or why she would specifically kill her own brother, Wilson.

I just wanted to go home.

Chapter 33
The Search for Answers

On the way back to Newport Beach, Louie and I decided we were ready to go public with our relationship. We had witnessed so much destruction; now we were ready to build something positive and loving as we worked to put this case behind us. We worried a bit about how everyone would react, but I assured Louie that I thought everyone already knew or assumed we were a couple. We would just be confirming what everyone suspected.

So when we got to my house that afternoon, we walked onto the patio holding hands. Beatrice, Colette, and JJ were all there, and as we walked in, they applauded. Well, they applauded for ten seconds and then wanted the full story of what had happened. After we told them, the discussion of everything that had happened—beginning to end—went on into the night. It seemed as though no one wanted to leave and have to be alone with their thoughts. Three key topics kept coming up—what is guilt, what should happen to the grandkids, and how could Miles really be innocent? We went round and round.

In the end, we agreed that there were at least two definitional streams regarding guilt. One was in the causal sense, in that a person participated in or allowed a crime or harm to happen. Another was as an emotional outcome to something. The people involved in this fifty-plus-year saga were responsible for appalling crimes, but only a handful of them had expressed emotional guilt.

Then there were the grandkids. The thinking was that there should be a penalty that would not affect their futures, perhaps some kind of meaningful community service for an entire summer or a semester: Being a full-time tutor in a school with low-income children? Helping Carlos get his agricultural research up and going again? Constructing a public playground in Lower Sierra? We had a lot of ideas, but mainly we wanted the hate to stop.

And regarding Miles . . . Was leaving him alive a reward for being innocent or a punishment for being guilty? His life and reputation as he'd known them were over. He would always be the one who survived to tell the story.

All of this discussion seemed to help, and we were finally ready to move on. JJ left to spend the night on his boat and to go fishing early the next morning. Colette had given Beatrice a guest room in her house, and she had already moved in. For the first time, Louie and I went up to my room together, and I was comforted at having someone to share it all with.

▲ ▲ ▲

Alex fell into a whirlwind of activity, so we didn't hear from him for a few days. I went back to work, and I was able to give it my full attention. The ten-week quarter was just ending, and I was busy with students' final presentations and papers, year-end reviews for my grants, and year-end reviews of the faculty and staff. Coming up, we had a three-week break for the holidays and then another week of being at work with no students. I didn't know what to expect for Christmas and New Year. We had an eclectic group of people that we considered family, so I was just going to let it all unroll naturally.

A week or so after the murders, I got a call from Alex. They had conducted searches of the houses, but they were clean. Alex said he was forwarding me a copy of a letter from Pricilla but that I should read it later because he had other things to discuss.

"Given the overall pattern of illegal activities, law enforcement from all sides decided to allow the grandkids to do six months of full-time community service. To count, the service must be approved ahead of time and monitored by a senior member of the community. There were some complaints about the disruption of school plans, but we decided to give them a choice—three months in jail or six months of service. They all chose service.

"The hardest murder to explain is Brittany's. Her fiancé told us she was hardworking and gracious, and everyone loved her. I asked him how long he had known her, and he said he had known her basically all his life, but they had just recently become engaged. Of course, the portrait I got from other people was quite different, and she was viewed by most as aggressive, competitive, and willing to do anything to win. This seemed to be a perfect combination for her career in journalism. Her boss and colleagues thought she would rise to the top of her field.

"We are at a dead end in terms of suspects. If you think of anything, let me know."

I agreed to do that and we ended the call. Then I opened Pricilla's note. To my surprise, it was addressed to me:

Dear Phoebe,

I am writing this letter to you because you will be the most pivotal survivor and you are the one who has suffered the most as we have tried to cover up our crimes. I am assuming I am now dead or in jail and that the police found this letter in my jewelry box. I expect, though, that I died at someone else's hand.

One thing you may be wondering about is why Brittany came at you so hard. Deborah had two daughters about three years apart. Her older daughter bought into the family narrative, and she did everything her parents asked of her. The younger daughter, Christine, was the source of the problems. She was a constant embarrassment to the family. She was particularly embarrassing to them once Miles went into politics. Her biggest trespass was that she became pregnant at fifteen and had Brittany while living with her parents. The father was a handsome senior who came from a family of migrant workers, and Deborah was beside herself with hate. She forbade them to be together, and somehow they managed to obey this one command. I imagine the boy was bribed in some fashion.

One day when Brittany was around a year old, Christine left

Brittany with Deborah so she could go shopping, but she never returned. Eventually, Deborah and Miles adopted Brittany. Her cousins have always been around her, and she thinks of them as her younger brothers. Living with Deborah and Miles, Brittany soaked up all her grandparents' hate and prejudices. She is the one who doled out tasks to the younger kids and guilted them into doing what she wanted. She always knew that Tony's great nephew would not marry her if her history and nature became public knowledge.

I have found it impossible to reconcile what I did as a child with the person I want to be now. Somewhere along the way I either outgrew or outlived the hate I'd felt for the "newcomers" to our area. The funny part is that they weren't new to me, as I actually didn't know the place before they came. But my parents did, and they taught me to scorn the poverty and desperation they'd brought with them as they settled in "our space." Every time one of "them" succeeded, especially when it was noted in the newspaper, they would go on tirades about how they'd won by cheating. This is what I knew from the time I was old enough to understand.

They hated your family, too, because your grandparents didn't share their beliefs about the dust bowl "dirt" and instead gave them opportunities. MG was the worst. We invited her into our inner circle, and she rejected us. Of course, she did it in her own sweet, passive-aggressive way, but she made it clear anyway. For years I feared and hated MG. I feared her because I knew she had evidence that would implicate us. I hated her because I knew at a deeper level, she was a better person than me.

Months after MG died from cervical cancer, I was diagnosed with breast cancer. I was dependent on my treatment being delivered by the sort of people I had always hated. They were the aides, technicians, and janitors who made the clinic function.

People I would not have talked to if I saw them on the street or in a line. They tended to me with compassion and acceptance. They didn't complain if I threw up on a clean floor or couldn't walk on my own.

My oncologist, Dr. Roan, talked freely about MG, and the affection he felt for her shone through his eyes. After a while, I grew to regret how I had treated her and then I grew to regret how we had killed so many innocents.

My regret grew into self-hatred and self-disgust. When the first body was found on your land, we all panicked. Unfortunately, one evening when we were discussing what to do, Brittany overheard us. She became the zealot of her generation and clung to the idea that our actions had been just and that we should wage an offensive war to save the family. Deborah egged her on.

So yes, the six of us—Deborah, me, Penny, and Wilson, led by Clover and Jay—killed all the girls and their babies. I think today it would be considered a hate crime, since we drew from only the lowest social class. Most important for the world to know is that Miles and Tony had nothing to do with the murders.

Penny came to us soon after school started that fall. Wilson was pretty sure he had gotten a girl pregnant, and he was crazy worried his family would not pay for college. Penny went to help with the murder because Wilson didn't have the stomach for it, but she lost her pep squad bracelet in the process. She went back a few days later, and the bracelet was gone. Our worst fear was that MG had found it, but she would never admit to it. When asked, she'd just smile and walk away. We even had the wild idea that the bracelet had fallen into one of the graves. Before she died, Maggie confirmed that MG had found it, but Maggie had no idea where it was.

All this time, Wilson pretended not to know if Penny was dead or alive or how to get in touch with her. In truth, he knew she was alive, and he knew about a post office that would forward letters to her. He sent her a message about the bodies being dug up and that MG had indeed found the bracelet all those years ago, but he never heard back.

That was when Wilson paid to have Clover and Maggie murdered by someone he found on the dark web. Clover, because her greed knew no end, and Maggie, because she was close to the truth. Wilson knew that Penny's lost bracelet would tie her to the crimes, and he worried that the spotlight on Penny would soon extend to him. But imagine wanting to kill her "best friend" over a scholarship that she didn't even win.

I have lived a life of lies up till now. A loveless marriage, indifferent children, and frightening actions. I will drink a cup of coffee while I look out over the Sierras. Having written this, I have my first real sense of peace. I am now ready, no matter what happens.

Pricilla

CHAPTER 34
I Know What Happened

A few days after reading Pricilla's letter, I was sitting on my patio having my morning coffee when Beatrice came through the wall door from Colette's. She was carrying a small pile of photographs and papers from the case. She put them down in front of me and then went to get a cup of coffee.

I started sorting through the pictures and stopped when I reached the one of the dirty half dozen. I was looking at the picture when Beatrice sat down to join me. She said, "I was looking at that picture earlier and it made me think about how families in small towns have their own identities."

"What do you mean?" I asked.

"Well, sometimes your identity is set more by your family's identity than your own characteristics. For example, in this picture, all the girls are popular and all of them were in cheer or dance squads. But looking at personal characteristics, Penny doesn't fit with what you'd associate with being popular and being on the cheer squad, as she was overweight and not particularly graceful or attractive. When I looked at the pictures of her squad, Penny was the one who was most often out of step. But her brother was a popular football player, as was their father, and their mother had been a cheerleader when she was in high school. I saw this dynasty effect over my own years of high school but not so much when I was a principal in Baltimore. In Baltimore, there was much more mobility, and it was rare in public schools to have parents and grandparents who were alumni. This was compounded by the constant redrawing of school boundaries."

I continued to look at the picture. Two of these people did not fit in—Penny and Jay—but Jay, was dead. On a hunch, I asked Beatrice if she had the pictures from Maggie's funeral on her laptop. She said she did and went back through the door to get it.

When she returned, she pulled them up, and we started going through them one at a time. The cemetery was at the base of a hill in Lower Sierra, and the grave sites went a hundred yards or so up the side of it. Most plots were on a flat stretch below, and that is where Maggie was buried.

I had an idea forming about the identity of the killer, but it was preposterous. Still, I knew that it would bother me unless I checked it out. We went through the pictures slowly; most showed people gathered around the burial site, but a few were directed toward the mountains to show Maggie's overall resting place. We came to a picture that included the hillside, and there were a man and a woman who appeared to be tending a grave halfway up the populated section of the hill. Beatrice had captured them in three pictures—in two of them they were looking down, and in one they were looking straight at the ceremony below.

The pictures featured an older couple in loose-fitting clothing. The man had a baseball cap hiding his face, and the woman had a scarf hiding much of hers. I held the picture of the dirty dozen beside the picture of them looking down the hill. Could this be Jay and Penny? Had they bonded over their love of killing? If so, had Jay's death been staged?

I quickly texted Alex to see if he had pictures from the other murder victims' funerals, especially the funerals held in the Lower Sierra cemetery. Two of the victims were buried close by to Maggie—Brittany and Deborah. I found what I was looking for in the ceremony for Deborah. A series of pictures showed the same two people pretending to care for a grave on the side of the hill. Two pictures showed the couple's faces. Beyond the extra weight and the fifty added years, the similarity to Jay and Penny was there. Especially telling was the flattened nose of the man.

Out of curiosity, I went through the pictures for Maggie's funeral again. This time I was looking for any shots of the parking lot or vehicles parked along the aisles. Mostly, I was looking for anything that didn't fit in. On the aisle closest to where the couple was tending the grave was a large trailer-truck combination. I couldn't imagine how the couple had managed to park there, and I wondered if they'd been ticketed. I quickly pulled up the pictures from Deborah's funeral. The same trailer truck was parked in the same place.

I turned to the websites for the local community newspapers and looked for stories about Jay Schmidt. After the stories of his wrestling glories was the murder of his wife. Then there was nothing for a few years until stories about his death came out. These were the stories I wanted to read. I copied them to a file and arranged them in chronological order.

There had been a fire in a cell with a single occupant. The occupant was burned beyond identification because there was an attempted breakout and a small riot at the same time. The guards couldn't get back to the cell that was on fire until the riot was quelled, and by then three men had escaped and one had died in the fire. The dead man was assumed to be Jay Schmidt because the fire had occurred in his cell.

Follow-up stories continued to say the victim was Jay, but there was no conclusive identification possible. Following practices of the day, in which poor people with missing, broken, or decayed teeth had all their teeth removed and a set of false teeth made, the fire victim had only a mangled set of teeth lying by the body. Forensics tests did not yet include sophisticated DNA analysis. Jay's family insisted that the body was his even though there was no documentation that he'd had his teeth removed. A final story recapped the situation and announced that two of the three prisoners had been captured. They both refused to confirm the identity of the third prisoner that had been with them. Through the years, there were no sightings or leads on the missing escapee. Thus, the assumption held that the dead prisoner was Jay and the missing prisoner was Michael Black, the only inmate who had not been found.

I quickly copied all the relevant pictures and stories into a file and sent copies to Alex and Louie. I asked them to let me know when they could conference call. In the meantime, I'd see if Louie's facial recognition expert could determine if her age-progression tool would support the identity of the unknown grave tenders as Jay and Penny

▲ ▲ ▲

Two days later, we had our conference call with Alex. Louie, Beatrice, Faith, and I were in the office conference room when Alex called in. I had not shared my theory with Faith, so to bring her up to speed I made a presentation using pictures and newspaper stories. Then I asked for reports and discussion.

Louie went first and told the group that the facial recognition expert reported a 95 percent probability that the pictures were a match. Using the age-progression tool on Jay and Penny resulted in faces that resembled those of the older couple. One flaw was that their hair was covered in the cemetery pictures, so it was difficult to know exactly what they looked like when out in the community.

Alex went next. "Well, cuz, you continue to give me headaches. But I guess they are good headaches because your theory has some support. The truck and trailer were in several pictures, and one picture provided a good shot of the license plate. I expected the plate would prove to be stolen, but I was wrong. The rig was registered to Michael and Sara Black in Riverside County. The address was for a semipermanent campground, where visitors could choose from a number of different-sized camping spots and camp for a night or indefinitely, as long as they paid in advance. According to the manager, the Blacks had been spending long stretches of time on a half-acre lot on the outskirts of the park. They led us to the site, but it was empty. We found footprints but no fingerprints or DNA so far.

"The manager told us they would not have noticed that they were gone until rent was due again in about a month. We will put out a nationwide search, but my guess is that they went underground in order to protect their identities.

"The manager also told us they did not seem to have jobs, as they often took off on random trips."

"Sounds like they turned a hobby into a profession. Do you think they do murder for hire?" I asked.

Everyone murmured yes. The question was, were these latest hits a freebie or were they paid?

I sat thinking about the conversation so far, then it hit me. "Why did Jay and Penny suddenly grow stupid? They had avoided detection for decades and then they led us on a path straight back to them. I think they were playing with us. I would bet anything they are off again with new identities, and that attempts to find them will all run into dead ends."

I thought about the last part of the message left at Pricilla's house. *And now it is done.* I wondered if they were announcing it was done because they had changed, they had regrets, or because they had new ventures ahead. I suspected I would never know unless they told me.

I had to admit that my feelings about Jay and Penny were a bit twisted. The murders of the girls and fetuses were incomprehensible and horrifying. Wilson Peterson seems to have been responsible for the murders for hire of Maggie and Clover, which were meant to protect his comfortable life. I wasn't sure how I felt about the murders of four of the dirty half dozen before they could be prosecuted. Clover and Pricilla had both expressed regret and remorse. My guess is that some of the others still believed what they did was not a crime—they were just taking out the trash.

Chapter 35
Time to Replenish

In the meantime, there was frantic planning for the James Taylor concert. There had been toiling over the guest list and then the party went to a full-day activity and then to a weekend. This was the itinerary: meet at Colette's on Saturday afternoon for a barbecue; go to the concert via a limo service; come back to Colette's for a midnight champagne dinner; sleep over (women at Colette's and men on JJ's boat); brunch the next morning at Colette's. Colette, Beatrice, and Faith had spent hours conference calling about every detail of the event. They acted more like teenagers planning for a sweet-16 party, but I knew they were engaging in active coping. Beatrice was never going back to live at the ranch, Colette was not going back to her relationship with Abe, and Faith had learned about the senseless reasoning behind the death of her sister.

Louie and I had planned for a festive evening too. We knew it would be too noisy to stay at my house, so we made plans to party on Louie's boat.

We couldn't get out of the James Taylor event because Colette was insisting we go to the barbecue before the concert. At the last minute, she told us the barbecue was black tie. What? I admit my experience was limited, but I had never heard of a black-tie barbecue. Louie had multiple tuxedos and sophisticated suits, so he was fine. That left Beatrice, Faith, and me in need of something to wear. Plus, I had the special need of finding something I'd be able to step onto the boat in.

Colette announced she was taking the three of us shopping at her favorite stores the day before the event. I would neither have found nor visited such exclusive shops on my own. Once I got to the first one, I went a bit crazy because it had both the kind of evening wear and casual clothing I had been wanting. I don't know if it was the egging on by my friends or my sudden desire to live life more fully, but I went home with a dozen outfits—easily three years' worth of new clothes. Beatrice joined in, and she came back with about half the number of outfits I'd bought. Colette went a bit overboard, buying outfits for both her and Faith so that everyone was included in the madness.

▲ ▲ ▲

The next afternoon I was looking through all my new clothes and finding it hard to settle on just one outfit. This was the opposite of my usual situation. Finally, I decided on a knee-length silver dress with a slit that went about twelve inches up the side. It was fancy but not over the top. I paired it with low-heeled black satin sandals and a black satin clutch. I looked rather good, and by three I was ready.

Louie walked through my back gate just moments later. Meanwhile, party sounds were building up next door.

Just as we were about to pull the door open, we heard someone tuning a guitar. As we walked through, we heard the first notes of "You've Got a Friend." And there he was, James Taylor, singing to us from the center of Colette's garden. I looked around and saw a handsome young man standing beside a handsome older man and a handsome middle-aged man. After I blinked, I saw that it was my son, my father, and my almost-cousin Alex. I turned to Louie to ask if he had known about all of this, and before I could do so, he shook his head no.

With the audience in the palm of his hands, and with the older people acting much younger than their age, Mr. Taylor sang another two of his best hits. Following that, his manager came out to escort him back to his limo. Before he left, he gave Colette a hug and a kiss on the cheek. As he left, the buzz grew even louder, and the music was cranked up to play a Spotify playlist of James Taylor and friends he had recorded songs with—including Carly Simon.

I didn't know who to greet first, Will or Colette. I chose Will and rushed over to give him a big hug. "What are you doing here?" Will had been living in Gainesville since November, at a condo JJ had found to sublet in Haile

Plantation, a small community a few miles from campus. There were more faculty than students living there, but it was easy to navigate to get everything he needed.

He simply said, "Florida is not the state for me. I can give you reasons why, but it starts with the politics." I just nodded my head to let him know I understood. I gave him my biggest hug, then turned and gave one to my dad. Louie and Alex joined us, and I looked around and saw Beatrice, Faith, and Colette talking animatedly, but every few seconds, Colette would stop and hug one of them. I inched my way over and stood beside them. Colette pulled me into a hug and whispered in my ear, "I made a donation to his foundation."

I whispered back, "How are you going to fit all these people into a single box for ten?"

She gave me a steady look and said, "I may have bought more than one box."

I noticed Colette was working hard to get Alex to stay for the party. Beatrice was working on Louie. Then I saw Will walking toward me with that wheedling look in his eye. I knew then we would be having a full night of James Taylor.

As Will and I turned away to join Louie and Beatrice, Colette ran up and whispered in Will's ear. They both laughed and gave me a look. After Colette flitted off, Will said with a shrug, "She told me Jackson Browne was coming to town this spring."

Epilogue

I often plan to do about three times the things I can actually accomplish when I am on break. It's partly because in academia we use the term break rather loosely, and for me it actually means a break from going to the office. I continued to putter around in my home office every day as I prepared for the holidays and the upcoming semester.

I had pushed hard to have a family meeting of JJ, Will, Beatrice, and me to discuss the future of MoonShots, my mother's company, and the ranch. It was a difficult discussion because it involved the possible dissolution of people's lifework, though I kept trying to reframe it as an evolution of what their lives had produced. We found we could all agree that we would go forward in stages, and it might take us a decade to sort it all out. Another thing we all agreed on was that we wanted to sell agricultural land that was not adjacent to or within one mile of the family home. After we made that first step, we would take another.

We also agreed that we wanted to honor all the girls who died—particularly Nina, since she was part of our community. To honor all the girls as a group, we endowed a scholarship at Lower Sierra High School to support a first-generation female student each year. The student would be fully funded for two years at any community college, and if she maintained a 3.0 GPA, she would be funded for another two years at any California college or university. We planned to put the money from the sale of the land into the fund and to name it the Canton Moon-Nina Scott Scholarship.

Carlos decided to sell his land in the same pattern as we did, and he would fund and structure a scholarship in the name of Miguel Sanchez, as we had done for Nina. Beyond that, he wanted to focus on sustainable farming practices. Knowing this, JJ had had his greenhouse rebuilt, and it was waiting for Carlos when he was released from the hospital. JJ was intrigued by the idea of feeding more people with fewer resources, and he made an agreement to sponsor Carlos's work if he could help out there part time. Of course, where JJ went, Will went also. He was toying with the idea of a new major. Surprise—it would be sustainable agriculture. He was looking around for a program that had both a national and an international emphasis. I was enjoying watching his process of self-development.

▲ ▲ ▲

I was starting to feel like myself again, optimistic and energized. I wasn't thinking about the deaths of the girls and their fetuses every minute of every day. Then Alex called to schedule a wrap-up meeting about the case. I was conflicted. I wanted to move on and start the new semester in a strong place. However, Alex had helped me so much that I knew I owed it to him to do the wrap-up.

The next morning Beatrice and I met Louie at his office and waited for Alex to call in. When he came on the line, he didn't look refreshed at all. He looked exhausted and in need of a break. He got started right away.

"Thanks for being available for this meeting. I have been trying to write a comprehensive report over the past few weeks. That has included working with Louie's team to align all the interviews and other evidence into one coherent report. Once that is completed, I will turn everything over to the CBI and let them decide what they want to pursue. I can't express my appreciation for all that your team did to unravel what was going on.

"It is difficult to understand how such heinous crimes happened over fifty years ago. We think of those as being the 'good old days,' but obviously there was evil then too. To summarize: All of this started as a way for Clover and Jay to make money for college. They killed four girls for money, and they threatened two others. After the murders, they continued to extort money until a total of five thousand dollars was paid for each murder. The exception was Penny, who fell short on her payment for Sharon.

"When Nina's body was found, it was Deborah and Wilson who panicked. They responded in two directions. First, they hired someone to kill Maggie and Clover. Maggie, because of her on-going investigation and the fact that she knew about the bracelet. Clover, because she knew the full story and she continued to want money. We believe Deborah got Brittany to send the threatening letters to Maggie and Clover before they were killed. Second, they hired the men to burn down the greenhouse and to conduct the break-ins. The men for hire will all be prosecuted accordingly. When their plan to intimidate and to steal the bracelet didn't work, Brittany brought in her younger cousins to help. None of them knew what they were doing or that it was criminal. They thought their parents were playing jokes on friends. They have all been given six months of full-time community service.

Finally, we believe that it was Jay and Penny who killed Deborah, Brittany, Wilson, and Pricilla. After talking extensively with Miles and corroborating his alibis, we found no proof he was involved with the current crimes. All accounts that we have from his peers stated he was not involved with the murders of the girls. That is probably why he was spared. The DNA of one fetus matched Tony Farr, one matched Wilson Peterson, and one matched Miles Curtis. Amy White declined to have her child tested. So, what I want to know from you is if this matches the facts as you know them."

No one spoke. For me it was a factual account that highlighted the bare bones of the story. I thought about Robert Jennings, Sonny Jennings, and Tony Farr. Would I feel comfortable sharing this story with them? Because they had paid for the crimes of the dirty half dozen for a lifetime, would it be enough to know that four of the six were dead without ever being held accountable? And that the other two may never be caught? Maybe I could talk that over with Faith someday.

Alex prodded us again: "Is it factual?"

I answered, "Yes, in a skeletal way, it is factual."

By this admission, I was not acknowledging it was a thorough explanation. The truth was so much more nuanced. I went back to my original desire to understand MG's role in the chain of unfortunate events. If she had warned Nina, either directly or through Maggie, would she still be alive? I couldn't be sure, but I don't think Nina would have believed it. First, because she loved Tony, and second, because she probably wouldn't have believed that so much evil existed. Yes, she had spent her youth being looked down on, but there had always been constraints in place. But somehow those constraints failed as the members of the group grew into more independence of action.

However, now we have instances of school violence that have been stopped before they transpired because someone spoke up. Slowly that is becoming a new cultural norm, to warn of dangers. But it was not the norm when all this happened. At that moment in the 1960s, the ultimate betrayal was to be a snitch. Technically, by blaming MG now, it would be a case of presentism, but I couldn't help myself. Because of her inaction, I could not say that MG was innocent. It was still too early to know how I would evaluate her long term, but I knew I would love her anyway.

▲ ▲ ▲

Louie and I had managed to carve out the last week of break to spend together. We were both so exhausted that we hadn't planned anything specific. On the first day of our week, we were still too exhausted to plan. We decided to flip a coin—beach or mountains. It came up mountains. Then we flipped for in state or out of state. It came up out of state. But the flip didn't reflect what I really wanted to do. I wanted to make a loop around California to speak with the families of the dead girls. I wanted to end my time with a visit to Tony Farr in Colorado. I wanted to tell him the full story, not just the highlights. And then we would toast the short life of Nina Scott.

About the Author

Barbara is a native Californian who attained her education at three UC campuses: Santa Barbara (BA, MA), Santa Cruz (PhD), and Irvine (Postdoctoral studies). After her training she traveled east to work at three schools of public health, starting with Johns Hopkins University. She advanced to becoming a full professor and department chair at the University of Florida and then she relocated to the University of Maryland. Her research and publications have clustered around cancer prevention, survivorship, and treatment decision making. She also worked to develop an instrument to measure occupational stress and the influence of stress on women's well-being. Barbara has written extensively in the academic research literature and her papers have been cited extensively both nationally and internationally. Upon her retirement she switched to writing fiction and *Last Orange Tree* is her second novel. Both this novel and the earlier book *Prism* feature her academic protagonist, Phoebe Moon, and cybercrimes expert, Louie Dawes. Her books feature an in-depth look at work life in a research academic institution associated with a fictional university in Southern California. Her characters solve murders within the context of a multigenerational team.

Barbara and her husband live near the historic town of Berlin, Maryland with their two dogs.

www.ingramcontent.com/pod-product-compliance
Lightning Source LLC
LaVergne TN
LVHW091126080826
845145LV00008B/2054